PARZIVAL
AND THE
STONE FROM HEAVEN

LINDSAY CLARKE

PARZIVAL

AND THE

STONE FROM HEAVEN

HarperCollins*Publishers*

FOR CHARLIE,

one day

HarperCollins *Publishers*
77–85 Fulham Palace Road
Hammersmith, London W6 8JB

The website address is: www.fireandwater.com

Published by HarperCollins *Publishers* 2001

1 3 5 7 9 10 8 6 4 2

©Lindsay Clarke 2001

Lindsay Clarke asserts the moral right to
be identified as the author of this work

A catalogue record for this book
is available from the British Library

ISBN 0 00 710813 3

Printed and bound in Great Britain by
Creative Print and Design Wales, Ebbw Vale

CONTENTS

t some point towards the end of the 12th Century, Chrétien de Troyes, a northern French poet writing under the patronage of the Count of Flanders, began to put into rhyming verse a mysterious story that he considered to be the best of the tales that were told in royal courts. Frustratingly, we know almost nothing about either the oral or written sources on which he was drawing, and – even more tantalizing this – the story was left unfinished at his death. Its title was *Perceval*,[1] yet Chrétien also referred to his romance as '*li contes del graal*', and through a fusion of ancient Celtic lore with the newly evolving courtly ideals of the amorous latin temperament, he created an appetite for a chivalric myth – the story of the grail – which magnetized the imagination of medieval Europe and has never since quite lost its fascination.

It seems characteristic of the elusive nature of the grail motif that almost everyone has heard of it and no one has ever come up with a definitive idea of what it is. Some of the confusion arises from the fact that so many other imaginations have improvized around Chrétien's themes that a complete account of the influence of the myth on European culture is probably now impossible. Any attempt would certainly have to take into account the work of such diverse figures as Robert de Boron, whose *Joseph d'Arimathie* solemnly christianized the once pagan vessel by associating it with the chalice used at the Last Supper and the vessel in which Christ's blood was carried from the cross; the Nazi war criminal Heinrich Himmler, who instituted his obscene SS as an order of 'grail knights' with its own lugubrious ritual centre at Wewelsburg Castle; and the Monty Python team, unforgettably urging on their invisible horses in quest of the further reaches of human absurdity.

When a symbol becomes so diverse in its application that it can be variously interpreted as a relic of an ancient pagan fertility cult, as a coded reference to the blood-line of Christ, and as an emblem of psychological integration, while journalists have come to rely on it as a useful cliché ('the holy grail of sustained growth and low inflation'!), then one might reasonably ask whether there can be any virtue left in it at all.

The reasons why I believe that there is, and that such apparent promiscuity reflects the undepletable generosity of its nature, will be explored in the essay at the end of the book. In the meantime it feels necessary to say something about what kind of book this is.

Of all the authors who have seized on the themes first assembled by Chrétien and put them to their own purposes, there is one – Wolfram von Eschenbach – who has long exercised a particular enchantment over my own imagination. This book is an attempt to re-tell his masterly version of the grail story, but in a form and language which may make it more accessible to a wider audience in our time.

Wolfram flourished in the brilliant first half of the Hohenstaufen period of medieval German culture around the turn of the 12th and 13th centuries. He was a knight *ministerialis*, bound in service to a feudal lord, whose family hailed from Eschenbach in Franconia but who considered himself a Bavarian. Writing under the patronage of the Landgrave Hermann of Thuringia, he was a highly accomplished poet who declared himself to be illiterate – though this may have been no more than an arch joke directed against the pretensions of some of his more learned rivals. In any case, the many qualities of his writing reveal a man with broad cultural horizons, and one whose highly developed sense of the integrity of the individual conscience was always enlivened by a wryly humorous vision of life that was widely tolerant in its sympathies.

As with all the significant poets of that evolutionary moment in western consciousness, Wolfram was imaginatively engaged with the problem of renegotiating the relationship between the masculine and feminine principles. His story of Parzival and Gawain is a lively exploration of ways in which the male talent for aggression might be converted to energy available for the cultivation of the feelings, and he is also writing out of a subtle awareness of the links between the erotic and the spiritual dimensions of our experience. At a time when the Holy Roman Emperor was resisting the claims of a corrupt papacy to political supremacy over Christendom, and when heretical beliefs were attracting large numbers of people, it's significant that the orthodox structures of the church have almost no part to play in a story which sets out to dramatize a knight's solitary quest for redemptive meaning in the world.

Wolfram's extraordinary poem was also written at the time of the Crusades, yet it takes a Muslim as one of its heroes and seems, at its climax, to seek a kind of gnostic *rapprochement* between Christianity and Islam under the mysterious aegis of the grail. And Wolfram's grail itself is no Christian vessel – in fact not a vessel at all, but a sacred stone in which the opposing powers of light and darkness are reconciled in creative tension.

This brief account of some of the issues raised by Parzival barely starts to do justice to a work of which Ted Hughes once wrote, 'this immense poem shaped the colliding and fermenting inexhaustible mix of materials and religious passions that coursed through Europe in the eleventh and twelfth centuries'.² Like all great art, however, *Parzival* transcends the age in which it was written. It's not surprising, therefore, that it has exercised a particular fascination for writers, artists and thinkers across the centuries, and that it has furnished the narrative underpinning for works as diverse as Wagner's opera *Parsifal*, Thomas Mann's novel *The Magic Mountain* and George Lucas's film *Star Wars*. Yet as one translator, AT Hatto, admits, Wolfram's verse is 'dense, sententious, and at times consciously gnomic',[3] and many passages lack even a clear syntactical structure. A faithful translation will reflect those qualities and no one should expect it to make for easy reading. But when you add to those stylistic idiosyncrasies, Wolfram's fascination with the heraldic detail of courtly life, his preoccupation with genealogy, and his delight in a multiplicity of minor characters with such exotic names as Poydiconjunz or Karnahkarnanz Leh Cuns Ulterlec, then there is a danger that readers who are neither scholars nor enthusiasts for the medieval period may too quickly lose heart and close the book on one of the great adventures of the western imagination.

It is for such readers that the present prose adaptation is intended, though my hopes will be best served if it encourages them to embark on Wolfram's far richer original. Anyone who does so, however, will find considerable differences between my version and his, and these should be explained.

The main narrative thrust of Wolfram's poem is embroidered with diversions and elaborations which once delighted the hearts of a patient medieval audience but will not be found here. Hoping that my version would appeal to younger readers as well as to interested adults, I decided to streamline the story, leaving out a number of incidents which, while interesting and entertaining in themselves, were not essential to the already complex interweavings of the main drama. This has resulted in simplifications and rearrangements which some lovers of Wolfram's story will find regrettable. I have also conflated the nature and deeds of some minor figures to those of single, more significant characters, and have taken the liberty of changing names, or the spelling of names, to attune them to modern ears. In order to avoid too much in the way of intrusive commentary, I have also relied more heavily than Wolfram did on dialogue to explore the issues and advance the narrative.

What follows is not a novel, with all that that implies of social, psychological and even 'magic' realism, but the telling of a tale – something closer in spirit to the Grimm Brothers than to Sir Walter Scott. I gave myself considerable licence to improvize, however, and as has always been the case with re-workers of the grail material, I have come up with inflections and variations that suit my own temperament and purposes. Those purposes include the desire to speak through the imagination to some of the dilemmas and possibilities of our own transitional time, as Wolfram himself was certainly doing for his. And though I may have altered the letter of his vision in many ways, I have tried to keep faith with what I take to be his essential, generous spirit as a true poet of the heart.

Some of the issues that have been briefly raised here will be explored more thoroughly along with related themes in the concluding essay. But for the time being, enough of facts, ideas and explanations – let's get on with the story!

Notes

1. *Perceval, The Story of the Grail,* Chrétien de Troyes, translated by Nigel Bryant (DS Brewer, 1982).
2. *Shakespeare and The Goddess of Complete Being,* Ted Hughes (Faber & Faber, 1992).
3. *Parzival,* Wolfram von Eschenbach, translated by AT Hatto, (Penguin, 1980).

PART ONE

THE

WOUNDING

Here begins the Book of the Grail.
Here begin the terrors.
Here begin the marvels.

(Perlesvaus)

CHAPTER ONE

THE

BLACK QUEEN

ver since he had first put his infant head inside the iron hollow of his father's helmet, he had dreamed of growing into a man big enough to fill a suit of armour. As a youth his greatest delight had been to practise knightly skills, learning how to wield lance and shield, to fight with sword and mace, and to inspire confidence in his mount so that it would swerve and leap at his command. And even when, as a young man, he watched his father die from a lance-wound taken in a violent clash of arms, his appetite for the kind of glory that can be won only through combat remained undimmed.

His name was Gahmuret. He was the second son of King Gandin of Anjou, and when a king died in that country it was the custom for the first-born son to inherit all his lands and titles. But Gahmuret was so loved for his noble nature and his command of all the knightly virtues that when the lords of the realm came to pledge allegiance to their new king, Galoes, they begged him not to leave his younger brother dispossessed.

So great was Galoes' love for his brother that he was ready to share half his kingdom with him. Another man might have accepted the offer and relaxed into a life of idle comfort, but Gahmuret was driven by a larger sense of destiny. Impelled by a proud spirit and a restless heart, he asked his brother for no more than four pages of noble birth to accompany the sixteen squires already sworn to his service. He declared that these twenty followers were all he needed, for his only desire was to ride out into the world at the head of that small band, resolved to gain honour and renown in foreign wars, and – if fate were kind to him – to win the love of a royal lady as his bride.

Galoes protested that such plans might leave his kingdom whole but by separating him from his brother they would cut his heart in two. Yet seeing that Gahmuret must go wherever his own adventurous heart might lead him, the King insisted on giving him far more than he had asked.

Five of the most spirited battle-chargers in the royal stable were put at his disposal, fine clothing and mounts were provided for all his company, and their panniers packed with gold and precious stones so that they need lack for nothing on their travels. Gahmuret's resources were increased still further by gifts valued at a thousand marks or more, urged on him by a noble lady whose infatuated heart ached at the thought of losing him.

Yet if that lady's grief was great, the grief of his mother was even more bitter. Already devastated by her husband's violent death, the queen was driven near to distraction by the imminent loss of her son. Clasping Gahmuret to her breast, she wept and pleaded with him not to go, not to leave her, not to put his precious life at risk in foreign wars. Was God blind that he did not see her suffering, she cried, or deaf that he did not hear her pleas? How else could he abandon her to sorrow as insupportable as this?

'May God in his mercy console you for the loss of my father,' Gahmuret answered her quietly, 'but that a son should go out in search of his fortune is surely no cause for grief.'

His voice was soft but it was also absolute. And when she looked up into his face, the Queen saw his father's reckless eyes smiling back at her and knew that a mother's tears would not dissuade him from his destiny. Composing herself as best she could, she pressed gifts of silk and samite on her son as offerings to his future bride, asking only that he name a date for his return. But Gahmuret would not grant her even that small relief. He told her that he had no knowledge of the distances he might travel, and little more of the foreign lands that lay beyond the horizon. Nor could he foresee the adventures that might befall him there. So giving thanks for the many rich gifts bestowed on him, he mounted his horse and rode out into the world, leaving his mother, his brother and the court of Anjou grieving behind him.

Eyes on the distant hills, his ears alert to the snap of banners in the wind, Gahmuret felt the pelt of his horse shivering under its coat of green silk blazoned with anchors of white ermine. He set out from his home knowing that he would mend his fortunes only by entering the service of a powerful lord. Being a proud man himself, and brother to a king, he was determined to serve only the most powerful lord of all.

The air tasted fresh at his lips. He knew himself on the vivid brink of things. And if this handsome figure did not once glance back where his friends and family watched from the parapet, it was because his ambitious heart had no idea that he would never see any of them again.

The months passed. Having jousted his way across Christendom, Gahmuret entered the service of the Caliph of Baghdad who ruled two thirds of the known world and counted many kings among his subjects. The knight and his company so distinguished themselves in battles for Babylon and Aleppo, Damascus and Alexandria, that this brave Christian warrior won the Caliph's own friendship. Out of loyalty to his lord and an insatiable appetite for adventure, his campaigns took him to countries as far-flung as Morocco, Persia and Arabia. Soon the fame of Gahmuret the Angevin had spread so far across the world's horizons that few dared challenge him to single combat.

With his fortune won and his reputation made, the knight decided that the time had come to visit his homeland in Anjou. The Caliph gladly fitted out a ship for him and Gahmuret put to sea with his company of knights, both Christians and Saracens among them now.

The voyage began well enough, but one afternoon huge anvils of cloud began to build over the African coast and by nightfall a storm was blowing far out at sea. Lightning flared above the bare poles of Gahmuret's ship. Soon it was toiling among loud billows as it ran before the wind for shelter.

By dawn the tempest had blown over and first light found the battered vessel riding at anchor in the quiet harbour of a Moorish port. When Gahmuret came on deck he saw the walls of the city as a white glare against the drenched blue of the African sky. Ranging far out across the desert beyond those walls, he made out the pavilions and banners of two armies camped around the city. Smoke drifted from their camp-fires. Soon would come the sound of drums and trumpets, and the creak of siege-engines straining beneath their load. Between the tang of salt-air and the dry smell of the desert Gahmuret caught the scent of war.

Shielding his eyes against the glare to assess the strength of the city's defences, he saw that he too was observed. A group of ladies with skins as black as grapes were standing together on the high balcony of a domed building on the seaward side of the town. He guessed that this must be the royal palace, and that these watchers in their bright silks, chattering together like weaver birds, were ladies of the court, pointing down at him, and doubtless wondering whether the commander of the ship that had entered their harbour overnight would prove to be a friend or yet another foe.

His eye was caught by movement below the wharf where a narrow pinnace put out into the harbour, making for his ship. Calling his master-mariner to his side, Gahmuret asked whether he recognized this port, but the ship had run before the storm all night and none of the crew could be sure where they had dropped anchor. So Gahmuret had to wait till the boat bumped against the ship's side, and a gaunt, bearded African clambered aboard. Limping from his wounds, the man informed him that they had made landfall in Zazamanc, that he himself was Marshal to the besieged forces of that city, and that his Queen was eager to welcome the commander of this well-armed vessel because she badly needed friends.

Gahmuret had seen as much in the old Marshal's haggard eyes. He also saw the light of hope return there when he told the man his name, for the fame of the Caliph's champion had reached across Africa and the Marshal had once been in the Caliph's service himself. He and Gahmuret had fought together at Alexandria. Perhaps they might be comrades again, he urged, for his city was in a desperate condition and could not withstand this siege much longer. 'My Queen still commands great riches,' the old man added eagerly. 'Come to her aid and she will open her treasury to you.'

'I already have more wealth than I need,' Gahmuret answered. 'Return to your queen and tell her that I will add my strength to hers merely for the love of battle, and for an old comrade's sake.'

All the inhabitants of the city were Moors, most of the men were wounded, many of them grievously, and as Gahmuret's relieving army processed on horseback through the narrow streets, sounds of wailing rose from houses where the women grieved over the dead and dying. The knight saw only signs of exhaustion and despair in the famished faces round him, yet the old Marshal welcomed him into the palace, declaring that their sorrows were now turned to joy because the gods had sent them the worthiest of champions. Then he brought Gahmuret into the presence of his Queen.

For a moment of rapt silence the Queen and the knight gazed at one another. Belakane was a woman of statuesque beauty, whose skin shone blacker than a moonless night, while the shy smile with which she greeted him was as modest as the moon by day. And the man who elicited that smile presented so striking a figure in his silks and iron armour that he instantly commanded the entire attention of her soul. As she would shortly confess, Queen Belakane had reason to reproach herself for keeping her heart closed for too long against the claims of love, yet in the presence of this stranger she could almost hear the sound of it unlocking now.

'I have heard much of your valour, sir,' she said.

'Command me,' he replied, 'and I will do what I can to ease your cares.'

So the Queen drew Gahmuret aside and told him how it came to be that two armies, one black, the other white, had laid siege to her city at the same time. The fault was her own, she insisted. Both armies were led by kinsmen of Prince Isenhart who had thrown away his life because of her timidity. For too long she had allowed him to protest his love for her, but a maidenly shyness had left her afraid to declare her own love in return. Isenhart had put himself at risk in ever more daring exploits, until at last, driven to desperation by his apparent failure to move her, and losing all desire for a life deprived of her love, he had gone into battle unprotected by armour, and taken a lance through the heart.

Overwhelmed by grief, Belakane had suffered as never before, while Isenhart's kinsmen blamed her cold heart for his death. They had raised armies against her in both Africa and Europe, and though her own soldiers had fought hard to defend the city only a miracle could prevent it falling now.

The Queen was in tears before her story ended. In awe of her beauty, aching for her pain, Gahmuret was now certain that his life could have no more noble purpose than to champion this lady against her foes. Holding her hand in his, he vowed that he would take the field next day and challenge any man who dared question the innocence of her heart to meet him in combat.

'Be of good cheer, Lady,' he gently sought to comfort her, 'I will uphold your cause or gladly die in the attempt.'

Gahmuret rose at dawn after a night made restless by his love for the Queen. Yet as he strapped on his armour, the gentle figure of the previous day hardened into a man of iron whose thoughts were fixed only on the coming fight.

Fish-eagles flashed white against the blue sky as he rode out into the field. Dust rose hot and dry under his horse's hooves. Briefly Gahmuret glanced up at the balcony where the Queen and her ladies watched, and raised his lance in salute. Trumpets sounded out his challenge. As always in such moments, his senses quickened at the imminence of death. The air shook in the heat.

The first champion to come against him took Gahmuret's lance squarely on his shield and went flying over his horse's cruppers to lie winded on the sand. The man got to his feet, found his breath, and would have drawn his sword, but Gahmuret wheeled his charger, ran him down and pinned him to the ground at lance-point. Forced to yield, the knight demanded to know who had bested him. Soon the name of Gahmuret the Angevin was passing like a wind off the desert through the besieging hosts.

Champion after champion rode against him that day. Each was unhorsed, each gave his parole to present himself for ransom if

Gahmuret emerged from the day unbeaten, and as knight after knight, black and white alike, fell under the shock of his lance, the cheers grew louder from the city walls. At last, in the stupefying heat of the afternoon, it became clear that neither army could find another contender willing to pit his strength against the Angevin.

Gahmuret rode back into the city to the acclaim of the crowd. In dented armour, still sweating and bruised, he presented himself before the Queen. And if Belakane's heart had once been cloistered like a nun, it was open and excited now as this man stood before her, vivid and bloody in his wounds.

'This armour hangs heavy on you, friend,' she said. 'Come, I will disarm you with my own hands.' Again their eyes met as she lowered the coif of chain-mail from his head. 'Today you have saved my city and freed my heart,' she whispered. 'It is only justice that both should fall to you. Yesterday you came to this land a stranger. Tonight, if you will have it so, you will be its lord.'

And so a great bed with a sable coverlet was prepared, and as Belakane delivered herself body and soul to him, Gahmuret came to believe he had fulfilled the dream of love that brought him from Anjou all those years before.

They were agreed that there is no god but God and his name is Love. So, the couple were wed soon afterward, untroubled by their different faiths. Acknowledged as King of Zazamanc, Gahmuret made peace with Isenhart's kinsmen. He urged gifts on them from the realm's prodigious treasury, released all his prisoners without ransom, and accorded their unlucky prince a royal funeral. After both armies had dispersed amid an air of festival, all the lords and emirs of Zazamanc came to pledge allegiance to their new king. Then the royal couple were left to enjoy their nights of love together, and the quiet, sunlit days of a peaceable kingdom.

Each morning Belakane woke in wonder that her life should have been so blissfully transformed. No longer a virgin, and more wife than queen, she felt such love for the man who lay, naked and white, beside her that it came very close to worship. She had not yet learned that there are men so infatuated by the glamour of their manhood, and so blithely unaware of everything except that which serves their glory, that to love them is to run the risk of going mad with grief and loneliness.

As for Gahmuret – the unfamiliar pleasures of love, and the rich light it cast across the ordinary world, kept him happy for a time. But if the whole of Christendom had been too small a stamping-ground to satisfy his appetite for adventure, how much smaller was to prove the black queen's bed! He lacked patience for long days spent in court, vainly trying to sort out the squabbles of his subjects. The daily release of riding far out into the desert with his hunting dogs, or pitting his falcon against his lady's sparrow-hawk, began to lose appeal and soon turned tedious. Each dawn the sun sizzled up out of the eastern sea and went down each night in a stupendous conflagration of clouds and sky over the western desert. During the hours between, nothing exciting or important ever happened in Zazamanc. It seemed that his own arrival had put an end to what passed for history in that torpid zone.

Meanwhile a cargo vessel would drop anchor in the bay every now and then, bringing news ashore with its merchandise, and rumours of war in foreign lands.

Three months after their first night together, Gahmuret walked out of a show put on for their entertainment by jugglers, acrobats and fire-eaters. When the show was over, Belakane found him, bored and restless, staring from a balcony at his ship where it lay anchored under the stars. Again and again he flicked the bristled tail of a fly-whisk across the palm of his hand.

For some time the Queen had been uneasily aware of her husband's brooding silences, but she had news for him now that must surely lift his heart. Her one concern was that someone might have spoiled her moment by displeasing him.

On the contrary, he answered, his every wish was met before he could utter it. Yet his tone was querulous, the words spoken as if in complaint, he was looking for an argument. Tenderly, a little anxiously, Belakane put her hands to his shoulders, seeking to ease the tension there, and asked him to come lie with her, but Gahmuret shrugged away from her touch, swearing that he was sulking like a caged hawk for lack of action.

'Then let us hunt together tomorrow,' she said. 'There are Arab horses in my stable that remain untried.'

'I've had my fill of your desert,' he snapped back at her. 'It wearies me.'

'My Lord?' Her voice reached out to him again.

Turning impatiently, he saw the puzzled hurt in her eyes. 'I'm a fighting man, Belakane,' he said more gently. 'I miss the din of lance on shield, the thrill of risk. It's where my heart beats fastest and most fiercely, it's where I know myself alive.' He turned away again, staring into the blackness of the African night. 'A life lived without the taste of death in one's mouth is no life at all. Lady, there is rumour of war in France. My skills are needed there.'

'Do not speak of it,' her voice broke across his. 'Have I not already suffered too much from pointless war and pointless death? Ask anything but this.'

'Then you refuse me the one thing I desire,' he scowled.

'Have I refused you anything else?' she protested. 'And if I cannot grant you this, it is with good reason. I am carrying your child. Is that not worth living for, my Lord?'

Gahmuret turned, bereft of speech, to gaze at her. For a moment he was all confusion and amazement, then he laughed out loud, his rage and frustration utterly dispelled by delight at the news. Soon afterwards he took her to bed and the night was made tender by his awkward care.

Yet only two mornings later Belakane woke to find the bed empty beside her. She heard the murmur of prayer from the faithful in the square beyond the palace walls. And then, far above it, the mewing of a hawk gripped her heart like an omen, and she was up, running through the chambers of the palace, calling out her husband's name.

Gahmuret was nowhere to be found. It was some time before Belakane saw the parchment he had left tied with green ribbon on her dressing table.

My skill is with arms, Lady, not with words, yet by this fond letter one great love salutes another, though like a thief I have stolen secretly away to spare our tears. For how could our happiness endure while war rages in Christendom and I lie fettered to a wife who is no Christian?

If our child should be a man, I know that he will be brave and true, for he too is an Angevin, and Love shall ever be his mistress, as you, dear Lady, are forever mine. Until my return, forgive me and farewell.

He had signed himself Gahmuret the Angevin, Son of King Gandin.

When Belakane went to the balcony overlooking the harbour, she saw through a blur of tears that his ship had weighed anchor and was gone.

Six months later, shouting and singing through the pain of her labour, she gave birth to their son. With cries of amazement the newborn babe was placed in her arms and Belakane gazed in wonder at the miracle performed by those first brief hours of married love. For this was no ordinary child.

As if the universe itself had sought to make a visible emblem of her union with Gahmuret, the infant's skin was parti-coloured, both black and white, a magpie child such as had never been seen before. So Belakane named her son Feirefiz, which was as close as her heathen tongue could come to the words *Vair Fils*, which meant 'Dappled Son' in the language of his vanished father, the Angevin.

Here, it was said by all who saw him, was a prince singled out for a special destiny.

CHAPTER TWO

THE

WHITE QUEEN

eanwhile, following his own impatient destiny, Gahmuret had entered the service of the King of France, and added so many victories to the tally of his achievements that his exploits stirred the French Queen's amorous heart. But those wars were over and won now, and the knight's thoughts had returned to the wife and child waiting for him in Zazamanc. He was planning to go back there, stopping to visit his family in Anjou on the way, when he heard news of a great tournament to be held at a place called Kanvoleis in Wales. All the most famous champions were gathering there to joust in competition for the hand and lands of Herzeloyde, that country's virgin queen.

Here was an arena where a man might test himself against the finest warriors in Christendom. If he returned to Africa at such a time he might never know how highly he ranked among their number. So telling himself that a month or two more away from his wife could make no difference, and that his brother would certainly be among the many kings assembling for the tournament, Gahmuret turned his horse's head around and made speed for Wales.

*

When the dawn mist lifted at Kanvoleis, a stately new pavilion was seen among the many already pitched in the meadow beneath the castle walls. Word soon spread that this magnificent array belonged to the King of Zazamanc, who had arrived by dark the previous night to add his name to the list of contenders – a list already gleaming with the names of kings from Ireland, Gascony, Aragon, Castile, Portugal, the German lands and realms still further afield.

For mere love of the sport, Uther Pendragon, the old king of the Britons, had come to take part in the tournament himself, but his son Arthur was absent from the field, having gone in urgent search of his mother, Arnive, who had been abducted by a magician. Uther's son-in-law, King Lot of Norway, also intended to break a lance or two, watched by his son Gawain, a boy still too young to fight though he was eating out his heart to do so. These and other champions were marvelling at the costly panoply of the newcomer that first morning, when the exotic splendour of his pavilion attracted the gaze of the Lady Herzeloyde.

Since the recent death of her father, the young queen had relied for guidance on her Marshal, the Lord Gurnemanz. It was he who informed her that the King of Zazamanc had once famously championed the Caliph of Baghdad, that his vast wealth was matched only by his prowess as a knight, and that he was in fact a Christian and brother to King Galoes of Anjou.

'Then we look forward,' said Herzeloyde, 'to meeting one who has such wonders to show and of whom so many speak in awe.'

Unaware of the stir caused by his arrival, Gahmuret was still resting in his pavilion when the contest began at noon that day. Two mounted champions had taken to the field under bright banners, followed by their troops of armed retainers, and he was roused by the din of the mêlée. Not yet armed he rode out to the field, holding himself aloof from combat while he assessed the skill of those already fighting there. With a cool eye he watched the splintering of lances and the flight of sparks struck from each clash of iron and steel. His horse snorted as its pulses quickened to the shouts and groans from the hurly-burly around the knights, and the passionate clamour of the crowd.

Trumpets sounded, more knights joined the throng. From a balcony on the castle walls, Herzeloyde and her ladies watched the fighting with excited hearts, but though she searched for his banner throughout the early afternoon, the young queen saw no sign of the King of Zazamanc among the knights contending there.

Beginning to tire of the noise and confusion, she was about to withdraw when a great moan went up from the crowd. A blow from the King of Aragon's lance had knocked Uther Pendragon out of his saddle, back over his horse's tail. As soon as the old king hit the ground his retainers rushed to make a stand above him, but they too might have fallen under the King of Aragon's next charge had he in turn not been thrust back over the cruppers by a tremendous blow from a knight in emerald green who bore the sign of the anchor at his crest.

'The African king has taken the field at last,' said Gurnemanz, smiling with gusto. 'Now we shall see some sport, if tales are true.'

The mêlée was joined with greater force. Herzeloyde sat down again. She saw heads broken there, great kings winded and bruised, their lances shattered, shields smashed, horses left injured and screaming in the din. One after another, knights retired from the field, limping and bleeding, to watch dizzy-headed from the sidelines as the clash of arms rang back from the castle walls. And as the afternoon wore on, it seemed that the King of Zazamanc loomed on his charger everywhere, fighting like a man inspired, and quite reckless of his wounds, as though carried through that violent affray by a vision of his own invincibility.

When Gahmuret withdrew to change his mount, he found an embassy of Frenchmen waiting for him. Carrying as credentials a ring that the knight had once given to the Queen of France, their leader urged him to open the sealed letter they had brought. Gahmuret wiped the blood from his lips and read, to his sorrow, that the French king had recently died. But his widow's letter was inspired less by grief than by her passionate complaint that she was on the point of death herself for love of Gahmuret. 'Forget your kingdom in Africa,' she entreated him, 'it is too small for a soul as great as yours. Forgo the Queen of Wales, for I am more beautiful and powerful than she. If you would requite a truly noble passion, then return at once to France, for there you shall receive at my hand a crown and sceptre worthy of your fame.'

The French ambassador smiled as Gahmuret looked up from the letter in amazement. 'My lady is eager for your reply,' he said. But the knight's head was still hot with battle. Hearing the renewed clamour from the field, he gave orders that the ambassadors be entertained in his pavilion, then donned his helmet, swung his body up onto a fresh mount, took a new lance and, heedless of everything but the fighting still to be done, galloped back into the fray. From all quarters of the crowd, applause and cheering greeted his return.

Herzeloyde caught her breath as she saw him thrust his way into the thick of the fighting. She was on her feet, shouting with wonder, when another famous jouster crashed to the ground under his onslaught. Turning to her friend and confidante, the Lady Sigune, she confessed that the knight's courage excited her heart and frightened her for him at the same time.

Gurnemanz heard the catch in her breath, saw the flame in her eyes. 'Indeed, Madam,' he muttered. 'I'm thinking that here might be the protector your lands will sorely need.'

'It was my thought also,' Herzeloyde whispered.

She watched Gahmuret fight on into the afternoon, delighting both in the skill that defeated his opponents and the magnanimity with which he treated his captives. Taking the Lady Sigune's hand, she said, 'Do you think this African champion speaks with the same passion as he jousts?'

Sigune, who was young and flirtatious, answered her with a teasing smile. 'They say that the Queen of France has quite lost her heart to him!'

'Yet should he prove the victor tomorrow,' said Herzeloyde, 'have I not the right to claim him for my own?'

'Such are the rules of contest, Lady,' Gurnemanz put in, but a great shout drowned his words as Gahmuret's iron mace brought down a knight plumed with ostrich feathers. He wheeled his charger, looking in vain for the next mounted opponent, but it was clear by now that the first day's fighting was done. Sweating and bloody, Gahmuret opened his visor and lifted his lance in salute to the royal balcony where Herzeloyde nodded in demure response.

'Then the hopes of Wales and my own fondest wishes will ride with him,' she said to her Marshal, though her eyes were still gazing down where both horse and rider were surrounded by those eager to praise and touch the champion. 'Command my herald to take this favour to the King of Zazamanc,' she added, unbuttoning her sleeve. 'Tell him we will dine in his pavilion tonight.'

Having invited all his vanquished opponents to a banquet that evening, Gahmuret returned exultant from the field. He had scarcely had time to wash the sweat from his body and bathe his wounds, when the French ambassadors presented themselves again, congratulating him on his achievements and pressing for an answer to the letter from their Queen. Still dazed by his success, the knight was wondering how best to respond when he saw a herald galloping towards his pavilion carrying an inverted shield.

At once Gahmuret recognized the royal arms of his family. Even before the herald had gathered breath to speak, he knew why his brother had failed to join the royal gathering at Kanvoleis. King Galoes of Anjou was dead, killed like his father before him in single combat. Along with everything else that had fallen to him that day, Gahmuret had now inherited the crown of Anjou.

Already exhausted and emotional from his triumphs on the field, Gahmuret was reeling with grief at the death of his brother, but that was not the end of the herald's news. Gahmuret now learned that the shock of losing her son had burst his mother's heart. She too was dead.

A day that had been bright with glory darkened around him like a shroud. Gahmuret retired into the seclusion of his tent, declaring that he would take no further part in the contest. He would have grieved alone there throughout the night had not word been brought to him that the Queen of Wales had come to his pavilion, wishing to offer her condolences for his great sorrow.

'Here in this pavilion you are host,' Herzeloyde said as he kneeled to greet her, 'and I am mistress of this whole land, yet grief rules both our hearts. You have lost your mother and your brother, and I my father. Shall we be friends in mourning then? Rise, sir, and if a kiss will bring you comfort, I assent to it.'

Gahmuret saw the young queen, tall and pale among the rich hangings of his pavilion. He took her hand and kissed it saying, 'Your beauty shines so brightly, Lady, that should all these candles expire we could still see by its light,' then the two of them sat down together, each taking comfort in the other's presence. In response to her gentle approaches, Gahmuret tried to share the burden of his sorrow with her, but his words were awkward and incoherent. Touched by his vulnerability, Herzeloyde spoke in wonder at his achievements on the field. He caught the scent of her perfume as she leaned towards him, he heard the tremor of her breath. When he conceded that he had been fortunate in arms at least that day, she told him lightly that she had heard rumours that he was also fortunate in love. 'Is it not true,' she teased, 'that the widowed Queen of France pines for your return? Must we soon lose the pleasure of your company to the allure of the French court?' And when Gahmuret was uncertain how to answer her, she saw that this man might be an angel of grace and fire on the battle-field, but he had much to learn in the tender realm of feelings. 'I see it was more than a nimble tongue that won the French Queen's heart,' she said, and threw him further into confusion.

At that moment her Marshal, Lord Gurnemanz, presented himself with a flourish before them, announcing that all the champions gathered there at Kanvoleis had been discussing the events of the day and had reached agreement. Each of them conceded that none could hold the field against the man who had come there as the King of Zazamanc and was now also King of Anjou. A victory attained in his absence from the fray would be a mere sham. 'Therefore the contest is over and won,' Gurnemanz declared. 'All assent to it, my Lord. The prize is yours.'

'But I fought for no prize save honour,' Gahmuret protested amid the loud clamour of applause from the assembled company.

'Yet you have won far more,' said Gurnemanz. 'The hand of our Queen is yours, great king. All her lands and titles will be added to your own.'

In the ensuing silence the Lady Herzeloyde got to her feet. 'Perhaps the news of victory after such great loss has left our noble champion amazed,' she said quietly. 'Or is it that you are pondering a richer prize in France?'

'My Lady has the prior claim,' Gurnemanz put in. 'The rules of engagement were plain. By lacing on your helmet you accepted them. Sir, you are the Queen's man now, to have and hold.'

'Peace, Lord Marshal,' Herzeloyde interrupted him. 'If I can be won only at cost to this king's fame, then let me take my leave.' She would have made to go from the pavilion then, but Gahmuret forestalled her.

'I would not have victory bring disgrace,' he began in confusion, 'yet ...'

'Yet the French widow urges her love on you,' said Herzeloyde.

'Madam,' he answered, 'my heart beats far more quickly here than ever it did in France. But there is another cause.'

'Then do you break hearts wherever you go, sir?' taunted the Lady Sigune.

'I have left a Queen behind me in Zazamanc,' Gahmuret answered at last.

'A Moorish Queen!' exclaimed Gurnemanz. 'It can have been no Christian marriage. There is no impediment.'

'Yet the memory of that lady wounds my heart,' Gahmuret confessed. 'It robs me of all thought of happiness elsewhere.'

'Then I wonder you should have left her,' said Herzeloyde quietly.

'She tied me too closely, Lady. In Zazamanc I had no room to breathe.'

Herzeloyde studied him a moment where he stood uncertainly before her. 'In a truer love you would find a larger liberty,' she said. 'You are a free man, sir. I trust you will honour all womankind in me by sparing me humiliation.' Then she turned and left the undefeated warrior utterly confounded amid the splendours of his pavilion.

Gahmuret hardly slept that night. It felt as though he was besieged by women on all sides, and that dishonour lay in wait whichever way he turned. How much simpler were the bloody conflicts of the battlefield!

Yet by the end of that long night certain things had come clear to him. Grieve as he might, his mother was dead and there was nothing to be done about it, so he put her from his mind. He had also recognized that after the glories and sorrows of this day, he could never return to the tedium of life in Zazamanc, so his African Queen was abandoned for ever now. As for the lovesick pleadings of the Queen of France, he had begun to weary of them even while her husband was alive, and found them no more alluring now that he was dead. So, the real and immediate choice was whether to spurn the love of the Lady Herzeloyde, or to submit to her beauty and thereby forfeit his freedom once again. By dawn he thought he had seen a middle way.

That morning he came to the chamber where the Queen had been anxiously conferring with Sigune. 'Your frown is grim, sir,' Herzeloyde said when she and the knight were alone. 'I think you have sought this private audience only to spare me public shame. But Sigune tells me I have made my love for you so plain that all the world will mock me when you leave.' She turned away, feeding with a trembling hand the songbird she kept caged in her chamber.

'Lady,' he said, 'I would do nothing to harm your name.'

'It is not my name I fear for,' she said. 'If you are here to break my heart, then do it quickly and be gone.'

Gahmuret's eyes scouted the chamber. He drew in his breath, came closer, put his hand to the gilded bars of the cage. 'This lark you keep in your chamber,' he said, '– it sings sweetly enough, but would not one who truly loved it, freely grant what it longs for?'

Herzeloyde held his gaze for a long moment, then she unlatched the small door of the cage and put her hand inside. 'See,' she said a moment later, 'I hold the bird in my hands.' With her palms cupped around the warm flit of feathers, she walked to the window, held up her arms, opened her hands, and watched the lark fly out into the day's blue light. 'Now be gone after it,' she said, turning away. 'I am too proud to keep you here against your will.'

'Grant me less, lady,' he said. 'I ask only the right to go whenever there are feats of chivalry to answer. If you can allow me so much freedom, then the rest of my life is yours to command as you will.'

Herzeloyde turned and stared at him through the blur of light in her eyes.

'Then you will stay?' she whispered, disbelieving. And when he nodded, she laughed out loud with sudden joy. 'Oh breathe easy, friend,' she cried, 'for the eagerness of my heart matches the urgent need of my land. And both are yours on whatever terms you choose.'

So once again Gahmuret celebrated the rites of marriage amid great revelry, and his new Queen – as ivory-pale in her slender nakedness as the first had been ebony-black – gave herself to him with all her heart. Nine months later a son was born to them, and Gahmuret held up the infant proudly in his arms.

'He's a strong boy, lady,' he said in delight to his wife. 'He has the makings of a fine knight. Oh yes, this fellow is his father's son. He'll be a great breaker of heads, and of hearts too, I promise you.'

'Give him back to me before you break him,' said Herzeloyde. She cradled the child at her breast. '*Bon fils, cher fils, beau fils,*' she crooned, and smiled up at her husband. 'Isn't that how you say it in your Angevin tongue?'

'It is, lady,' said Gahmuret, and then a further play on words occurred to him. 'But we'll call my son Parzival, which means "to pierce through the middle" – so that like his father he'll always remember to seek the middle way.'

For a time it seemed that the infant Parzival must become the centre of his father's life, but the child was only a few weeks old when news came from the east that the Babylonians had risen against the Caliph of Baghdad. Gahmuret eagerly recalled his vows of loyalty and friendship, and was making preparations to go to the Caliph's aid when his wife sought to deter him. Surely, she insisted, an old pledge of friendship had less claim on his heart than the needs of his wife and child?'

'Remember your own promise, madam,' Gahmuret tersely counselled her.

'I do not forget it,' she answered, 'but there was no babe tugging at my breast when I made that promise.'

'Yet pledges are made to be honoured.'

'Is your passion for honour greater than your love for your son?' she asked.

'Without honour,' said Gahmuret, 'a man is nothing. Our son must learn that lesson.'

'Is it honour you seek,' Herzeloyde demanded, 'or mere excitement?'

'Peace, woman.'

'You command me to peace,' she answered, 'while you lust after warfare as your whore? There are gentler lessons I would teach our son. Can you cultivate no deeper feeling, my Lord, than this boorish appetite for violence?'

'Madam, let me freely leave,' Gahmuret said, '– or drive me away.'

'So now you threaten to abandon us, as once you abandoned your heathen paramour? Can't you see?' Herzeloyde cried, 'I love you more than my life. I can't live without you now. I'm terrified that I'll lose you in this stranger's war.'

'There is only one way you risk losing me,' he answered, refusing to argue with her further. 'Take courage, madam, and avoid it.'

So Gahmuret rode off to war. Ten weeks later came word of his death in a bloody skirmish on the Baghdad road. A lance-thrust through the brains had put out his light, and farewell gallant Gahmuret!

When news of her husband's death was brought to Herzeloyde she went mad with grief. She seemed to take comfort only in holding her infant son, though even then her mind rambled with dreadful memories of a dream that had come during her pregnancy, a dream in which a serpent had rent her womb and a dragon had suckled at her breast before taking flight. One afternoon she was weeping in the arms of the Lady Sigune when a letter arrived from the Caliph, telling her that Gahmuret the Angevin had been given a glorious funeral in Baghdad and that he would be forever mourned by the Saracens. But the letter merely deepened her misery. Only with great difficulty did the Lady Sigune prevent Herzeloyde from trying to kill both herself and her child that night.

After that they tried to take the baby away from her, but the mad queen raved so wildly in her resistance that she terrified Sigune and the other ladies. Gurnemanz gave her such rough comfort as he could, though he too was cowed by her savage anguish. When he urged her to keep her grief within reason, Herzeloyde cried out, wild-eyed, that her reason was lost and scattered in the desert where her husband had died. 'But they shall not take the child from me,' she cried. 'I will not let them take my child.'

'Your son will be kept safe, my Lady,' Gurnemanz said. 'We must all care for him now so that he grows to be a valiant knight worthy of his father's name.'

'Never!' Herzeloyde snarled back at him. 'Let him be anything but that. Let him be a coward or a fool, anything but a man of iron.' Clutching the babe tightly to her breast, she said, 'You shall not break heads, *Bon Fils*, no, nor hearts either. I'll find means to make a loving man of you, I alone shall be keeper of your heart.' But when Parzival wailed in her arms at the smothering fervour of her love, Gurnemanz reproached her for frightening the babe.

'I shall keep him from fear,' Herzeloyde spat back. 'I shall take him from this violent world to where I know he will be safe. Come, *Beau Fils*,' she said to the howling child, 'we will live in the innocent woods, away from harm, away from those who take pride only in death and killing, and know nothing of the heart. No one shall come between us.' Cunningly she stared back at Gurnemanz and Sigune with a gleaming she-wolf's glare. 'I'll be both mother and wife to him,' she said. 'I shall be all the love he needs. Never shall this child hear the cursed name of knight!'

Shaking his head, Gurnemanz said that this was madness indeed. But the lady proved as good as her mad word. Taking advantage of an unguarded moment, she stole from the castle by night, relinquishing a courtly world that held no further hope of peace or joy for her.

Deep in the unpeopled woods she raised the infant Parzival like a fawn.

CHAPTER THREE

THE

PERFECT FOOL

erzeloyde's flight to the forest with her child left both Wales and Anjou without a king. When Gurnemanz failed to discover their hiding place, he rallied Parzival's kinsmen to protect the domains of the vanished heir, but powerful and ambitious lords smelled weakness and soon both lands were ravaged by civil war.

The hideous clamour of that time went unheard in the woodland glade under the Welsh mountains where Herzeloyde raised her infant son. By the time seventeen winters had passed that child of simplicity had grown into the perfect fool. Lithe and muscular, he was a half-savage creature, alert to every motion of twig and leaf, his nose sensitive to the spoor of stag and boar, his eyes quick to spot the best basking-places of trout and tench. He knew nothing of his father or of the seasons of blood and smoke raging across his lost lands, or even that those lands were his. And he knew nothing of love either – except a mother's love that kept him in his ignorance, jealously hidden from the world. Yet there were hours – especially on hot Spring afternoons – when he watched the cloud-shadows drift across the empty hillside, or sat staring into the cold depths of a tarn, when he felt obscure yearnings in the stirrings of his heart.

On one such day his mother came looking for him and found him listening to the song of a pair of larks scaling the tall blue sky. Remembering how she had once freed a lark herself, Herzeloyde watched her son with sadness in her own woebegone eyes, a sadness that intensified to grief when she heard him release a heavy sigh. 'Why do you sigh so, *Bon Fils?*' she asked.

'The song of the birds,' said Parzival. 'It gives me feelings I don't understand.'

'And they make you restless, these feelings?'

Parzival studied his mother's anxious face, puzzling how to name the ache inside him. 'They fill me with a kind of ... loneliness,' he said.

'Then come,' said his mother, clapping her frail hands together, 'we shall drive them away from here.'

Parzival watched in baffled dismay as she shouted and clapped her hands, smiling at him with crazy satisfaction when the sky emptied of all sound except the white clatter of a nearby waterfall. 'Why did you do that?' he asked.

'Only to spare you pain, *Beau Fils.*'

'But the birds meant no harm,' he said, 'and there was beauty in that pain.' He stood before her, tall in his rough hide-clothing, his big hands resting on the crown of his tousled head as he swayed a little, staring up at the vacated sky.

Frowning, he said, 'I wish you hadn't done that, mother.'

The boy had never previously reproved her for anything. For a moment a cranny opened in her madness and Herzeloyde saw that he was no longer a child. She saw her own behaviour through his bewildered eyes, and became a stranger to herself again. Worse still, in the suddenly bleak light of the afternoon she saw how those years in the wilderness, bereft of other company, might have turned her into a kind of canker, stunting her son's green life.

Her heart chilled with a kind of panic then.

'Forgive me, forgive me!' Tugging at a strand of the grey hair that hung by her gaunt cheeks, she turned away from the reproach of his puzzled stare, muttering to herself. 'Oh my God, my God, is the boy right? Have I done wrong? Am I trying to thwart your will?'

Parzival was baffled by her words. They were clearly not addressed to him, yet there was no one else to hear them on the bare hillside. 'Who are you speaking to, mother?' he asked. 'Who is God?'

'You ask me who is God, *Cher Fils*?' Herzeloyde's heart lurched again. She gave a mad little chuckle. 'Oh my son, have I forgotten to teach you about God?'

Parzival looked about him as though expecting to detect some presence that had hitherto escaped his senses. 'I see no one here,' he said.

'We cannot always see God,' said Herzeloyde, 'though he took on man's form and shines in glory brighter than the sun. God is the threefold Lord of Light, *Bon Fils*. You must pray to him and his angels for help whenever you might need it. You must love and fear him with all your heart, and shun his foes, the devils of hell and the Dark Lord of Despair. Do you understand, *Bon Fils*?'

'He is a great light, you say?'

'Yes, a very great light. And you must always follow that light for it is the gentle way of love. Will you promise me that, *Beau Fils*?'

'Oh yes,' the innocent fool answered eagerly, his heart exulting at her words as though they opened up a radiant new horizon, 'when I see that light I will surely follow it.'

Another summer passed, and a harsh winter followed. Already expert with his javelin, Parzival kept them supplied with meat, carrying home unquartered deer from his hunting expeditions deep into the forest. Then, one hazy Spring day, as he stalked a white hart through the thickets, he came out into a grassy ride cut through a stand of beeches and the great world caught up with him.

At first he was alerted only by a distant, thunderous sound, though it seemed to be beating upwards through the earth rather than falling from the sky. He felt a trembling beneath his feet, was aware of a blackbird chattering out its warning cry, and sensed that something new and terrible was about to happen. The sound grew louder, he heard a crashing among the bracken, and then, for an astonished moment, he was conscious only of the light. The sun's rays shafted down through the beech boughs and glanced off a complicated, gleaming presence like nothing he had ever seen before. It was bearing down on him at speed through the woodland's smoky haze and his eyes were dazzled by that sudden radiance. He blinked, opened them again, and the glittering cavalcade of light resolved itself into three brilliant figures, taller and larger than men, hurtling through the woods like a cascade. They were almost upon him when Parzival fell to his knees, threw his arms wide open, and cried out loud, 'Help me, oh God!' Above his head he heard a shout of 'Whoa, Gringolet,' as the first of the three armoured knights reined in his horse to a halt only a moment before its huge hooves would have trampled the tousled-haired youth to the ground.

The other two riders reined in beside their leader, sunlight glinting off their helms and hauberks, as their horses snorted and steamed. Unflinching, Parzival gazed up at each of them in turn with an expression of rapt wonder on his open face, until one of them, the burliest, shouted, 'Get off your knees, dolt, and let us pass,' as he struggled with his startled mount.

'From the sound of your approach I thought devils were coming,' said Parzival, 'but now I see you are the threefold God of whom my mother spoke. And she was right, she was right. Oh God, you are beautiful!'

'These stupid Welshmen lack the brains of brutes at pasture,' said the burly knight, bringing his horse back under control. 'Be off with you, boy.'

Parzival stared up at him in dismay, wondering what he had said or done to displease this brilliant figure. 'But I love you,' he cried. 'I must follow your light.'

'I think this churl mocks us, Gawain,' the burly knight growled, reaching to knock the boy aside with the butt-end of his lance.

'Hold your hand, Kei,' the first knight answered. 'It would be a pity to blacken those pretty eyes. Look, the lad is trembling.'

'I have been taught to love and fear you, God,' said Parzival.

The third knight snorted at that. 'Gawain's no god, bullcalf,' he said, 'though there are women who worship him as though he were.'

Utterly confused now, Parzival got to his feet, reaching his hand to the soft muzzle of the first knight's horse. He frowned up into the friendlier gaze of the man who sat high in his saddle, holding his lance upright, with a golden pentacle painted on the green ground of his shield. 'You are not God?' the youth asked uncertainly.

'Faith, no!' the figure laughed, 'I'm a knight.'

'A knight?' said Parzival, who had never heard the word before. 'What is a knight?'

Again Gawain laughed, flashing a quick incredulous glance at his companions.

'A knight, Sir Innocence,' he said, 'is a champion of courtesy and honour.'

Parzival felt his heart thumping at his ribs. He could scarcely draw breath, such was the splendour of the figure smiling down at him. 'Then a knight is more beautiful than God,' he gasped. 'I will be a knight. Make me a knight as you are.'

Again Gawain laughed. 'Only the High King at Caerleon could work that miracle. And he's waiting for us. So come now, unhand my bridle. Let us pass.'

But Parzival's eye had been caught by the knight's lance. He gestured at it with the point of his javelin, demanding to know what it was.

'Do you know nothing?' Gawain asked, as amused as he was incredulous. 'This is a lance. For teaching my enemies to kiss their mother.' Gaily, he laughed out loud at Parzival's baffled stare. 'I mean the earth, boy.'

'Do you throw it?' Parzival asked.

'By no means,' Gawain answered. 'Do you take me for a peasant? A knight fights on horseback, lance against lance.'

'Then this javelin I made is better,' Parzival said. 'It can bring down a quarry nearly at a bowshot's length.'

'A clodhopper's weapon!' Kei growled from his charger. 'Out of the way, oaf, or I'll run you down.' He dug his spurs into the horse's side so that it reared above Parzival, flashing its great hooves. In a reflex of self-protection, the youth fell back. Gawain's companions pushed their mounts past him as though he were a mere obstacle and, laughing with derision, galloped away among the trees.

For a moment longer, Gawain smiled down at this wild boy who had a striking nobility in his bearing despite his unkempt hair and the rough clothes he wore. 'If you had wits in your head, youth, you would lack for nothing,' he said, shaking his handsome head. 'God save your sweet ignorance. Farewell!' Then he too dug his heels into his horse's flanks and rode speedily away.

Forgetful of the white hart he'd been hunting, the youth wandered the woodland in a daze of wonder for hours afterwards, and when he returned at last to his frantic mother, Herzeloyde sensed at once that her world was at an end. Parzival came back to their bothy as dusk

34

was falling, though his face was still radiant from the wonder of what he'd seen. A torrent of words poured from his mouth as he tried to share the exhilaration of the experience with her.

'They were so beautiful the sight made my heart sing,' Herzeloyde heard her son enthusing. 'You told me that God's light shines like the sun, and though they said they were not gods, I think they must have been touched with the same splendour, for they are the brightest things alive. They are called knights.'

'Dear God, prevent this,' she whispered fervently to herself, but her son chattered on, insensitive to her distress.

'They told me there is a High King at Caerleon who makes these noble creatures. The fairest of them said that if I go to that place this king will work a miracle that will make a knight of me too.'

'Listen to me now,' she sought to interrupt him, 'listen to me, *Bon Fils*. Oh dear God, help me, help me now.'

'But, mother,' said Parzival unheeding, 'I've seen what I was meant to be.'

'Be silent,' she cried. 'Be silent and learn. Your father was such a knight as this. There was none prouder in all the world. And where is he now? Dead, *Bon Fils*. Dead in his blood these many years, and food for worms.'

'But I am alive,' Parzival protested.

'And I would keep you so. Your life is mine.'

'But don't you see, mother? It was as if these knights were made of light. I think that God has shown me his light to follow. And if my father was such a man ...'

'No,' she interrupted him with ever more anxious urgency. 'Didn't I tell you there were devils too? These knights are devils, boy. They bring death to one another and madness to all. They madden the hearts of all who love them. I beg you not to think of them. Your place is here with me.'

Parzival studied her in silence for a time, weighing her distress against the excitement of his heart. It soon came clear to him that, not having shared the splendour of the experience, she simply could not understand. 'No, I have seen my way at last,' he said. 'My life has been yours mother, and I thank you for it, but I must make my own life now. Tomorrow I shall follow God's light as you yourself once told me I should. I shall follow it till it brings me to the High King at Caerleon, and he will make a knight of me so that I too will shine like the sun.'

Neither mother nor son could know that, many years earlier, though in very different circumstances, the boy's grandmother had once begged her son Gahmuret not to go forth into the world like this. Herzeloyde's tears were as bitter as that long dead lady's had been and no more effective. Unwittingly she herself had planted a vision in Parzival's innocent mind and nothing she could now say would come between him and his desire. She might as well have tried to argue with his father's ghost.

Herzeloyde lay awake all that night, and by the time her son woke at first light, eager to leave for Caerleon, her mad brain believed that it had found ways to make the world send him back to her. 'If you would enter the orders of chivalry,' she said, 'you must have a mount to ride.'

'A horse! yes,' he cried, 'I must have a horse, like Gawain.'

But, as Herzeloyde knew, there was only one horse available – the swag-bellied nag that had drawn their simple cart for years, and was old and broken-winded now. 'And if you are to appear before the High King in his court, you'd better have the proper finery too,' she said craftily. 'Let me see what I can do.'

So she set to, cutting a tabard out of old sackcloth, and – at Parzival's insistence – making a cowl for it that he could draw over his head like a coif. Then she shaped a rough pair of buskins out of calf-skin for him, which she dignified with the courtly name of sollerets as he shoved his feet into them. 'And you must have a plume, such as knights wear on their helmets,' she said, threading the stems of holly leaves through the crown of his cowl so that he looked like a savage greenman from the woods when he stood tall before her, glowing with self-approval, and wholly unaware how preposterous his appearance.

She could have wept to look at him, for she remembered enough of the court's cruel ways to know how wittily those lords and ladies would mock this bumpkin figure when he rode his nag into their elegant presence. But if the shock of humiliation brought him quickly back with his tail between his legs, so much the better! She would rather have her son mocked as a living fool than mourned as a gallant corpse.

Parzival was aware that his new apparel lacked the sheen he had so admired, and that his horse had seen better days. But he was confident that a glittering suit of armour and a fiery mount would come with his knighthood. In the meantime, he knew that his javelin was a better weapon than a knight's unwieldy lance, so he swung himself up onto the nag's back, and tugged at its rope-halter, eager to leave. His mother let out a heart-rending cry then and ran towards him, grabbing the rough bridle, looking for means to delay him.

'Wait,' she cried, 'there are things a knight must know.' Panting with anxiety, thinking quickly, she filled the lad's head with all the crazy advice that came to her distracted mind. 'Listen to me, *Beau Fils*, you must always wear these clothes I've made for you. Let no one take them from you. And greet everyone you meet, saying "God protect you, good sir," then they are sure to treat you well, for the world is full of wickedness and greed. But if grey-haired old men give you counsel, listen to them closely, for they know how to survive. What else, what else?'

'I understand,' said Parzival impatiently, 'let me go now, mother.'

'Wait,' she gasped. 'You must learn about women first. Women are frail creatures. If you see one in need of help, you must grant it, for when a knight fails to heed ladies his honour dies. And you may give them kisses, yes, have kisses of them, but I forbid you to take more. For love of me, my son, leave her only with a kiss. Though if she has a ring for you to win, you may take that of her in all innocence. And if ... Dear God, if you meet such men as those who killed your father ...'

But her voice broke down at that thought and tears streamed from her eyes. Parzival leaned down to put his big hand tenderly to her cheek. 'My javelin will avenge him, mother,' he promised quietly, and was astounded by the torrent of woe his words released. Wanting only to be gone now, he tried to pull gently away. But, 'Kiss me, my son,' his mother cried, dragging at his hand. 'Ah dear God, no, I cannot bear this. *Beau Fils, Cher Fils*, I beg you, do not abandon me.'

Parzival tugged his hand free, more urgently now, pulled the old horse's head round, dug his heels into its sides, and rode slowly off out of the glade without a single glance back at his wretched mother. 'Don't go, don't go,' she pleaded, falling to her knees among the leaves and beech-mast, watching the white sway of the mare's haunches and tail as her son rode away. Like the strike of lightning across her breast, she felt the searing anguish of a breaking heart. 'My son, my son, do not abandon me,' she moaned, but now her breath was breaking too. Filled with hope, exalted on his nag, the youth heard only a summoning to glory in the sound the wind made rustling through the boughs.

Parzival rode through the forest for two or three hours, and when he came out through the trees his eyes were momentarily dazzled by the gleam of sunlight off a river running among stones. Then he made out the vivid gold and purple stripes of a pavilion pitched on the far bank where a flat stretch of meadow ran down to white water. Wondering what this marvellous spectacle could be, he urged his mare into the shallows.

Once on the far side he dismounted, leaving the nag to drink while he walked round the pavilion until he saw the half-open flap of its door. Peering inside, he saw a figure with shining black hair splayed across a blue velvet cape, lying asleep among fat cushions. The air in there was heavy with a fragrance such as he had never smelled before. It quickened his senses and stirred his heart. The figure was sleeping so peacefully he felt he should leave without making any disturbance, but then he remembered that this was a woman lying before him, and that his mother had given him clear instructions about how women should be treated. And so, undoing the last of the tent-flap's toggles, Parzival stepped quietly through onto the richly woven carpet.

Trembling a little, his breath tight in his throat, he knelt down beside the still sleeping woman. He saw the emerald green glint of a ring on her slender hand. In the stillness of that cool pavilion, he watched the rise and fall of her breast, took in the fragrance of her perfume, lowered his cowled head to hers.

'My mother says I might have a kiss from you, lady,' he whispered then, and pressed his puckered lips to her slightly open mouth.

The lady stirred sleepily at his touch. Without opening her eyes, she gave a little moan of pleasure, smiled, and said, 'Orilus, what are you doing?'

'God protect you, Lady,' said Parzival. Delighting in the sweetness of her breath, he pushed his mouth at hers again, but the lady's vivid eyes had shot open at the unfamiliar voice. She saw a strange face looming over her in a sackcloth cowl with a bobbing tuft of holly leaves. Her lithe body stiffened in recoil. 'What? Who are you?' she protested, struggling under the nuzzling weight of this coarsely clad oaf who smelled of animals. 'What are you doing? Get off my hair, you brute. Get off!' She was pushing at Parzival's shoulders fiercely now, kicking with her little feet. 'I am the Lady Jeschute,' she spat out at him, 'lover to Duke Orilus. He'll kill you for this when he comes back.'

'Let him come,' Parzival gave her a good-natured grin. 'No man shall stop me kissing you as my mother bade me. This kissing is a sweet thing.'

Jeschute pulled her head away from his approaching mouth. 'Are you mad?' she gasped. 'You're frightening me.' Parzival pulled back a little, startled by the terror and fury in her eyes. 'Do you mean to force me?' she panted up at him.

'I wish to heed you, Lady,' he said, 'for when a knight fails to heed ladies his honour dies.'

'A knight! What are you? A simpleton?' His odd response had dispelled her first shock. Jeschute's pride and courage were returning now. 'I think you must be,' she snapped. 'Get away from me. Go home to your mother.'

'She told me I might take a ring as well as kisses. You must give me your ring before I go.'

'My ring? No,' Jeschute shook her head, 'no one takes my ring except by force.'

'If you say so, lady,' said Parzival, seizing her pale wrist with one big hand and tugging at the emerald ring with the other. When it stuck at the knuckle, she howled that he was hurting her, but he pulled harder and the ring slipped off. 'There, I have it,' he said. 'I wish you well, Lady.'

Parzival got to his feet, putting the ring into the wallet that hung from his rope-belt. He looked round the tent and for the first time took in the table with its silver salvers and platters, the pair of fine goblets and a flagon of wine. Realizing that he was very hungry, he crossed the carpet to lift the lid of a dish.

Jeschute was saying, 'Please don't take my ring. It was a gift from Orilus. If he finds it gone ... it will cost you your life, I promise you.'

But Parzival's mind was already on other things. 'I see there is food here. I have a great hunger on me. May I take this pie?'

'Take what you like,' she answered, 'but leave me my ring, I beg you. Orilus is mad with jealousy. He'll think I've given it to another man.'

'But you have, Lady,' said Parzival, munching on pastry, 'and I thank you for it. And for this most excellent pie. I shall repay you for it one day, when I can.'

And with that, the youth ducked out of the pavilion, called his horse, and cantered away, happily ignorant of the trouble he was leaving in his wake.

Towards early evening, Parzival was riding through a dusky grove when he heard the sound of sobbing on the quiet air. Reining in his mare, he made out two figures in the shadow of a great yew tree. A woman with dishevelled hair was sitting on the ground, cradling in her lap the head of an armoured knight who lay in an ungainly posture with one arm stiffly thrown out to the side. At Parzival's approach, the woman raised a lovely face that had been ravaged by pain and sorrow.

'God protect you, Lady,' the youth greeted her solemnly. 'Can I help you?'

'There is no help for us,' the lady sighed. 'My love is dead.'

Dismounting from his horse, Parzival saw that the iron plate on the knight's breast was smashed and buckled, and that the torn vestments beneath were clotted with blood. When he asked whether a javelin had caused the wound, the lady looked up from her weeping, white-faced, saying, 'No, my love died an honourable death.'

'Another knight struck him directly then,' said Parzival, '– lance against lance.'

'He was a noble prince,' the lady moaned through her tears. 'He gave his life fighting against Duke Orilus for another's cause.'

'It grieves me to hear it,' said Parzival, leaning forward to look more closely at the wound. He saw the knight's handsome face, gaunt and pale, and stained with blood where it had trickled from his mouth. He saw the livid gash where a lance point had broken through the ribs and punctured the lungs. 'Yet he is dead, Lady,' Parzival said, 'and we should bury him.'

'No, don't touch him,' the lady cried. 'He is mine. You shan't take him from me.'

Parzival looked on in dismay as she clutched the dead knight in a fierce embrace, weeping and berating herself for having kept him from the joys of love while he was alive and protesting that he would never leave her arms again. Everything about this grievous scene felt wrong to Parzival, but his mother had told him always to heed what ladies said, so not knowing what else to do, he softly muttered, 'I have great pity for you, Lady,' and turned back to his horse.

'You have a kind heart,' the lady cried after him. 'God give you better fortune than ever my prince found. Tell me your name and I shall pray for you.'

'I am called *Bon Fils, Cher Fils, Beau Fils,*' he said.

'What?' the lady exclaimed in sudden amazement. 'Who gave you that name?'

'My mother,' said Parzival, 'who else?'

'Come closer,' the lady demanded. 'Let me look at you. Dear God! I know your mother. She is the poor mad Lady Herzeloyde. You must be my cousin Parzival. And rightly called because your mother's heart also was pierced through the middle by the death of her love. Her heart and her wits too. But does she live still, cousin?'

Confused by this outburst, Parzival told the lady that his mother was alive and well and living contentedly in their hut in the wildwood beyond the river.

'And you have left her alone there? In times like these! How could you have done that?'

'Because I am following God's light,' answered Parzival proudly. 'It will bring me to Caerleon where the High King will make me a knight.'

'A knight! But you are a great prince, cousin, and heir to many kingdoms.'

'I know nothing of this,' said Parzival.

'Then learn it now, Parzival, of your cousin Sigune, who loves you – even though it was for your sake my love gave his life.'

'For my sake?'

'He died upholding your claim to Wales. And you knew nothing of it.' At that Sigune's tears flowed again, she clutched the dead knight to her bosom, and when Parzival declared that he would avenge his death, she stared up into his simpleton gaze and cried out that he should not even think of it. 'Go back and take care of your mother,' she urged him. 'Your lands are lost. This world is too cruel. There is no place in it for an innocent fool such as you.'

'But God wants me for his knight, Sigune,' Parzival insisted.

'Would you be killed too?' she cried. 'Hasn't there been enough killing all these years? I beg you, Parzival, leave the knightly world to its madness.' She gazed up into his youthful eyes, saw the tenderness and perplexity there. 'Honour your own gentle heart,' she urged. 'Find some kinder way to be a man.' Then she returned to weeping over the decaying corpse of her lover, and the youth could get no further word out of her. So, baffled and confused, trying to make sense of all that he had learned, he remounted his nag and rode on in search of Caerleon.

CHAPTER FOUR

THE

RED KNIGHT

or a day and a night Parzival travelled across a land
ravaged by war. He saw smoke rising like grief from
the roofs of sacked farms where kites fed off unburied
corpses. His greetings met with fear and suspicion in
the eyes of the few people he passed. Only reluctantly was he given
guidance and shelter.

His mood lifted when he saw the towers of Caerleon, tall and
formidable, on the crown of a hill. As he approached the gate, his
pulses quickened again at the stirring sight of a knight in vivid red
armour galloping towards him on a sorrel charger, with a plume of
crimson feathers dancing at his helm. The horse's trappings were
of crimson samite, the reins, lance and shield that the knight gripped
in one hand all gleamed bright scarlet, while in the other hand he
flourished a goblet of red gold. Shaking out its fiery mane, the
charger came to a halt alongside Parzival. The youth reined in his
own weary mount, stunned with wonder at this flame-like vision
dazzling his eyes.

'If you're going in there, lad,' the knight called to him, 'tell Arthur
I wait for him here. And if he dares not defend his honour himself,

tell him I'm ready for any champion that comes.' Parzival nodded, awe-struck, and would have ridden on, but the Red Knight wheeled the restive charger across his path. 'Wait,' he commanded, and then, more softly, almost in apology, he said, 'Tell the Queen that in snatching this cup from the King's hand, I had not meant to spill wine in her lap. Tell her I intended no dishonour. Now go.'

Breathless, desirous of nothing now except to have the Red Knight's gorgeous armour for himself, Parzival entered the castle. At that moment, amid the loud barking of hounds and the squawk of startled hens, a door flew open across the courtyard, and a small, hunched figure in cap and bells tumbled out into the dust. The heavily-built man who had thrown him out loomed over him for an instant, shouting, 'Out, fool, and don't show your face till you think of a jest that better pleases the king.' Then he went back inside, slamming the huge wooden door behind him.

With a rude gesture at the closed door, the man on the ground got to his feet, shouting, 'I'll make you rue this, Kei, you brainless ox!' Groaning, he dusted himself down, then noticed the lad on the bandy-legged mare gazing down at him. 'What are you staring at, mooncalf?' he demanded.

'God protect you, good sir,' said Parzival. 'I'm looking for the High King.'

'Then take my advice,' the jester scowled, 'and come back on a better day.'

Parzival met the scowl with a smile. 'I think there can be no better day for him to make me his knight and his champion.'

'What?' The jester stared up at the simpleton in amazement. There was a jingle of bells as he used his motley-coloured hat to fan himself.

'When I've beaten his enemy out there,' Parzival assured him, 'the king shall grant me that red armour for my own.'

For a moment the jester gawped at him in amazement, then a crafty grin crept across his face as he spotted an opportunity. 'I see, I see! Then let me show you in, gallant sir. Together we'll sweeten the temper of this miserable court. Dismount, I pray you.'

'The knights I met in the forest did not dismount,' Parzival replied. 'No more shall I.'

'Of course not. What was I thinking? I crave pardon, brave sir. Stay right where you are in all your incomparable dignity.' Turning away with a chuckle, the jester banged on the door. 'Open up there, Seneschal. Open up, I say.' He gestured to Parzival to bring his mount closer, the door opened to a further barking of dogs, and the burly Kei brandished his fist saying, 'If you value your head, fool ...' But he stopped there, astonished by the extraordinary sight of the youth in his holly-plumed cowl, sackcloth hauberk and buskins, mounted on a fly-blown nag.

Taking advantage of surprise, the jester grabbed the mare's halter, pushed past the stupefied seneschal, and led Parzival into the great hall, shouting, 'A champion! A champion is come at last! Salvation is at hand.'

The shout echoed round the vaulted silence. In the light shafting down from high windows, Parzival was aware of a colourful assembly of knights and ladies ranged around the bannered walls, and of two uneasy figures, whom he took to be the High King and his queen, seated on a raised dais under an awning at the far end of the hall. The air of the place felt tense and brittle. No one said a word, though a vague murmur of astonishment began to stir as the jester turned to Parzival and said, 'Speak up, lad. Tell them what you want.'

Encouraged by the fact that everything was happening so easily, Parzival took a breath and raised his voice. 'I have followed God's light to this place,' he said. 'Now I would have the High King make me his champion that I might win the Red Knight's armour for myself.'

Utter silence met his declaration. The jester chuckled nervously. 'What, no laughter, lords?' he gulped. 'Are you ashamed that this spring green has heart enough to meet the Red Knight on the field of honour while the pack of you have no more balls than it takes to beat an honest fool?'

Kei strode towards the jester and grabbed him by the scruff of the neck, growling, 'Antenor, I'll have your guts for this!' But at that moment, the High King got up from where he sat frowning on his throne. 'Peace, Kei,' he commanded, and then smiled a little wearily at Parzival. 'Come forward, youth.'

'Are you the King?' Parzival demanded.

'I am,' Arthur answered, more amused than annoyed by the lack of deference.

'Then make me a knight at once that I might serve God and defend your honour on the field.'

By now a trickle of amused laughter had begun to pass around the court. A fair-haired man dressed in gorgeous green silks got up from a chair close to the throne, where he sat surrounded by ladies. He gestured towards Parzival with his goblet. 'I know this youth,' he said. 'I met him in the woods the other day. He's a pretty enough fellow but I fear he lacks the wits of an ape.'

More laughter greeted the remark. Gawain was about to turn away, back to his admiring ladies, when Parzival said, 'And I know you, Gawain, and took you for a man of honour as I am myself. My mother is a Queen, look you, and I have a rightful claim to many kingdoms.'

'As is evident, my Lord Simplicity,' Gawain retorted, 'from your most regal appearance. Faith, you outshine us all. Tell me, where can I find your tailor?'

Unabashed by laughter he did not understand, Parzival said proudly, 'My mother made me these clothes.'

'Then she is truly fashion's Queen!' said Gawain to amused applause.

Aware now that things were not as he'd thought, Parzival surveyed the court with a colder eye. 'I did not come here to be mocked,' he said, but his air of baffled outrage only provoked more laughter until King Arthur raised his hand.

'Indeed you did not, sweet youth,' he said. 'You have a holy innocence about you. It puts us to shame, sirs, that we should scoff at it.' Then he smiled gently up to where Parzival sat on his fat mare, plumed in holly leaves. 'Were it not merely to waste your young life, I could find it in my heart to grant your wish.'

'Then do,' Parzival demanded, 'for I want that red armour for my own.'

'If you want it so badly,' growled Kei, 'why don't you go and take it? This cockscomb shall be your squire.' With the tip of his boot he kicked the jester onto the flagged floor at the hooves of Parzival's mare. A further burst of derisive laughter filled the hall, but it faltered to a halt when the king again raised his hand – all except for one voice, that of a young woman with braided hair who stepped forward to stand beside Kei, laughing uncontrollably as she looked up at Parzival – a light, chuckling ripple of sound that had no edge of scorn to it, only the helpless joy of pure mirth.

'Be silent, Cunneware,' growled Kei, 'be silent, damn you.' But the lady laughed on regardless until her increasing gaiety so exasperated the angry knight that he raised his hand and slapped her across the face. 'How many noble knights have passed through this hall since your brother betrayed us,' he demanded, red-faced and furious, 'yet you laugh in the presence of this buffoon?'

Holding the palm of her hand to her reddened cheek, yet evidently untroubled by the blow, the Lady bubbled into a further fit of giggles. 'Yes, I laugh, I laugh,' she cried amid tears of merriment.

Parzival looked down on her in dismay. 'Do you mock me also, Lady?'

Helpless with laughter, the lady could only shake her head in denial, and it was Gawain who answered for her. 'Indeed she does not, youth,' he said with an uncharacteristic note of wonder in his voice, 'for this is the unhappy Lady Cunneware of whom it was said that she would never laugh again until she set her gaze on the noblest knight of all.'

But Parzival was learning to doubt the sincerity of this sophisticated world. 'Is this true?' he asked the lady. Convulsed with laughter still, Cunneware could only nod her head. Arthur came to her aid. 'To our great wonder it is,' he said. 'Since her brother turned traitor to our court, this lady has not laughed even for Gawain himself.'

'Then I am your servant, Lady,' said Parzival, and turned his proud eyes on Kei. 'I shall have recompense, sir, for that unmanly blow you gave her.'

'I accept no challenges from feckless Welshmen,' Kei blustered. 'Win arms if you can, fool. Then seek me out.'

Parzival studied the seneschal coolly a moment. 'This fool thanks you for a timely lesson,' he said quietly. 'I had thought the King's court a place of courtesy where valiant knights would honour ladies as my mother taught me. Now I see how truly ignorant I was. But I *shall* win those arms, sir, and you *shall* answer to me.'

With that reproach, Parzival pulled round the head of his mare and rode out of the hall amid the abashed silence of the court. Astounded by the events he had unleashed, Antenor the Jester got to his feet and scampered after him.

Parzival rode his mare out into the tall blue day. After the shady light of the hall, the field outside the castle glowed luminously green. His ears were stinging from the jibes he'd taken, his heart banged against his ribs. When he looked up from patting his mare's neck he saw the Red Knight waiting, visor-down, lance raised, the sorrel charger fretting in its steam.

Parzival dug his buskined heels into his mare's flanks but she crossed the field in a weary amble, refusing to be urged.

Impatiently the Red Knight raised the visor of his helmet. 'Will the coward carry a lance against me, boy,' he shouted, 'or has he found a champion amongst those fops and braggarts?'

'You must answer to me, traitor,' Parzival shouted back. When the knight only frowned at him in dumbstruck astonishment, he raised his voice again. 'In the king's name, lay down your arms.'

'What? Does Arthur mock me?' the Red Knight growled. 'Out of my way, churl.'

And with that he wheeled his charger and fetched Parzival such a blow about the head with the side of his lance that the youth rocked in his saddle. For a stunned instant his brains were ringing like a belfry, then he recovered his balance, saw the knight shimmering before him in a scarlet haze, and without thinking, in a hot reflex of rage, he lifted his javelin and let it fly with such unerring force that it smashed through the socket of the Red Knight's eye and stuck there quivering.

It happened so quickly that the Red Knight never knew what killed him. Staring sightlessly at Parzival from the other, undamaged eye, he sat there, supported by his saddle, for what felt like an age. Then, sensing a lack of tension on the reins, his charger snorted uneasily and vigorously shook its neck. Pulled to one side by the weight of the javelin, the dead knight crashed to the ground.

Parzival's heart jumped at the din. He was staring down at the man in a trance of dismay when the jester came running up to stand beside him. 'Great God, an ignoble death for a noble knight,' he panted, 'but as good as any for one who would have cuckolded the King! What is it, lad? You're white as a woman.'

'I've never killed a man before,' said Parzival.

'Well you've done it now,' said Antenor with a dry chuckle. 'And all Caerleon watches from the walls. Don't let them see you trembling. Dismount, lad. Take up this armour that you've won.'

Numb with shock still, seeking refuge in obedience, Parzival slid down from his mare and bent down over the dead knight. He put his hand to the crimson breast-plate and tugged at it, but nothing moved. Nor could he shift the great fluted pauldron at the knight's shoulder. He looked up, white-faced at Antenor.

'It won't come off,' he gasped. 'I'll have to cut him to bits to get at it!'

Shaking a disbelieving head, Antenor said, 'Have you never seen buckles before? Here let me.' Unceremoniously he heaved the knight over, and began to undo the vivid suit of armour piece by piece. 'A good job your dart took him through the brains,' he said as he worked. 'There's not a spot of blood on this fine silk.' He unlaced the tunic the knight wore beneath his armour, pulled it off and offered it to the trembling youth. 'Now you can get rid of those farmyard clouts you're wearing. Come on,' Antenor encouraged as Parzival stood there, rigid, shaking his head, 'this is all yours now.'

'My mother made me these clothes. I'll not change them.' Parzival picked up the breastplate and tried to fit it in place across the dusty folds of his sackcloth hauberk. 'The armour is all I want. That and my javelin.'

Tutting with disapproval as he helped the boy strap the armour on, Antenor said, 'You can't use that again. It's a peasant's weapon. No, it's the lance and sword for you from now on. And I can't say I care much for the idea of you going back into court dressed like a clod for Gawain to scoff at!'

'I'm not going back,' Parzival answered in a hoarse whisper. 'I don't belong in that place. Not yet. Not ever perhaps.'

Antenor studied the youth shrewdly, in awe of such invincible honesty. 'Well, maybe you're right,' he said. 'But where will you go? What shall I tell the king?'

Parzival stared down at the glittering red helmet he held in his hands. His fingers softly caressed the plume of scarlet feathers. 'Tell him I know myself for a wild thing still,' he said, 'and that part of me at least is glad of it.' Then he plucked the holly leaves from his cowl and lifted the helmet over his head. He felt its weight. The encasing darkness closed round him. When he spoke again his voice sounded hollow and metallic. 'Tell him he won't see me again till the world knows me for a true knight.'

Watched by the jester, Parzival crossed to where the sorrel charger shivered and steamed near the body of its former master. He took hold of the red bridle, calmed the animal by breathing into its soft nostrils, then gripped the pommel. Feeling the unfamiliar weight of the armour on his limbs, he pulled himself into the saddle. From there he looked down where the body of the dead knight lay in an ungainly posture with blood oozing from his ravaged eye. It was not the first corpse he had seen since leaving home, but this one was his own creation. He had done this thing himself and it could never be undone. Only a few minutes earlier the knight had been filled with spirited and virile life. Now he was a dead, stripped, half-naked lump of carrion because Parzival had made him so.

The youth's head dizzied inside the dark helmet. He thought of the father he had never seen, dead in his blood like this, and food for worms. Inside that bright blue day a vortex of darkness had begun to spin. Staring into it, Parzival would have swayed and fallen had the high cruck of the saddle not held him there. He thought he would be overcome by nausea. So he closed his eyes against the sight of the corpse, and shook his head to clear it.

Somewhere high above him he heard the piercing sound of a buzzard's mew. He felt the horse's breath shudder under him. Then he pulled its great head round, grabbed the scarlet lance and shield that Antenor offered up to him, and without so much as a glance upwards to where the King and his court gazed down at him from the high walls of Caerleon, he dug his newly won spurs into the charger's flanks, and galloped away down the green hillside.

He had no idea where he was going. He rode quickly, stretching the limbs of the horse as though its speed might carry him away from the hideous picture fixed in his mind. Eventually the shock of knowing himself a killer began to pass. It was displaced by a hectic sense of exhilaration at the power he commanded. He had done what none of Arthur's knights had dared to do. He alone had challenged the Red Knight to battle and won his horse and scarlet armour for himself. By killing a man he had proved himself a man. It was that simple. The whole wide world would have to answer to him now.

Towards evening he was crossing a broad meadow and beginning to flag from the hard day's ride, when he saw an old lord watching him from where he stood in the failing light with a hawk at his fist. Parzival reined in his horse and cried, 'God protect you, Good Sir.'

'And you too, Sir Knight,' the lord answered. 'Have you taken a wound?'

'No,' Parzival replied, puzzled by the question.

'Then you've a damned lax way of swinging your shield,' the old lord reproved him. 'You should grip it firmly – so.' He made a rigid gesture with his free arm.

'I'll remember that,' said Parzival, nodding. 'My mother told me always to take advice from grey-haired old men.'

Thinking this a curious response, the falconer grunted, then asked, 'Whose service do you ride in, lad?'

'I ride only in God's service, sir.'

With a tinkling ring of its jesses, the falcon stretched and fluttered its wings. The old man soothed its fierce head with a finger-tip. 'A good enough cause,' he said, '– if a lonely one. And God knows, there's no other Lord to be trusted these days! You're welcome to guest with me tonight,' he smiled, '– if an old man's gossip won't weary you.'

'I'd gladly do so,' Parzival answered, 'for I've ridden far and hard today, and I'm unused to the weight of these arms.'

Raising his eyebrows at the admission, the falconer said, 'You've a frank enough way with you, friend. Tell me, how shall I call you?'

'My mother calls me *Beau Fils*, but I've lately learned that my true name is Parzival.'

For a long moment the old man gaped at him in silence. Then – muttering, 'God be praised!' – he knelt down on one knee and bowed his white head. When he raised his face again, a smile of both sorrow and wonder wrinkled his eyes. 'I am Gurnemanz, my Lord, who was once Marshal to your mother, the Lady Herzeloyde, and your own true man till death. As were my three sons,' he added sadly, 'who gave their lives fighting for your cause.'

Night had not yet come, but again Parzival felt as though he was staring into an impenetrable darkness. 'It seems too many have already died for me,' he said.

'But your lands, my Lord,' Gurnemanz sighed, shaking his white locks, '– your lands are all lost. We couldn't hold them against the might of Duke Orilus.'

Parzival saw the sorrow in those ancient eyes. 'Lands can be regained,' he said, 'but you have suffered more grievously. This Duke shall answer for it.'

Gurnemanz glanced up where the lad sat proudly on his horse. For a moment his veteran heart lifted, then he took in the clumsy way the rough sackcloth stuck out here and there under the scarlet armour. He recalled the gaucheness of the boy, the inexperience that made a mockery of his fine equipment, the madness of his mother, and – over against all this – the terrible nature of the times.

'Yes, well ... I don't doubt it, Lord,' he muttered. 'But come, you are weary. We shall bathe and dine you in my house. Our condition is less comfortable than once was, but my daughter and I will care for you as best we can.' Gurnemanz lifted his arm and released the hawk. With a tinkling of bells from its jesses, the bird circled the darkling sky, then flew homeward to announce its master's imminent return.

Liaze, the daughter of Gurnemanz, came with her maids to disrobe Parzival that evening. All of them were impressed by the youth's fair and open face, his clear eyes and honest features, the broad shoulders and the lithe, muscular strength of his limbs. All of them were appalled by the sackcloth jerkin with its rough cowl that were revealed when they removed his armour. Their muffled giggling turned to dismay when, with fierce blushes of protest, he refused to take them off.

Amused by his bashful pride, Liaze had a quiet word with her father, who came to see Parzival in his chamber. 'My daughter tells me you refused the raiment I sent you from my son's own wardrobe, lord,' he said. 'Did it not please you?'

'Forgive me, Gurnemanz,' – Parzival blushed again, remembering how the maids had giggled at him – 'but my mother made me these clothes. She told me not to part with them.'

'Hmmm, I see. Well, your mother is a good woman, Lord, but ...' Gurnemanz faltered there, sensing this innocent could have no understanding of how far the Lady Herzeloyde's wits had gone astray.

He thought for a moment, then began again. 'Did she never speak to you of your father?'

'I have no father. My father is dead in his blood and food for worms.'

'I know it. I watched him ride out to his death when you were but a fortnight old. But it's been a sad lack, Lord. A youth needs a father's guidance.'

'Yet my mother has given me good advice.'

Gurnemanz grunted. 'Could she teach you how to hold a shield?'

'No, Gurnemanz, but she ...'

'Enough of your mother, boy,' the old Marshal interrupted testily. 'Will you wear these bumpkin's clothes till they stink? Come, my Lord, it's time you dressed like the prince you are.'

'But my mother told me ...'

'Always to take a greybeard's counsel!' Gurnemanz silenced him. 'If you mean to win back your lost lands ... well, that's man's work, boy, and you'll find it takes manly knowledge. Only a man can give you that. One who knows how this world wags. Tell me, are you skilled in the use of the arms you won with that damned javelin? No, I thought not. Then try to raise a lance against Duke Orilus, where he presently advances against my Lady Blanchefleur's citadel at Belrepaire, and he'll crush you in your armour like a snail!'

Not at all discountenanced, Parzival sprang to his feet, hotly demanding to know where he could find that place, as though he would be ready to ride there that night as soon as he had eaten.

Gurnemanz gazed up at the lad, shaking his head with a rueful smile. 'You've got your father's blood in you all right. But you stand in sore need of counsel. And of some hard training too.'

'Then you must help me, Gurnemanz.'

'Did I not say I was your man?' The grizzled veteran sighed at the lad's rash confidence. 'Very well, stay with me a while, Lord, and I'll teach you everything I know.' Half in despair, he laughed at the eager light in the youth's eyes. 'Damn me, we'll see if your mother's old Marshal can't make a proper man of you.'

So, for many weeks, Parzival lived in the house of Lord Gurnemanz, and the Marshal was as good as his word. Day-in and day-out he drilled the youth in the skills of lance and shieldwork, watching him tilt at the quintain first, then against an experienced jouster, who unseated him again and again till Parzival began to learn from his bruises to keep his eye fixed, his balance steady, and his head cool. There were the arts of horsemanship to be learned too, and the dexterous use of sword and mace, both from horseback and on foot, together with the names and use of all the engines of war.

Each day made Parzival more conscious of his ignorance, so he battered his mentor with question after question, never letting a problem slip till he felt he'd got the measure of it, then immediately turning to some other area where his knowledge was deficient. Each question seemed to father another in endless eager interrogation until Gurnemanz almost exploded with impatience, for not all of them were to do with straightforward matters of fighting and war.

Parzival had not been lumbering about the house for long, for instance, before everyone saw how badly he needed instructing in the rudiments of polite behaviour. With the help of Liaze, who took an amused and affectionate interest in the ups and downs of the young man's belated education, Gurnemanz set about doing what he could to improve the lad's table manners, dress sense, and the more refined aspects of courtly accomplishment. Their laughter at his awkward efforts sometimes left Parzival feeling glum as an ox, but when Gurnemanz despaired of him, Liaze would pull him out of the dumps, and tease him into believing that if he brought the same enthusiasm to learning courtly behaviour that he did to fighting on horseback, he might have the makings of a gentleman.

By high summer his perseverance began to show remarkable results, and as Parzival's confidence grew so did his restlessness. One evening he sat at dinner with Gurnemanz, unusually silent. Wondering whether the lad's spirits had sunk again, the old Marshal congratulated him on the neat way he'd thrust his sparring partner back over his horse's cruppers in the tiltyard that afternoon. 'I'm beginning to think there's nothing much more we can teach you there,' he said.

Parzival nodded silently. He emptied his tankard of ale, drew a deep breath and looked up at his old friend. 'I have another question.'

'God, spare me!' groaned Gurnemanz. 'I was beginning to hope I'd heard the last of your damned questions for one day at least. Well, fill me this tankard first.' Parzival crossed to the barrel, filled the tankard, and put it down in front of Gurnemanz, who took a swig, wiped the foam from his beard with the back of his hand, and sighed, 'All right, what is it?'

'Am I not ready?' Parzival asked.

Gurnemanz took another drink. 'Ready?'

'To go forth and reclaim my lands. I've had enough of practising in the tiltyard. I'm eager to break a lance with that traitor Orilus.'

The more deeply he'd grown attached to the youth, the more Gurnemanz had come to dread this moment. 'I hear your father's voice there, Parzival,' he said.

The youth shrugged, glanced away. 'You are all the father I've ever known,' he declared quietly. When he looked back again, he was surprised to see a damp glint in the old man's eyes.

Gurnemanz reached his hand across the table and laid it over Parzival's clenched fist. 'Then would you rather not bide here till I die?'

Smiling, the youth shook his head. 'I think there are many years left in you, old warhorse. But if something is not done soon, then Belrepaire must fall.'

'I know, I know,' Gurnemanz said gruffly, 'yet the world out there is near to hell, boy. It may beat you down as it has beaten me. I couldn't bear to watch that happen. Listen a while, I beg you. My daughter is unwed. She's yours if you'll have her. Stay and make a life with us rather than courting death out there.'

'You honour me, old friend,' said Parzival, 'but you forget I have a light to follow. I think my life depends on it.' He smiled into the Marshal's uncertain eyes. 'As to your daughter – Liaze is obedient and will do as you ask, I know. But I very much doubt that you have asked her. And if you did, and she spoke true, I know you would find she cares for me, but only as a sister cares for her brother. I think if I am to have a wife, I must win one for myself.'

Gurnemanz studied the young man in silence for a long time. Already having buried three sons, he was reluctant to risk losing Parzival now. Yet he knew that everything the lad had said was true. 'Well, you have strength and heart, and a noble will,' he said at last, 'and God forbid I should come between a true knight and his destiny.' The old Marshal sniffed loudly, pulled himself together. 'So – to answer your last question then: I suppose you're as ready as any man I know. It's time for me to let you go.'

Both elated and humbled to hear himself called a true knight at last, Parzival said solemnly, 'I vow you shall be proud of me.'

'I'm that already – though God knows there's one last important lesson you've yet to learn.'

'What's that?' Parzival demanded eagerly, and was taken aback by the old man's answering chuckle. 'Tell me, what is it? What do I still need to know?'

'Not to ask so many damned questions!' laughed Gurnemanz. 'You still make too frank a show of your innocence. Once you're out in the world, remember this – only fools and spies ask questions.' He tapped the table with his finger, adding, 'A wise knight never willingly reveals his ignorance.' Then his grizzled old face crackled into laughter again as he saw Parzival mentally digesting his words.

'I'll not forget it,' the youth promised, then he too was laughing, laughing with a wry mixture of affection and dismay at the ignorant young oaf he'd once been. 'With God's help,' he declared, 'and after your good instruction, my dear Lord Marshal, no one shall ever again take Parzival for a fool!'

CHAPTER FIVE

CONDWIRAMURS

o once more Parzival rode out into the world, though with every mark of a noble knight about him now.

A day's journey brought him to where the besieged citadel of Belrepaire stood on a narrow headland overlooking the sea. Looking down on the city from the brow of a nearby hill, he saw a small force sally out across the drawbridge in an attempt to end the siege by capturing the traitor Duke. Taken unawares, the besieging troops momentarily gave ground under the onslaught, but the Duke quickly rallied them, the attackers were pushed back on to the defensive, and soon they were caught up in a desperate struggle to regain the bridge.

Shouting the battlecry, 'For God, Lady Blanchefleur and Belrepaire,' Parzival lowered his visor, dug his spurs into the horse's flanks and galloped down the hillside to their aid. The force of his unexpected charge carried him through the Duke's soldiers into the rout at the bridgehead where his lance shattered against the helmet of a mounted knight, unseating him and almost taking off his head. A blow from the broken haft knocked down a foot-soldier who came at him with an axe, and then his sword was out of its scabbard and cutting to left and right with a skill that needed neither space nor time for thought. From high on his huge sorrel horse, his scarlet armour shining in the windy light off the sea, Parzival commanded the fight like a man possessed by his destiny. Blanchefleur's men regrouped under his protection, falling back towards the bridge. Only when the last of them had crossed did Parzival wheel his horse and follow them over the moat into the city. He heard the sound of a windlass whirring in one of the bastions as the iron portcullis crashed down behind him.

With a hand pressed to an open wound on his arm, the captain of the company dismounted and came to salute him. 'God bless you, Sir Knight,' he panted. 'Had you not made your stand, I fear the enemy must have forced the bridge.' Then he turned to a herald, saying, 'Escort this valiant gentleman to our Lady. She will have seen his exploits from the tower and will wish to thank him.'

As he was led through the streets of the beleaguered city, Parzival's eyes smarted from the smoke drifting from burned-out houses. Some were in flames still, others mere shells of blackened timber where blazing missiles of sulphur and tar had been hurled by siege-engines across the city walls. Women and children lay famished among the ruins, bewildered monks muttered over their beads, and the groans of the injured and dying made those buildings which had been turned into rough hospitals seem places of terror rather than relief. Parzival had seen death and suffering before, but not on this scale. By the time he was brought into the presence of the Lady Blanchefleur his heart was banging at his chest with pity and rage. Yet at his first sight of the Lady it stood quite still.

Slender and proud, with all the gauntness of a young face that had chosen to share the grief and hunger of her realm, she came towards him, holding out her hands to take his, almost as though they were old friends re-met rather than strangers encountering each other for the first time. 'I could wish you found us in better state to welcome you, sir,' she said. 'But such scant comforts as are left to us are yours, for I and my city stand greatly in your debt.'

As if from a high and breathless distance, Parzival heard himself saying, 'Lady, I would rather bear great hardships for your sake than live in luxury elsewhere.'

'Then Belrepaire will be sadly to your taste,' she answered with a wan smile. 'Duke Orilus presses us hard. We scarcely have strength to withstand another day.' A sigh clouded her face. 'You have come to us bravely, sir, though not wisely, I fear. But come, let us disarm you. Tonight you shall dine at my side.'

To the sound of sad music they ate a frugal meal together in the great hall, and though the company of lords and ladies sought to cheer them as best they could, Blanchefleur was oppressed by the thought of the coming day, and Parzival was strangely silent. In part he was hampered by the old Marshal's advice not to ask questions, and his native shyness made him slow to answer those that were put to him. Blanchefleur was too discreet to press her guest and, when others tried, no more than a flustered mumble passed his lips. The truth was, that after the fine, impulsive flourish of the first words he had spoken to her, Parzival found himself dumb-struck with love for the Lady of Belrepaire.

That night he lay tossing and turning in his bed, furious at his failure to utter the love that was burning inside him now. It was as though a bright shaft had pierced his eyes at the first sight of Blanchefleur, and he could have cried out loud for the agitation in his soul. Yet his inability to speak had left him stranded alone on a cusp between ecstasy and pain from which he had no idea how to release himself, nor any certainty that he wished to do so.

At last he fell asleep from sheer exhaustion, but he had not been sleeping long when he was woken again by a muffled stirring in the room. His eyes were still closed when he recognized the sound of weeping, and when he opened them, the room was dark. He called, 'Who's there?'

As though summoned through the night by the urgency of his need, a woman's voice – the voice of Blanchefleur – quietly answered him through its veil of grief. 'Gentle knight, have pity on me.'

At once Parzival was up from his bed and crossing the dark room to where she stood in her white gown with her hands clasped softly together at her mouth, saying, 'Do not think badly of me. I haven't slept for many nights now. Good sir, I need a friend.'

'You have a friend in me, Lady,' he answered hoarsely. 'A loving friend and a servant unto death.'

'But I don't want your death,' she turned away, sighing. 'There has been too much of death and dying. My people starve. Arthur sends us no aid. I know my city must fall tomorrow, and then death will dance everywhere. Duke Orilus will take me, and all the dying will have been in vain.'

Parzival reached out and took her hands in his. 'Do not think so, Lady,' he whispered. 'It may be that God has sent you better fortune than you think.'

'I pray so, for my people's sake. Were it not for them I would kill myself rather than let Orilus take me.'

'Take heart,' said Parzival. 'I mean to challenge him tomorrow.'

'No, I pray you,' she protested. 'Orilus is terrible in battle. No one can stand against him. Do not throw away your life for me.'

'I have my own cause against him, Lady ... though, believe me, I will fight all the harder now because of the love I feel for you.'

The two young people stood together in silence for a time, veiled by darkness, scarcely able to breathe above the clamour of their hearts, scarcely daring to believe the care and hope that each was finding in the other now.

'Dear friend,' sighed Blanchefleur at last, 'there is so much I want to say. But the night is short, it will soon be light and, if you truly mean to do this thing, then I must let you rest.' Reluctantly she turned away from him, but he would not release her hand. Holding on to its soft warmth, sighing at such imminent loss, Parzival said, 'May I not first have a kiss?'

'With all my heart,' she answered.

Their lips met, tenderly and shyly, in a soft, mutual exchange of spirit, and for those rapt moments it seemed that the night held still around them. Gazing down into the eyes of Blanchefleur, Parzival whispered, 'Henceforth, my Lady, I shall call you Condwiramurs, for you have led me into love.'

'I shall bear that name joyfully,' she answered, 'before all the world. But if we are ever to know that joy, you must rest yourself now.'

'I shall rest better this night,' he said, 'if you do not leave me.' He heard the indrawn catch of her breath, felt her uncertainty. 'In my mother's name,' he reassured her, 'I ask no more than kisses of you.'

Blanchefleur stood across from him, caught between the claims of modesty and those of her heart's desire, but the deeper she gazed into his entreating eyes the more clearly she recognized the purity of the heart reflected there. 'If it is your wish,' she said at last.

So all that night they lay chaste as infants in each other's arms, falling deeply into innocent sleep, and deeper still into the patient innocence of their love.

The next morning, Duke Orilus was planning his final assault on the city when he was called from his pavilion by a fanfare of trumpets from the walls. Anticipating an offer of surrender, he smiled at his companions and went out to hear the voice of a herald carried on a stiff breeze off the sea. To his amazement he learned that the Lady Blanchefleur of Belrepaire had found in the Red Knight a champion willing to fight with him in single combat.

'This whole city falls to me today,' Orilus shouted back, snorting with incredulity. 'Why should I take such a risk?'

He saw the scarlet glitter of the Red Knight's armour, and was answered by another voice. 'Because Parzival of Wales brands you coward if you do not.'

Put out of countenance by this unexpected show of resistance, Duke Orilus turned to his lieutenant, demanding to know who the devil Parzival of Wales might be. 'My Lord,' the lieutenant answered, 'I think he is the mad queen's son.'

'You owe me lands, traitor,' Parzival shouted down from the walls. 'You have slain many who fought in my cause, and now use force against my Lady of Belrepaire and her fair city. Do you dare to take the field in final quittance of this and all other disputes, or will you have the world mock you for a craven knave?'

'The youth must be crazy himself,' scoffed the lieutenant.

'But he challenges my honour,' said Orilus, 'and the world is listening. Bring me my lance and horse.'

At that moment a young woman in dirty and ragged clothes who had been listening to the exchange came running towards the Duke and threw herself down at his feet, panting and tear-stained in her bedraggled finery. 'No, Orilus,' she cried, 'the risk is needless.' The Duke tried to shrug her off, shouting, 'Get this whore from my sight.' Immediately his companions came to tear the woman away. Once free of her, Orilus glowered back up at his challenger. 'You'll get no more than your length in land from me, Welshman,' he shouted. 'Come down and fight me if you dare.'

The wind blew among the tresses of Blanchefleur's hair as she watched Parzival ride out to meet the Duke in combat. He was wearing her favour of white lilies for a plume. They gleamed, white and brave, against his scarlet helmet as he raised his lance in salute to her before crossing the drawbridge. Then her heart shook like a banner in the wind as she watched the Duke ride out from the cheering throng of his troops, formidable in his black armour, his huge stallion tossing its head. With a grim smile, he too raised his lance to her before snapping shut the jutted snout of his visor and wheeling his horse for the charge.

At the shock of the first onset both lances shattered and both horses came ungirthed. Thrown to the ground in the same instant, both knights were winded and staggering a little as they got to their feet. Dimly aware of the shouts coming from the crowd around him and the anxious watchers on the walls, Parzival raised his shield just in time to fend off a swingeing blow from the Duke's mace. It was followed instantly by another. The clang of metal on metal rang in his ears. The impact shook his bones and dented his shield, but he swerved lithely aside, found space to draw his sword, and held the Duke's next assault at bay. Uttering a dismissive snort, Orilus tossed his mace and shield aside, drew his own huge, double-handed sword from the scabbard at his horse's flank and, with a gesture of his gauntleted hand, muttered, 'Come then, coxcomb, let's see how red you are on the inside now!'

Slicing the air with his blade, he strode towards Parzival, who gave ground, biding his time, hearing the sword swoosh through space he had just vacated or parrying its force with the edge of his own sword. He could hear Orilus grunting inside his helmet, and knew that if the Duke's strength was mighty, his own was younger and fitter, and just as formidable once unleashed. So he waited, shielding himself from strike after strike, until his opponent was unbalanced by the momentum of his own assault. In that critical moment, he seized the chance to come back with a blow that smashed the Duke's visor off its hinges, and was almost powerful enough to strike the whole helmet from his head. Sparks brightened the air. Orilus staggered beneath the impact. For a dizzy second or two, he stood reeling, and then, overwhelmed almost as much by shock as by the vigour of the next blow that Parzival brought down across his casque, he crashed backwards to the ground.

Instantly Parzival was over him, the point of his sword at a crack in the Duke's gorget, demanding that he yield.

Panting and breathless, hearing the wind buffeting against the sudden silence of his army, Orilus shook his head. 'No,' he groaned. 'You must finish me, knight.'

Wondering at the grim, obstinate light in the man's eyes, Parzival said, 'I would rather put you at the mercy of this city.'

'The mob would tear me to pieces,' Orilus glowered. 'As you are a true knight, give me honourable death.'

Uncertain, panting himself, a little dazed by the suddenness of victory, Parzival might have been alone in the universe with his fallen enemy. He was remembering Sigune's murdered lover, the three dead sons of Gurnemanz, and all the wounded, dead and dying inside the walls of Belrepaire. He was thinking of Blanchefleur gazing down on him from those walls, of the tenderness of her heart, and of the great harm this man would have done her. Orilus smirked up at him with a kind of grim, indifferent disdain, then closed the lids of his eyes.

Even as Parzival drew in his breath and tightened his grip round the haft of his sword, he became aware of a woman at his side, reaching to stay his hand with a beseeching arm. Her clothes were no more than blowing rags. Her pallid face streamed with tears. 'Spare him, Sir Knight,' she was pleading quietly. 'For pity's sake, I beg you.'

'Would you shame me, whore?' Orilus growled up at her.

'Who is this lady?' Parzival asked.

But the woman spoke for herself. 'I am the Lady Jeschute. For the love of this man I cry you mercy, knight.'

Puzzled by the familiar ring of the name, Parzival looked at her more closely. He saw how those eyes might once have shone, how that pale face might once have been glamorous with paint. He caught the memory of a vanished fragrance.

'We have met before, Lady,' he said. 'In a rich pavilion one day, when this torn gown you wear was beautiful. It was I who rudely stole your ring.'

Jeschute stared in amazement at the vivid, scarlet figure confronting her. 'It's not possible ...' she began, but when Parzival lifted the helmet from his head, she too found something familiar in the face that smiled at her. 'Great God,' she cried, 'then you are the cause of all my wrongs. This Duke spurned me when I lost that ring. He forbade me to wear anything but these rags till he had taken vengeance on the youth he thought had made a cuckold of him. If you have any pity, defend my honour, sir. Tell him I am no man's whore.'

Parzival looked down at his truculent foe. 'What she says is true. The fault is all mine.'

'What difference does it make?' Orilus scowled up at him. 'You've just robbed me of my honour another way. Spare me the shame of living without it.'

But now Parzival shook his head and looked back at Jeschute. 'Did I not say I would repay you, Lady? If you ask me for this man's life, I cannot refuse it. Get up, sir,' he said, sheathing his sword, and offering a hand to the fallen man.

Scorning help, Orilus got to his feet. 'In all honour, you should have killed me, knight,' he said. 'Where shall I go now? How shall I show my face?'

'Go with this lady to Arthur's court,' said Parzival, 'and submit yourself in my name to the Lady Cunneware.'

'What!' Duke Orilus snorted. 'Cunneware is my sister!'

Remembering that lady's laughter, and laughing himself now with amazement at such wizardry of circumstance, Parzival glimpsed in that triumphant moment how lasting peace might be restored only through an active generosity of the heart. 'Then tell your sister that in my ignorance I wronged you once,' he said, 'and that Parzival of Wales bids King Arthur show you honour.'

Only then did he become conscious of the loud cheering and shouting of his name from the walls of Belrepaire, and as he turned to gaze up to where the Lady Blanchefleur waited to lead him further into love, there came another, more distant cry of 'A sail, a sail!', and the air was loud with the ringing of bells as the ship that Arthur had sent to the relief of Belrepaire scudded before the wind into the harbour.

And so, in one brave day, the unruly power of Duke Orilus was overthrown, the siege was raised, a time of plenty returned to the famished city, and amid great feasting and rejoicing Parzival and his Condwiramurs were wed.

That night they were led in state to the bridal chamber where they lay together on a silken bed. Parzival gazed down in wonder at the beautiful young woman who was now his wife. 'Only yesterday,' he said, 'I would have thought it heaven simply to touch the hem of your gown.'

'And now, my lord,' Blanchefleur smiled back at him, 'I am entirely yours.'

Eagerly their two bodies moved together, but even as Parzival's arms closed round his bride in the warm embrace of their kiss, he heard the voice of his mother instructing him that he might honour ladies with kisses but was forbidden to take more. So caught between obedience and desire, he held his lady tenderly in his arms, kissing her about the lips and eyes and cheeks, until weariness overcame him and he slept.

In the morning Blanchefleur woke to find herself a maiden still. Yet she knew Parzival for her husband and that she herself was deeply his wife, so she tied her hair in a fillet such as matrons wear, and publicly invested Parzival with all her lands, so that all the country recognized him as her lord and prince. And again, on the second night, she meekly waited for more than the loving kisses that he gave her. Again, making no further demands, he fell asleep in her arms.

On the third night, however, as Parzival bestowed his last affectionate kiss on his wife, and bade her sleep well, Blanchefleur asked quietly, 'Do you not love me, my lord?'

'With all my heart,' he answered.

'Yet you desire no more than kisses of me?'

'I do, Lady,' he said uncertainly, 'but I think it would be a great shame to force more from you.'

Perplexed by this, Blanchefleur leaned over him. 'What need is there for force, my dear, when such sweet pleasures are the whole of my desire?'

'But the Lady Jeschute once considered me a beast and a brute for taking so much as a kiss from her,' he said uncertainly.

'Yet was there any delicacy of feeling such as trembles between us now?'

'How could there have been? I had no love for her as I love you.'

'And do you not know what love allows between a woman and a man?' she asked him, smiling.

'I know what my mother taught me.'

Gently she laughed at his bewildered innocence. 'Mothers are very dear, my love,' she said, 'but they are not always wise. Let go of her now. Come here and hold me close, like this.'

So Blanchefleur drew her husband down into the warm clasp of her embrace, and that night their bodies met in a long, waking dream of tenderness and passion. And when, later, Parzival saw his wife smiling as she slept, he felt that he held in his arms all that a man could hope to know of happiness.

Over the following weeks Parzival and his Condwiramurs began work on the restoration of their city, intending that Belrepaire should be even more lovely than it had been before the siege. One day as they stood on a high balcony of the palace surveying the progress of the work, Parzival found himself wondering aloud about his good fortune, how he had won the fairest of brides by following God's light, and how if his mother had had her way, he might still be alone with her in the wilderness, living an impoverished life filled with obscure yearnings. 'It seems,' he said, 'that she was wrong about many things.'

'Yet can it be God's will that she remain alone in the wild?' Blanchefleur asked, suddenly aware of the contrast between their own happiness and the wretched condition of her husband's mother. 'Should she not come to us here?'

'Then she might see that the world is less a place of suffering than of joy!' Parzival exclaimed.

'Oh yes, my dear,' his wife answered, 'let her be sent for at once.'

But Parzival remembered how timidly his mother had always shied from strangers, keeping both herself and her son hidden like grouse in the bracken whenever anyone passed by. He told Blanchefleur of the terror in her eyes when she had learned of his chance encounter with Arthur's knights. 'I fear,' he said, 'that she will come at no one's bidding but my own.'

'You are wiser in this than I,' Blanchefleur answered quietly, 'though I can scarcely bear the thought of parting from you. And the world beyond Belrepaire is full of dangers still.'

'Yet am I not Parzival,' he said, 'who slew the Red Knight and defeated Orilus? See how God protects and favours me.'

'And before God I am your own true wife. Yet there are fears in my heart.'

'Then let my strength allay them.' He pulled her into his embrace, smiling down into her troubled eyes. 'Don't you see? – I am God's own knight. I need only follow his light and no one can stand against me. Our love is sacred, my Condwiramurs. The world holds nothing strong enough to prevent my swift return.'

And so, true wife and husband, true lovers and true friends, they wept at parting, and the knight rode out alone into the wilderness, proud and confident, and utterly unaware of the anguish that lay in wait for him.

CHAPTER SIX

THE

RICH FISHERMAN

nce across the border of his own kingdom, Parzival passed through a terrain still laid waste by war. Autumn was coming but no harvest stood in the blackened fields. The day was silent and sultry. Even the sky itself seemed famished for light among dense clouds, and a torpid mist hovered over the dreary marshland through which he rode. By late afternoon he could scarcely see his way through the fog, and it wasn't long before he had lost all sense of direction, so he loosened his grip on the reins, trusting his horse to guide him across the grey dream of these wastes.

After a time, a light breeze blew the fog to thinner rags. It cleared still further as he came out through the trees to where a fading misty glare still hung across the shadowy span of a mere. Not far from the shore a boat idled at anchor with two men aboard. One lay patiently asleep beside the shipped oars. The other, a gaunt figure in fine clothing with a plume of peacock feathers shining on the crown of his hat, sat fishing from the prow. His line hung limp in waters so still that the boat floated on a perfect reflection of itself.

'God protect you, good sirs,' Parzival called across the water. 'The day grows late and I am weary. Do you know where I might find shelter for the night?'

Unsurprised, the angler stared back at him for a moment, then spoke in a voice that sounded hoarse with pain. 'I know of no house around this lake for thirty miles or more, save one.'

'Then I pray you, direct me there.'

The angler gestured with his free hand. 'Follow the crag by the shore till you come to a cleft in the rock. Ride through, and from the summit you'll see a mansion between the river and the woods. Bid them drop the bridge for you.' Then he returned his gaze to the motionless float of his line where mist had begun to thicken across the lake again.

Parzival thanked him and turned his horse's head in the direction to which the angler had pointed. He was about to ride on when the voice behind him said, 'Take care, knight. There are paths that will lead you astray in the failing light.'

'God willing,' Parzival answered, 'I'll be there before night falls.'

'Find the right way,' said the angler as the mist closed round him, 'and you shall have royal entertainment of me there.'

Again Parzival called out his thanks, though he could see nothing now of either the angler or the boat, so he followed the track at the foot of the crag until he came to the mouth of a gorge where a river sluiced over rocks into the lake.

The gorge rose steeply through the crag. He heard the sound of his horse's hooves on the rocks and the cawing of rooks as the dusk thickened round them. Otherwise, apart from the clattering of water among stones, the day dwindled into silence.

The climb took longer than he expected and by the time he reached the high ridge of the crag the light was almost gone. Parzival strained his eyes to peer into the gloom between the river and the wood but there was no sign of the promised house. Thinking he must have missed his way, he cursed his luck, and was preparing himself for a cold night out under the stars when a pallid shaft of moonlight gleamed through a gap in shifting clouds. Its radiance glimmered on the waters of a moat, and suddenly, as if condensing on the mist, a noble house appeared.

Parzival dug his heels into his horse's flanks and approached the moat. The bridge was drawn up over the gateway. Stone bastions rose high and windowless above him. There were no banners at the turrets, no sentinels anywhere in sight. The place might have been quite deserted, but he had been promised entertainment here, so he cupped his hand at his mouth and shouted up into the darkness, 'Let down the bridge, ho!'

'At whose bidding?' a voice demanded, echoing across the moat.

'My name is Parzival of Wales. The angler on the lake bids me shelter here.'

'Then if the Rich Fisherman sends you, friend,' came the voice through the gloom, 'be welcome here at Montsauvage.'

Amid the creak of a windlass and the clanging of iron chains, the bridge was lowered across the moat. Parzival rode over and dismounted in the dark courtyard. Eagerly, as though he had been long expected, four pages hurried to meet him. While one of them stabled his horse, the others led him through into a chamber where they disarmed him and prepared a bath for his aching limbs.

Parzival lay soaking in the warm water for a long time, wondering at the strange atmosphere of this place where everything had been prepared for his comfort, yet each move he made was watched with a kind of wary apprehension.

When he got out of the bath to dress himself he found that his clothes and armour had been taken away. He was standing naked in the chamber, about to call for a page, when one of the young men who had greeted him stepped out of the shadows, holding a robe that was finely woven from Arabian cloth-of-gold. 'My mistress Repanse de Joie bids you wear this mantle, sir,' he said, 'It is lent to you directly from her own person since no clothes have yet been cut for you.'

'Then for her sake,' Parzival answered, a little bemused, 'I shall wear it gladly.'

He slipped the mantle over his broad shoulders, leaving it unlaced at the neck. The page nodded his approval. 'If you will come this way, sir,' he said and led Parzival out of the chamber. Their footsteps were echoing down a long passage when a knavish fellow with a satirical glint in his eye stepped from behind a pillar and scoffed out loud as Parzival approached, saying, 'Who is this pretty fool in woman's clothing?'

Flushing, Parzival said, 'Take back that insult, sir,' but the man merely stepped to one side, leering at him with a cocked head as though he were a passing kitchen maid. 'Tell me, my sweet,' he whispered, 'what manner of bauble do you hide beneath that robe?'

Parzival reached to where the sword should have been hanging at his side. Had it been there, he might have cut out the man's impudent tongue, but he was left with only his bare hand to raise against him. He had already lifted it to strike when the page came between them. 'Stay your hand, sir,' he said. 'This fellow is a licensed fool. Bear with him. The Rich Fisherman awaits you.'

Parzival was still disturbed by the low chuckle behind him as he mounted a flight of stone stairs at the page's bidding. They brought him through into a high vaulted hall where a grave company of knights waited for him, reclining on couches in the heat thrown from a fire that blazed in its marble hearth with a scent of bitter aloes. Chandeliers dangled from the vaults and more candles burned in sconces on the walls. By their flickering light Parzival saw where the lord of the house lay on a bed that had been made up for him close to the fireplace. Wearing a mulberry-coloured hat over the locks of his iron-grey hair, and wrapped in a sable robe, he supported himself awkwardly on one elbow as he raised his other hand in greeting to the guest.

'Forgive me,' he said, 'if I do not rise to meet you.' The handsome face was gaunt with pain, and his smile of welcome hardly more than a brief, wincing grimace.

'I pray you, sir,' said Parzival, 'do not disturb yourself.'

But the man gasped with sudden pain as he shifted his position. 'Come closer to the fire,' he said. 'Sit by me. Tell me where have you ridden from today.'

'At dawn this morning I left my dear wife in Belrepaire.'

'Then you have travelled far to reach Montsauvage. Your welcome shall be all the warmer.'

'And I am truly glad of it,' said Parzival. 'This day has been strange.' He saw his host wince again as he moved once more. The man's whole body might have been no more than a twisted instrument of pain that could find comfort nowhere, but he offered no explanation of his condition. Host and guest smiled at one another in silence. A log shifted in the blaze, sending sparks up into the dark.

'You were angling on the mere,' said Parzival, '– was your catch good?'

'Just the one, sir,' answered his host. 'But the first in a long time.'

At that moment a bell chimed, thrilling the candle-lit air with its bright pang of sound. As though at its summons, a page entered the hall, bearing a sword upright before him in its brightly jewelled scabbard and belt. He came to a halt at the bedside. 'My Lord, that fair lady your niece sends you this sword as a gift,' he declared. 'It is of such fine steel that it can be broken only by a means secret to all save he who tempered it. Should you choose to pass the sword on to another, my Lady would wish it used well by him on whom it is bestowed.'

Without reaching to take the sword, the Lord smiled at Parzival. 'Dear guest, I think this gift was destined for you,' he said. 'Try the weight of it, I pray you.'

Astonished by such generosity, Parzival got to his feet, took the richly-wrought scabbard from the page, put his hand to the hilt of the sword and drew it. The steel hissed into the air. He flourished the blade, watching it gleam in the candlelight, feeling its perfect balance in his grip.

'Do you approve it, friend?' asked his host.

'How could one not? This is a truly noble sword.'

'Then gird it on.'

'But, my Lord ...'

Grunting with sudden pain, the Lord silenced Parzival's protest and once more shifted position on the bed. 'You are our guest, sir,' he urged. 'The sword is yours.' There was such a wincing edge of impatience in the voice that the words sounded more like a command than a grant.

Gazing from his host's anguished face to the magnificent sword, and back again, Parzival whispered, 'This is a gift of great price. I thank you humbly for it.'

Preoccupied with his own pain, the lord groaned quietly to himself, then said, 'Remember my niece's wish. She would have the sword used well.'

'I swear it shall be, sir. In God's service and your own.'

'Good,' the man sighed, nodding his head. 'Good.'

Parzival was about to say more when the bell chimed again. At the far end of the hall a door was thrown open, and the whole assembled company began to murmur in a low, grieving sigh of lamentation that echoed from the vaults in a hollow moan. Distressed by the sound, wondering what it could portend, Parzival saw another page enter the hall, carrying a lance before him. The moaning of the company grew louder, like that of sleepers deep inside a troubling dream. Then, for a hot instant, Parzival's heart stopped in shock as he saw that the point of the lance was leaking blood. Bright gouts of it were streaming down the shaft and dripping onto the page's hands as he circled the grieving company, brandishing this vivid emblem of pain.

Astonished by the sight, Parzival turned to the Rich Fisherman open-mouthed. He was about to ask what the meaning of this mystery might be, when a warning voice sounded inside his head – the voice of his friend and mentor, Gurnemanz. 'Remember,' it said, 'only fools and spies ask questions.' So he kept silent and when he looked back the page with the lance had gone. From some high gallery came the solemn yet heart-exalting sound of music, and a stately procession of maidens entered the hall through another great door. They wore green gowns clasped with girdles of gold, and their hair was garlanded with flowers. Two of them held elaborately fashioned candlesticks. Behind them, came two others carrying a table made of some rare substance through which light was seen to shine, and these were followed by yet more maidens, bearing platters and knives, and a gleaming silver dish. When the table had been set down before the crippled fisherman, a ninth maiden, even more beautiful than the others, entered the hall dressed in white brocade of Araby. On a rich cloth of green and gold, she reverently set down that radiant stone which men call the Grail.

Already deeply stirred by these sights and sounds, Parzival gaped now as a bounteous feast seemed to fountain forth before him – hot foods and cold, foods both cultivated and wild, sweet and savoury dishes such as might please every palate; and whatever drink one might wish for was poured by the power of the Grail, which is the bliss and sacrament of every heart's desire.

'Eat, dear friend,' said the Rich Fisherman, and again and again as the banquet of joy unfolded round him, Parzival wanted to question his host about the great mystery of the Grail, and the abundance it served, and the beautiful maiden who seemed to be its guardian. Yet his mind and senses were spellbound by the very radiance of the Grail itself, and each time he was moved to speak, the words were stopped in his throat by the cautioning voice of his old tutor, Gurnemanz. 'Remember,' it said, 'a wise knight never willingly reveals his ignorance.'

So he sat on, marvelling in silent stupor, and when the feast was done and the Grail was borne away, another smaller door was opened, and through it Parzival glimpsed the serene figure of an old man lying on a bed in an inner chamber. The glimpse lasted an instant only – a mild shimmering of light off hair that glittered like hoar-frost about the kindly, ancient face – yet it filled the knight's heart with such tender longing that he felt that this must be among the most moving sights he would ever be privileged to see.

Then the door closed again. The music ended. In the vast silence of the hall, the Rich Fisherman said in a voice filled with sadness, 'You must be weary.'

Bewildered by all the wonders he had chanced upon in this strange place, Parzival felt himself overcome with sudden drowsiness. 'Yes,' he agreed, 'I need to sleep. There is much upon my mind.'

'Then your bed is ready for you.'

Parzival heard the pain in his host's voice, but he also caught the note of bitter disappointment. He tried to clear his head, struggling for consciousness of some offence he might have given, some distress he had unintentionally caused, some fault in himself. But he could think of nothing, and sleep was tugging at his senses, so he got to his feet, saying, 'I thank you for this entertainment, sir. I thank you with all my heart.' Then he was led out through the strangely silent company, back to his chamber, where he fell immediately into a thick and troubled sleep.

In his dreams Parzival heard the voice of Sigune beseeching him to find some gentler way to be a man, he heard the angler on the lake warning that there were paths that might lead him astray in the failing light, and he saw Gurnemanz across the table, quaffing ale and advising him to keep his mouth shut. Harassed by their repeated, conflicting demands, he woke with a lurch from this long and evil sleep to the wail of his mother's voice crying, 'Do not abandon me.' He heard himself shout out aloud that he was God's true knight. Then the morning light was cold and empty round him.

He got out of the bed, shouting for a page, but no one came. When he went to the door and shouted again, only his own voice echoed down the passage. Turning back into the room, he saw where his clothes and armour lay waiting for him. Someone must have returned them while he slept.

In puzzled distemper, his head still aching from the night, Parzival dressed and armed himself, girding on both his own sword and the sword which the crippled fisherman had given him. Then he walked back through into the hall and found it bare and empty. All trace of the grave company had vanished. There was no sound of servants stirring in the kitchen quarters, no food waiting for him. The house might have been derelict for many years.

Thinking that this was strange entertainment after the warm generosity of the previous evening, he passed back down the stone steps and out into the courtyard. The day glinted chilly and drear. The misty yard was utterly silent but for the caw of rooks and the snort of his horse that waited, harnessed and ready. His shield and lance had been placed beside it. The gate stood open, the bridge over the moat was down. Parzival gazed up at the high parapet on the walls, at the towers and balconies. Nothing moved. There was not a soul in sight.

Of all the mysteries he had encountered in that strange house, this was the most disturbing. He felt lonelier in that moment than at any time in his life. Yet in the same deranging instant he felt as though he was being watched, though he was sure by now that there was no one left in the house to watch him.

How long had he slept? Unnervingly he had no idea. He couldn't even be sure that this was the next day, that he hadn't lain for much longer than a single night in a drugged sleep on that bed. Nothing felt certain any more.

'Come, old fellow,' he said to his horse, 'let us leave this ghostly place.'

Parzival put his foot to the stirrup and climbed into the saddle. With a last, uneasy glance about him, he rode towards the open gate. The horse's hooves clattered against the cobbles. They resounded on the planks of the bridge. And then, as though the noise of his departure had disturbed the house where all his shouting had failed, the bridge began to lift as soon as he had crossed over it. Behind him, the gates clanged shut.

Startled by the noise, Parzival wheeled his horse to gaze up at the walls.

Still he saw no one, but a bitter voice shouted down through the mist rising off the moat. 'Begone, sleeper. May sunlight curse you where it falls. Do you lack a heart as you lack a tongue? Could you not ask the question?'

'What question?' Parzival shouted back, reining in his uneasy mount. 'What question should I have asked?'

'Look around you, fool. The hour is lost, the land lies waste, hope withers with it. And you who might have aided us have forfeited the greatest prize of all.'

The words echoed hollowly across the moat, and then were gone. It was as if the house itself was reviling him. Mist rose from the stagnant water, swathing the walls so that they seemed to shiver out of focus and dissolve before his eyes.

'I don't understand,' the baffled knight protested. 'Show yourself there. Come down and speak to me. Answer me, damn you!' But the only sound was that of the bridge banging shut against the gate.

Parzival's horse reared and snorted. His mind raced as he struggled to bring the uneasy animal back under control. In what way had he failed to aid his host? What had he done that he should be cursed like this? He could recall nothing in his manner or behaviour that merited such treatment.

Then the thought crashed across his mind that the assembled company must have ridden out to fight some desperate battle while he lay sleeping like a drunken fool. He could conceive of nothing else to account for their disappearance and the bitter charges that his unseen accuser laid against him. Perhaps it was not too late? Perhaps there was still time to bring aid to their cause?

Digging his spurs into the flanks of his horse, he galloped down from the ridge through the damp fog of a desolate landscape that seemed to parch and wither round him. The bleak air felt harsh and empty at his throat. He stopped by a slab of gaunt stone, stilling his horse, straining his ears to catch the din of battle. All he heard was the vague soughing of the wind. He pulled his horse's head round, galloped off in a different direction. The fog thickened. Soon he had lost all sense of his bearings.

CHAPTER SEVEN

BLOOD ON SNOW

or several hours Parzival urged his horse down treacherous screes, among a maze of fallen boulders, and in and out of the surrounding forest till he found it impossible to believe that he had not covered all the wild terrain in the vicinity of the castle. Yet he had seen no sign of anyone.

Baffled, heavy-hearted, he was following a trail through gloomy woodland when his ears caught a faint noise that made him pull his horse to a stop. After a moment he recognized the pitiful sound of weeping.

Urging his horse forward again, he turned into a glade. In the misty glare among the elms, he made out the figure of a young woman cradling an armoured knight in her lap. She glanced up at his approach, her face drawn and pallid, her eyes nervous. He saw that the crown of her head was quite bald but for a few wisps of frail white hair. 'Forgive me,' he said, dismounting, 'but I'm seeking the battle that must be raging somewhere around here. Was this knight injured in that affray?' Looking down to see what aid he could give, he realized that the man was strangely motionless.

'I know of no battle,' the lady said.

'But this man is dead, lady,' Parzival exclaimed.

The woman's tear-filled eyes looked down lovingly at the knight, then back up at Parzival as if refusing to admit the truth of what he had said. 'Where have you come from?' she asked vaguely.

'From the castle that stands over ...' – Parzival looked for the sun and could not see it – 'that way, I think. I've lost my bearings in this fog.'

'Who are you?' the woman demanded then with anxious eyes. 'Why do you lie to me? There are no houses in this waste for thirty miles or more.'

'But I swear to you there is such a place,' Parzival sought to reassure her. 'It stands on a crag between the mere and the woods. I came there by chance last night. The house is called Montsauvage.'

The woman drew in her breath, her eyes widened. 'Come closer,' she said. 'Let me see your face.' And when Parzival did as he was bidden, she gasped out loud. 'Do you not know me, Parzival?' she said. 'I am your cousin, Sigune, and this is my love who died for your sake.'

Parzival pulled back from the haggard face in shock and dismay. 'Dear God, Lady,' he said, 'what has become of you? Your hair ... when I saw you last, it fell about your shoulders, and now ...'

'Gone, cousin, all gone,' she answered, 'like the beauty of this knight. Look on us and judge of the great grief that God has given me.' With a frail arm, Sigune lifted the head of her dead lover so that Parzival could see his face. The wizened features of a rotting head bared its teeth at him. No more than scraps of skin clung to the skull, and blood-clotted hanks of hair. Parzival gagged as an odour of decay sickened the air he breathed. 'Lady,' he urged in a horrified whisper, 'we must bury this man.' Thinking to dig a grave, he drew from its scabbard the sword that the Rich Fisherman had given him, but the Lady recoiled in panic at the gesture, grasping the dead man more tightly.

'No, he is mine,' she cried, 'I will not let him go!'

'But cousin,' Parzival's eyes pleaded with her, 'the flesh rots on him.'

Sigune looked up and saw the jewelled hilt of the drawn sword gleaming over her. Again her eyes widened. 'I know that sword,' she gasped, white-faced. 'It will hold good for a time, then break in the hour of greatest need. How did you come by it?'

'My host gave it to me last night,' he said. 'But, Lady, I beg you, let me ...'

'What of Anfortas?' Sigune asked, wide-eyed. 'Is his wound then healed?'

'Do you mean the Rich Fisherman? Is that his name?'

'Yes, yes. But the wound? Tell me, I beg you.'

Parzival stood over her, shaking his head. 'I saw many wonders last night,' he said, 'but the healing of a wound was not among them.'

'But if you came to Montsauvage, if you saw the wound of Anfortas in the presence of the lance and the Grail ... Was that not how it was?'

'It was, but ...'

'Then in God's name, you must have asked the question?'

Again, as under the walls of Montsauvage, Parzival's head reeled in bewilderment. 'What question? Tell me, cousin, what should I have asked?'

Sigune stared up at him aghast. 'O sweet Jesu,' she whispered then, 'could you not see for yourself? Did you not see his suffering?'

'Yes, of course. I saw him suffering grievously at every movement.'

'And you could not find it in your heart to ask the cause of such great pain?'

Parzival's mouth grew dry. He felt the dumb beating of his heart inside his armour. His face flushed with shame. 'Lady,' he confessed, 'I did not ask it.'

'Then it has gone,' Sigune cried out, distraught. 'The Grail has vanished again, and all hope with it.' She lifted a hand to the bald crown of her head. Again her face was streaked with tears. From where he stood above her, Parzival was protesting that he did not understand, but she was gazing down at the death's head face of her lover, sighing, 'Do you hear him, my love? Do you hear this dumb fool for whom you threw away your life?'

'Speak more kindly, cousin,' Parzival said quietly. 'If I have failed you in some way, I shall strive to make amends.'

Sigune laughed at that, a brief, mirthless scoffing that rankled with despair. 'Dear God, do you think such a fault can be mended? To have come into the presence of the Grail, and failed! No, that can never be put right. Montsauvage has gone back into the mists. The chance is lost and gone. The land must still lie waste.' She glared fiercely up at him. 'And the fault of it is yours.'

As amazed and disturbed by her passion as he was convinced of his own innocence, Parzival said, 'You are unjust to me, cousin. I have vowed to serve the Rich Fisherman in every way I can.'

'Yet you lacked the heart to ask after his suffering!' Again Sigune uttered a brief, bitter laugh. 'I see it now. I could not believe it at first, but now I see it was true what they said about you.'

Suspecting some dire insult to his honour, Parzival demanded to know what had been said about him, and Sigune spat back her reply. 'That your heart must be as cold as stone to let your mother die of grief and loneliness.'

'What are you saying, woman?' Parzival gasped. 'Only yesterday I set out to bring my mother home to Belrepaire. My mother lives.'

Sigune shook her withered head. 'Have I not wet her grave with my own tears? She is long dead. Her heart broke in the moment that you left her.' When she stared back up at him the woman's eyes were merciless with grief, her voice cold flame. 'Your mother is dead. And you killed her, Parzival the Wretched. You killed her with the same cold heart that made you fail before the Grail. I cry woe for her, and woe for Anfortas. And I cry shame on you. I cry shame for ever on your wretched name.'

For a long moment Parzival stood like a stone. It was as if the words had reached him long before their meaning, as if something in his mind had stopped with shock. No one ever spoke to him like this. He was God's knight. Goodness and light were on his side. This wasn't possible. There must be error here. But then the ground was swaying under him like water. His entire disbelieving being was shaken first by the shock of sudden grief, then by brutal aftershocks of guilt and shame. He stood, the blood gone from his face, panting at the injustice of what was happening, at the intolerable pain of it. Then he closed his eyes against a world he no longer understood, threw back his head and, through the black gash that had opened in his life, uttered a single, drawn-out, countermanding cry of 'No.'

Nothing changed. The glade was swathed in mist still. Boughs dripped into the silence. The faces of Sigune and her dead knight stared up at him. The sword hung in his hand. He looked down at it as if deciding whether to throw his body on to the blade, then the face of his wife flashed into his mind. He pushed the sword back into its scabbard, yet even as he did so his mind was seared by the memory of the boast he had made on leaving her. Here he was then, God's own knight! The fool who'd claimed that nothing was strong enough to prevent his swift return! The man who had killed his own mother.

Time and space blurred round his rigid form. Darkness whirled inside him. Then shock at his loss, shame at his failures of the heart, and rage against the evil fate that had brought him to this pass – all combusted in a frenzy of despair.

Parzival took to his horse and rode away. He rode without hope or direction, pushing his horse to the pitch of exhaustion, seeing nothing, hearing nothing, aware of nothing but the dark blizzard raging in his mind.

Weeks passed and a harsh winter fell that year, covering all the hills and moors in snow. On the day before Christmas, sunlight glinted across the white wastes, and at Caerleon, King Arthur rode out through the glassy air with a party of friends to try out a peregrine falcon that had taken his fancy.

They came to a place by a frozen lake where a skein of geese crossed the winter sky, and when he saw the peregrine spread its wings at the sound, Gawain wagered that the king's bird would be first to the kill. Proudly Arthur unhooded his falcon, whispering to its fierce head and popping a gobbet of meat into its eager beak.

'You'll spoil a good bird, my lord,' Sir Kei, his seneschal, protested. 'Fatten her up like that and she'll not return to the lure.'

'Those who love me always return,' said the King. 'Watch!' He raised his wrist, loosed the falcon from its jesses, and the bird rose, climbing quickly, wheeled and soared again, then vanished beyond the trees.

Confident that his bird would deliver a kill, Arthur stared up at the sky, but as the other hawks struck and returned, the king grew impatient and dismayed. It seemed that Kei had spoken truly, for though the falconers called and swung their lures for a long time afterwards, there was no sign of the errant falcon.

By dusk the bird had roosted in the forest. Drawn by the light of a fire, she perched on the branch of an oak overlooking the glade where Parzival lay huddled in his frozen armour. She remained there, watching him throughout shivering in his sleep. Famished, near to death with cold, the knight woke at first light, got stiffly to his feet, pulled himself up onto his horse, and rode mindlessly on through the drifts. After a time he became aware of the falcon that followed him, flying from bough to bough as he made his way through the forest. For the first time in many weeks he felt a sense of companionship.

His horse stepped out between the last of the trees and Parzival was looking down across white meadows that fell away towards a frozen lake. High on the still air he heard the honking of geese, and when he looked up he saw the wavering chevron of their skein against pale sunlight. A moment later the peregrine soared out of the wood. The knight followed its flight as the bird wheeled eastwards, climbing all the time until she was high above the skein of geese. Then she swooped out of the sun.

With frantic cackles of alarm the geese scattered across the sky, but the falcon had already struck. Her talons pierced the flesh of a fat goose almost directly overhead. Three drops of blood fell out of the sky, staining the surface of the drift where the crazed knight watched from his saddle.

Parzival looked down. He saw the scarlet shine of blood against white snow. And as he watched the soft suffusion there – the bright blood paling in the snow, the snow blushing to the touch of blood – he saw an emblem of his beloved wife's forgotten beauty. Yearning seized his heart. It held him there, bereft of all other thought, in a trance of love and longing.

All the world vanished around him. Seen from outside, his gaze was fixed on blood on snow, and so intently that he might have been a marble statue of a mounted knight, or a figure overtaken by a storm of ice and left permanently frozen there. Motionless, unblinking, he stared into the snow as into the loving gaze of his wife's eyes.

So deeply was he enraptured by his vision of love that he neither saw nor heard the peregrine's return, nor did he feel her perch upon his shoulder. Still less was he aware of the approach of a mounted falconer across the drifts. He heard nothing when the man called out to him, 'That falcon belongs to the King, Sir Knight. I bid you return it.'

Parzival sat motionless, staring in adoration at three drops of blood on snow.

'Do you hold the King in contempt, sir?' called the falconer again. When he still received no answer, he shouted, 'His companions shall hear of it,' and pulled his horse's head round to canter away across the drifts, making for Arthur's camp, where he brought news of this strangely silent act of defiance.

Always proud and ready to take offence, it was bluff Sir Kei who vowed to avenge this insult to the King.

By now a wind had got up and it was blowing a spume of snow across the drifts as Kei crested a rise and saw the figure of a knight in scarlet armour waiting across the meadow, holding his lance upright, utterly motionless. 'What, is it you, Red Knight?' he bellowed, riding closer. 'Are you grown so proud after your triumph over the traitor Duke that you think you can mock the King and go unpunished?'

Kei's voice was loud across the blowing drifts. Behind him came the sound of Arthur and his companions cresting the rise to watch the coming affray. But still Parzival heard nothing. Nor did he move or speak.

'Answer me, dolt,' Kei shouted. 'Dare you ignore me, boy? This is Kei who speaks.' By now he was within a lance-length of the stationary knight, though unaware of the bloodstains in the snow which had transfixed Parzival's gaze.

'Are you asleep there?' Kei demanded, urging his horse closer. 'Did you not once vow vengeance for a blow I gave? Then take another at my hand.'

Standing in his stirrups, he swung his lance and fetched Parzival a clanging blow across the helm. 'Perhaps that'll wake you,' Kei guffawed, wheeling his horse away, and when he turned, readying to make his charge, he saw that the Red Knight was looking about him now, dazed and wondering, like a man woken from a strange dream. 'That's put some life into you, eh?' Kei shouted. 'Come on then, lower your lance. Defend yourself.'

Uncertain where he was or what was happening to him, Parzival saw the burly mounted figure bearing down on him across the snow, lowering his lance-point as he charged. Reflexively, he gripped his own lance, raised his shield, and dug his spurs into his horse's flanks. Still dazed, eyes watering from the blow to his head, he managed to deflect Kei's lance with his shield, but the shock of the collision almost pushed him from the saddle as the knight swept on past him, his horse's hooves skidding in the snow.

Arthur and his companions had watched this first pass from the rise, and murmurs of 'Parzival' and 'The Red Knight' gave way to cheering and shouts of Kei's name now.

'A good strike, Kei,' Gawain called across the snow, 'but my Lord Simplicity keeps his seat.'

'I found him sleeping in the saddle,' Kei shouted back. 'Now I'll bed him in the snow.' Lowering his lance again, the burly knight growled, 'Come again, bumpkin,' closed his visor, and urged his horse to a second charge.

Coming to his senses now, Parzival was readier for the onslaught. His own horse was on the move at the same moment as Kei's, his lance more firmly couched in his grip. All the concentration he had given to the blood on snow was focused on the coming impact. He saw the steam at the approaching horse's nostrils, he glimpsed the narrow gap between Kei's shield and breastplate, and struck that place with such force that his lance shattered. Kei's mount was thrown off balance and fell screaming in the snow. Lifted out of the saddle and knocked backwards by the thrust, Kei crashed to the ground with his right arm so twisted under the weight of his body that the bone inside it snapped.

'Look to Kei there,' said the King. 'That was a heavy fall.'

Crying, 'Well struck, Parzival!', Gawain spurred his horse. Bells jingled on its bridle as he crossed the drifts. He dismounted by the fallen knight who lay groaning and cursing in the snow. Kei howled with pain as his friend tried to turn him over. 'Wasn't this the arm with which you slapped Cunneware?' Gawain asked. 'It looks as though the lad's broken it for you, Kei.'

But the seneschal shrugged off the offer of help, and walked away, gingerly nursing the broken bone.

Gawain smiled up at Parzival. 'So now you avenge two blows with one, my friend – and against one of the King's doughtiest champions. Faith, you're rapidly becoming the wonder of the world!'

Dazed and panting still, uncertain of his surroundings, Parzival failed to recognize the man who stood beside him. 'My wife ...' he muttered, 'my Condwiramurs ...' He was about to turn his horse and ride away when Gawain caught at his halter, saying, 'Whoa there! Easy, friend. Are you all right?'

'My lance,' said Parzival. 'Where is my lance?'

'You just shattered it against poor Kei,' Gawain laughed. 'Has his crass blow dizzied your brain?'

Parzival gazed down anxiously from the saddle. 'Who are you, sir?'

'Come, you know me. It's Gawain! Your friend. Let me bring you to the King.'

But Parzival stiffened inside his armour. The shadow of some obscure, cruel memory darkened his mind. 'The King?' he gasped. 'No, I cannot see the King. There is great shame on me.'

'Shame? What shame can there be?' said Gawain, laughing again. 'Faith, since you sent Orilus packing back to Caerleon we've heard nothing but glorious reports of your deeds at Belrepaire. No, if there's any shame here, it's mine. I beg you to forgive the discourteous way I mocked you once.'

'I cannot remember well ...' Parzival frowned. 'Yet I thank you for your kindness, sir. But my wife ... where is my wife? I saw her a moment ago ...'

'Not here, lad,' Gawain answered, mystified by his friend's distracted behaviour, '– though God knows you have the look of one sorely stricken with love.' He might have said more but at that moment King Arthur rode across the drifts to join them.

'Welcome, dear friend,' the King smiled, offering his hand. 'We have longed for your company at court. You shall be received with great rejoicing there.'

'Forgive me.' Parzival shook his head. His breathing quickened, he glanced away in agitation. 'I am unworthy.'

'I know of no one worthier than Parzival of Wales,' the King exclaimed.

'No, not so,' the crazed knight answered. 'I am Parzival the Wretched.'

'Let none dare call you that in my presence,' said the King. 'There were those who scoffed when you first offered yourself as my champion, but since that day you have won the admiration of the world. Come, friend, you shall pass Christmastide with us.'

And so, still dazed, and troubled by a nameless sense of shame, Parzival was brought back amid joyous celebration to the King's court at Caerleon. In other circumstances it would have been the proud fulfilment of a dream. Yet, with his memory gone, and his mind tormented by terrible, uncertain shadows, the bewildered knight was left with almost as little understanding of the honour that was done to him as he had once possessed of the true nature of King Arthur's court on his first arrival there.

CHAPTER EIGHT

THE

SORCERESS

n Christmas Day the whole company of Caerleon gathered to celebrate their revels. Bright with banners and tapestries and the wild holly boughs that were festooned about the walls, the hall was made still brighter by the richly embroidered garments of the assembled lords and ladies. A great fire blazed in the hearth close to the throne where Arthur sat in state with his Queen beside him. To the King's right sat his nephew, Gawain, surrounded as usual by a bevy of ladies, and the former traitor, Duke Orilus was also there, reconciled to the King, to his sister Cunneware, and to his wronged Lady Jeschute who sat happily at his side.

Parzival was ushered into this noble company still wearing all of his red armour except the helmet, and even that he carried in the crook of his arm. Arthur's pages had tried to coax him into more comfortable clothes, but it was as if the knight was afraid that such fragile sense of identity as he possessed might dissolve altogether were he stripped of his familiar iron gear. Perhaps in some recess of his mind he recalled that he had first come to Arthur's court in quest of knighthood. Well, it seemed he was a proven knight now and it was only in a knight's armour that he felt secure among the festive chatter of that company.

At the bidding of his friend Gawain, Parzival came uncertainly before the throne, where King Arthur greeted him warmly, insisting that he and Parzival should seal their friendship with a kiss. Guinevere gladly welcomed the knight with kisses also, and made a delicate point of forgiving him for the great sorrow he had given her when he slew the Red Knight with his javelin. Yet Parzival received these gracious courtesies in such a bemused state that the Queen asked with gentle concern if there was something troubling him.

'My heart yearns to return to my wife,' admitted Parzival at last.

'And so you shall, so you shall, as soon as you have shared our Christmas feast,' laughed the King, '– though be advised, it is the custom at Caerleon that none dines at Christmas until some new adventure has befallen us.'

'So we're looking to you for some excitement!' quipped Antenor the Fool from where he crouched at the king's feet among the dogs.

'Peace, knave,' said the King and kicked the jester lightly with his heel. Then he turned, smiling, to Gawain. 'Nephew, do you stand ready to sponsor this knight?'

'With all my heart, uncle,' Gawain replied with his own vivid smile, 'for though I am the elder by some years, I've come to think that we are twin souls, he and I.'

'Then I have a duty to perform that gives my heart great pleasure.' The King rose to his feet, commanding, 'Bring me my sword Excalibur.' A page wearing a tabard emblazoned with the red dragon stepped forward from a line of attendants, with the great scabbarded sword lying across the palms of his hands. Arthur took the sword by the hilt and unsheathed it. The blade glinted in the light. 'Sweet friend,' the King smiled at Parzival, 'your wildwood dreams of inno-cence come true, for against all likelihood you knew it your destiny to be my champion. And now, with all due ceremony, I would make you truly my knight.' Raising his noble head, the King commanded, 'Let the trumpets sound.'

From a balcony high above the bannered hall a fanfare clarioned its salute. The bright echoes faded among the vaults. Stunned with wonder, Parzival heard the royal voice declaiming in the silence of the hall, 'Parzival of Wales, rightful King of Anjou and Lord of Belrepaire, I, Arthur, High King of all the lands and isles of Britain, bid you kneel and swear fealty to me and companionship of chivalry with all the Table Round.'

In bewildered obedience Parzival dropped to his knee before the smiling King. His eyes caught the sweeping gleam of light as Excalibur was raised above him. He lowered his head, conscious of the pent breath in his throat, and was waiting for the touch of the sword at his shoulder when the reverential silence of the court was shattered by a coarse crying of the King's name that screeched across the air outside.

'Arthur! Arthur!'

Discountenanced and angry at this violation of a solemn moment, the King demanded, 'What noise there? Who dares disturb the King's peace so?'

'Where is the Pendragon's son?' screeched the voice. 'I would have words with him. Make way.'

At that moment the great doors of the hall crashed open, and the whole murmuring court fell silent as the most loathsome female figure they had ever seen rode into the hall. Dressed in a crumpled bridal gown, she sat with a crooked back on a bony mule, clutching a whip in her right hand. A long plait of coarse hair dangled from her head across the scabby pelt of her mount, but it was her face that appalled everyone to silence. Or was it a hideous mask she wore? For the squinting eyes and the fierce tusks jutting at her mouth resembled less the features of a woman than the savage, bristled snout of a wild boar. The dogs cowered at her approach. Antenor the Jester ducked behind the throne.

Struggling to conceal his own horror, the King found voice enough to demand, 'By what right do you interrupt us, madam?'

'By what right do you desecrate the sovereignty of Britain, King?' she retorted instantly. All the assembled knights stirred at the insult, but from where she sat on her ungainly mule the woman withered them with her stare. 'I, Cundrie the Sorceress, say that only men of proven virtue should sit at the Round Table, not base recreants that defile its name.'

Gawain had stiffened at this last utterance, now he leapt to his feet saying, 'I counsel you to speak more fairly to our King.'

'Be silent, Gawain,' the sorceress commanded with a glower so derisive that it made the knight blanch, 'or keep your twitterings for the painted creatures at your side.'

By now the King had recovered from his first shock and strove to regain control of the situation. 'I forgive you, madam,' he said, 'for I assume from your manner that you are not always in possession of your mind.'

'My wits are truer than the traitor heart of one here, King.'

'Then be forthright, Cundrie,' the king demanded. 'Who among my friends do you dare name traitor?'

'Who else,' the sorceress spat back, 'but that canker Parzival?'

Outraged, the King spoke over the shocked murmur of the court. 'Cundrie, that knight is among the worthiest of my companions.'

'Then you are betrayed by his fair manner,' the sorceress answered, 'and his fair face. You think *me* monstrous, King, but I tell you that the base wretch who kneels before you is more monstrous far than I. Does he not foul the honour of the arms he bears?'

'Those arms were won defending *my* honour,' Arthur declared.

'Peace, fool,' Cundrie came back. Again the court gasped to hear the hag dare to insult the King so, but she was staring at Parzival when she added, 'Do you think I don't know that he slew the Red Knight and by what ignominious means?'

Staring at his accuser in grim dismay, Parzival opened his mouth to speak in his own defence but no words would come. Cundrie snorted at his silence. 'Do I not also know that the Red Knight was kin to your father, and a man of your own blood?' she cried. 'Yes, it was your own kinsman that you killed – though you are unworthy to wash the feet of his dishonoured corpse.'

The whole assembled court was staggered by this revelation. There was a flurry of commotion then the hall became a vast, impatient silence in which Parzival stood alone, stammering, 'I swear ... I swear this was unknown to me.'

'Swallow your tongue, Sir Ignorance,' the sorceress commanded, 'for it wags when you should keep silent, but when you *should* speak – ha, what then?'

Parzival quailed under the impact of the question. His eyes widened. He lifted a hand to his head. Standing next to him, the King heard the indrawn hiss of his breath as though in sudden pain, but the knight said nothing.

'Speak plainer yourself, madam,' Arthur demanded.

'Then you shall know it, King. You shall know the terrible truth of it.' Cundrie's mule stirred restively under her. She tugged at the reins and pointed at Parzival with her whip. 'This wretch was admitted to the presence of the Grail at Montsauvage. He sat at the wounded side of Anfortas, and dined with him off the bounty of the Grail – yet he failed to put the question that would have freed the Rich Fisherman from his pain.'

The shocked silence of the court had been dense before but it closed now like freezing fog around the place where Parzival stood in turmoil. The hand at his side was trembling. It moved to his head where, like pain reawakened in a frozen wound, memory returned. 'But I didn't know,' he was gasping, 'No one told me. I would have asked ... I wanted to ask, but ...'

'But what, worm?'

'I have been told not to ask questions. A man who was as a father to me counselled me against it.'

'And do you only do as you are told?' Cundrie scoffed. 'Is obedience the only wisdom? Has the heart no knowledge of its own? Or were the sufferings of Anfortas not grievous enough to move a heart that must be made of stone?' Again she wrenched round the head of her mule. 'Do you lack all compassion, wretch? Pah! What else to expect from one callous enough to cause his own mother's death?'

Appalled by this further dreadful accusation, the King asked quietly, 'Can this be true, Parzival?'

Parzival said nothing. It felt as though his heart and lungs were on the point of bursting, for he was like a diver returning from black, unfathomable depths, and the harsh light of the surface above his head was lidded with ice.

'Do words fail you again, fool?' said Cundrie. 'Yet look into his face, King. See the guilt that stalks his eyes. I think memory returns. I think he begins to know himself for the unfeeling thing he is.'

Appalled by what the hag was doing to the friend he had just sponsored before the court, Gawain moved to his aid. 'Speak, Parzival,' he urged. 'You must defend yourself.'

'Sooner expect speech from a stone,' scoffed Cundrie. 'This mumchance dunce is ignorance incarnate. Why, he even has a brother he knows nothing of – a man mottled like a magpie, black and white. Yet that elder son of Gahmuret has won greater honour with his dappled skin than this simpleton of light has ever known.'

'Parzival,' the King commanded, sterner now, 'you must speak.'

And still the knight stood locked in silence. His hands had fallen back to his sides. They were trembling violently now.

'How should he speak,' said Cundrie, 'for the Sword was put into his hand, and the Lance and the Table were shown to him, and the hallowed Grail itself, yet he uttered not a word?' Cundrie transfixed the knight with her squinting, boar's head gaze. 'His silence condemned him then and it condemns him now,' she declared. Then she raised the harsh screech of her voice against him. 'I cry great shame on you, Parzival the Wretched, in the eyes of all the world, for the wound still festers at the Grail King's thigh and his land still languishes through your bitter fault.'

A charred log shifted in the hearth sending a flight of sparks into the chimney's black throat. Despite the crackle of the blaze the hall grew cold.

His voice hoarse with anxiety now, King Arthur asked, 'How shall this grave fault be mended, Cundrie?'

'It cannot be mended,' came the absolute reply. The mule shook its bony head, the bridle jingled. The beast stamped a hoof against the flagstones of the floor. Then Cundrie spoke again. 'Not unless the right man finds his way to Montsauvage.'

Since her dreadful cry of shame had stirred the echoes of Sigune's accusation in his mind, Parzival had recoiled ever more deeply into silence. His half-crazed cousin had first plunged him into despair. Now this hideous witch had cursed him with still more terrible force. But in those last few words – words uttered almost as an afterthought, a reluctant concession to the vagaries of fate – he thought he glimpsed the faintest shred of hope, a possibility that Sigune had denied to him. He grasped after it.

'I'll go back there,' he said. And stood, trembling. 'I have failed once, but I shall not fail the test again.'

'You've thrown away your chance, fool,' said the witch dismissively. 'The Castle of the Grail does not wait at every comer's beck and call. Such is its elusive nature that Montsauvage withholds itself from all who deliberately seek for it.'

'Still I shall seek it out,' Parzival declared, staring in baffled defiance at his accuser, seeing no chance of redemption but to commit himself before the King and the whole court to this desperate cause.

'Then see what comes of your arrogance,' said Cundrie. With a derisive snort she turned her tusked head from side to side, surveying the silent company. 'Yet if there are any left of courage and honour in this court,' she cried, 'there are deeds that might still be done!'

'Name them, Cundrie.'

It was Gawain who had spoken. Cundrie squinted across at him from the saddle of her mule. 'I know of four queens and a host of maidens whom the magician Klingsor has imprisoned in the Castle of the Marvels,' she declaimed. 'All adventure is vain compared with the honour that might be gained there by one who released them through acts of noble love.'

To the immediate consternation of the adoring ladies who sat about him, Gawain declared, 'Then I will undertake this quest.'

Again Cundrie snorted in contempt. 'I spoke of *noble* love, Gawain. What do you know of that, whose faithless way with women mocks honour out of court? You are incapable of love, false knight. I cry shame on your name too as traitor to the heart.'

'Take back that insult, hag,' Gawain demanded, but it was clear from the pallor of his handsome face that the barb had found its mark.

Cundrie cackled in his face with derision. Tugging on the reins, she pulled round the head of her mule. Its hooves clattered on the stones as she shouted, 'I'll hear no more of the fool Parzival and the philanderer Gawain. Send a *true* man after me, King, if there is one to be found in this vain company. And my curses on you all if there is not.'

With that threat scalding the silence behind her, the sorceress dug her heels into the sides of her mule and cantered out of the hall. Dumbstruck, the King and his court watched her go. As of their own volition, the great wooden doors slammed shut at her back.

As soon as she was gone the hall was all commotion. Shrugging off the hands of the women who sought to detain him, Gawain stood before the King, saying, 'Give me this adventure, Lord. The sorceress has shamed me before the court. How else shall I regain my honour?'

White-faced and suddenly haggard-eyed, as though it had consumed all his strength to make a stand before Cundrie, the King stared at him in dismay. 'If you ask it, nephew,' he said, 'I cannot refuse. I pray you may be fortunate and find the Castle of the Marvels and endure whatever ordeals await you there.' Then Arthur's anguished gaze shifted to Parzival who stood alone in that great company, breathing quickly, his head held high and pale on his broad shoulders. 'But you, Parzival ...' Arthur shook his head and glanced away. 'It seems that your failure has shut the doors of Montsauvage against you for ever. Your quest is without hope. My heart grieves for your lost honour.'

Parzival stared at the King, wild-eyed, unspeaking.

'Yet I stand beside you in your shame,' Gawain declared. 'We were brothers in honour, Parzival. We shall be brothers still in our adversity.'

Moved by his nephew's loyalty, the King looked for some gesture of consolation. 'And in this unhappy hour,' he said to Parzival, 'you have at least learned that you have a true brother somewhere in the world.'

'Oh yes,' Parzival answered bitterly, ' – a brother whose reputation condemns me for the unlucky fool I am! Ha, were it not for the sweet love of my wife, I would swear there is no meaning left in this unholy world. No meaning at all – only madness and despair!'

Queen Guinevere reached out a hand to console the knight, but he recoiled from the touch as though he might contaminate her. In the same moment Antenor the jester sprang out from behind the throne where he had been observing events with a wry eye. 'Well, your Christmas rule has been met, King,' he said. 'We can feed our faces now.'

'Peace, fool,' Arthur commanded. 'There is a great shadow fallen over us.'

Again Guinevere made a tender approach to Parzival. 'I think you should return to your wife, friend,' she said gently.

'But don't you see?' he cried, '– that's the true hell of it! How can I show my face at Belrepaire with my honour gone?'

'Blanchefleur will not deny you,' the Queen sought to reassure him.

'But I deny myself,' Parzival retorted. 'There can be no thought of happiness for me till I have found the place of the Grail again.'

'Did you not hear what Cundrie said?' King Arthur gravely shook his head. 'As long as you look for that place it will elude you. The quest is vain.'

'Yet still will I look.'

In a quiet voice, Gawain said, 'If I can aid you, friend, I shall do so gladly.'

But Parzival was beyond reach, in a cold place where no comfort could touch him. 'My shame is mine alone,' he glowered. 'Only I can redeem it.'

Patiently Gawain shook his head before the rebuff. 'Then we must both look to God in his goodness for a favourable outcome.'

'God?' laughed Parzival bitterly. 'Ha! Would you speak to me of God, Gawain?'

'As I look to him for my own salvation,' Gawain answered. 'I too have been a sinner. Yet as true knights we remain God's servants, you and I.'

'I will not serve him.' Parzival stood, jutting his chin in defiance. 'Once I thought myself his true knight, but now I find I've only been

God's fool. Well, no longer. I turn my face against him as his is turned against me.'

Gawain raised a protesting hand, 'Parzival, my friend ...'

But the knight spoke over him. 'No, let me counsel *you*, Gawain. Do not put your trust in God. He will only play you false.'

'May God forgive you,' said the King, crossing himself.

'I don't want his forgiveness,' Parzival shouted. 'Nor shall he have mine.' Inside the iron case of his armour, the knight might have been standing alone before the universe. Then he shook his head and turned again to Gawain. 'Believe me, beyond your lance and sword, there's only one thing to be trusted in this world, which is the truth of a woman's love. If you would live wisely, friend, then learn to value that.'

The two knights gazed into each other's eyes for a long moment, then Parzival turned on his heel and walked towards the great outer door of the hall. The silent company parted to either side, watching him go like a man walking to perdition.

'Parzival,' shouted the King, 'you cannot leave like this.'

The knight halted a moment by the door. 'There is no other way,' he said. 'I wish you well, friends. I do not know if we shall meet again.'

Then, shouting for his horse, he strode out into the world.

PART TWO

THE

HEALING

Hic lapis exilis precio quoque vilis
Spernitur a stultis, amatur plus ab eductis

'This insignificant stone may seem a trifling
prize, Though much despised by fools it will
be cherished by the wise.'

(Arnold of Villanova: *Rosarium Philosophorum*)

CHAPTER NINE

THE
CHESSBOARD
CASTLE

o both Parzival, the holy fool, and the sophisticated courtier Gawain were shamed before their peers, and the whole of Arthur's court was thrown into lamentation by the evil turn that events had taken. Nor was Parzival's departure the last shock of that dramatic Christmas Day, for shortly after he had left, a heavily armoured knight rode into the castle demanding to be brought into the presence of Arthur and Gawain. The stranger's head was helmeted, no one recognized his scutcheon, and all were amazed when he accused Gawain of foully murdering his lord, the King of Ascalun. Gawain immediately protested that he knew nothing of the matter, but the knight was sure of his ground, claiming that Gawain had treacherously struck down the King under the guise of giving friendly greeting.

'If you have any honour, you will come to Ascalun in forty days', challenged the stranger knight, 'and answer to me there in a duel of single combat.'

Gawain knew himself innocent of the crime, but his good name could be redeemed only by accepting this new challenge as well as the perilous charge that the witch Cundrie had already laid upon

115

him. And so, lamented by his lovers and friends, he mounted his charger Gringolet and set out in search of Ascalun and the enchanted Castle of the Marvels.

Gawain's long travels over high moors and hills brought him many adventures – and left at least one more heart aching in his wake – before he came one afternoon upon a company of knights out hawking. Their leader was a handsome young Lord whose hair shone in the windy sunlight with a strange radiance. The man had been eagerly following his falcon as it pursued a heron over a swamp when his horse missed its footing in the bog and he took a tumble into the muddy water of the fen. Gawain rode up just as his friends had pulled him from the mire, yet the lord smiled up at the newcomer with a bright enthusiasm that seemed undampened by his fall.

'I've ridden far in search of the Castle of the Marvels,' said Gawain. 'Cundrie the Sorceress has challenged me to come to the aid of four queens and a host of maidens held captive there by the magician Klingsor. Do you know if this is the right way to that place?'

'I know nothing of this Klingsor, sir,' the Lord answered, 'but your tale will make good company. My own castle stands on the next hill. If you wish to lodge there tonight, ride on.'

'Will you not accompany me, friend?' asked Gawain.

'As you see, my sport is here,' laughed the Lord. 'I'll join you when I've had my fill. But that fair lady my sister Antikonie is at the castle. Tell her I bid her use all her charms to make you welcome.'

Intrigued by this invitation, Gawain rode on alone and, when he crested the rise, he saw a magnificent, turreted castle gleaming on the next summit. Warmly received there by the steward, he was taken to a chamber where pages relieved him of his weapons and armour, then he was led up a flight of stairs to a private chamber in a tower where a young woman rose from her chair to greet him.

Quite as beautiful as her brother had promised, and evidently a little bored by life in this remote outpost, the Lady Antikonie was instantly enlivened by the stranger's arrival. 'I am unfamiliar with the ways of the great world, sir,' she welcomed him shyly. 'You must judge for me whether it would it be proper to receive you with a kiss.'

Delighted by such refreshing candour, Gawain answered that there could be no fairer welcome. He took her tenderly into his embrace, Antikonie offered up her lips to his, and when her eyes opened again they were shining. 'I see you are a knight of gentle courtesy,' she whispered a little breathlessly as she disengaged herself from his arms.

Gawain smiled down at her. 'Say rather that it is your rare charm that softens my rough ways.'

Antikonie blushed and smiled. She gazed down at her hands, then put them together to prevent them trembling. 'And you, sir ... You bring fresh life to the tedium of this lonely place.'

'As you do,' Gawain replied, 'to my own dull senses, lady.'

Disconcerted, unsure of herself, yet feeling more alive than she had done for a long time, Antikonie gazed back up at him. Her small breasts rose and fell under her dress as she took in the captivating intensity of his smile. 'Your face is pale, sir,' she whispered, glancing away. 'You have come far. I think it must be from great weariness.'

'There is a deeper reason,' said Gawain. 'The truth is that my heart falters to find you even fairer than your brother led me to believe.' Gawain reached out to take her hands in his. 'Another kiss would strengthen it.'

A moment later, Antikonie found herself deep inside his embrace again, her mouth opening to his, her eyes closed, her mind and pulses racing. She felt the tips of his fingers softly caress her cheek, then they moved to touch the delicate skin about her ear. Flame rose in her throat. After a long moment savouring her sweet breath,

Gawain relaxed the hand he held at her back. Antikonie withdrew a pace or two in a fluster of desire and dismay.

'I pray you let me breathe a little,' she said, turning away, aware how flushed her cheeks as she lifted a hand to her hair, trying to compose herself. 'Tell me, Sir Knight, are you not already sworn to some lady's service?'

For a moment Gawain temporized. If he was amused by her lack of sophistication, he was also slightly taken aback by it, and it took him a moment to realize that the question had not been a flirtatious gesture on the girl's part after all, but a sincere enquiry designed to protect her heart from the possibility of disappointment. And in the same instant Antikonie must have seen the hesitation in his eyes for she raised her chin and stared at him directly as she said, 'If you deny it, sir, I don't think I shall believe you.'

Thinking quickly, Gawain answered, 'Then I confess that I am.'

Antikonie strove to still the beating of her heart. 'And no doubt she grieves at your leaving?'

'She wept sorely when we parted,' Gawain admitted.

'Did she so?' Antikonie walked away from him, holding her hands together high at her bosom, with one finger touching her lower lip. Then, as if in mere polite enquiry, she turned to ask, 'Tell me, who is this lady?'

'Her name is Obilot,' said Gawain. 'Her father sought my aid in defence of his city as I travelled this way. I would have refused him because of the great urgency of my mission, but Obilot beseeched me to help his cause. She asked in ways that melted my heart, and for love of her, I could not deny him.'

'I see,' said Antikonie, glancing away to conceal the jealousy and disappointment in her face. She stood with her back to him now, biting the lip that had so recently kissed this devastating stranger.

'She named me her own true knight,' Gawain confessed. His voice was solemn, yet he was smiling as he admired the fall of shining tresses at Antikonie's long back, and her narrow waist. 'And I have a vulnerable heart.'

'Doubtless this lady is very beautiful!' Antikonie said to the wall, appalled to hear how hoarse and dry her voice had suddenly become.

'She is indeed!'

'And gave you a mark of her favour, I suppose?'

'She did, most eagerly,' said Gawain. 'I wear it always.'

But this was too much for Antikonie, who turned on him then with a cold and haughty glare. 'Then I must think you faithless, knight.'

'By no means, Lady. I keep her safe here in my heart.'

'Yet you press me for kisses, sir!' Antikonie protested, outraged and hurt, and wishing that she had more poise, more experience in such matters, a more practised talent for deception and disdain. Then she caught the glitter of amusement in Gawain's eyes. 'Or are you making sport with me?' she cried, turning away again, by now at the brink of tears.

'I am,' Gawain laughed gently, 'but not as you think, Lady.' He put a comforting hand to Antikonie's shoulder. He tried to make her turn and face him, but she would not move. He began to explain. 'The Lady Obilot is ...'

But Antikonie shrugged away, saying, 'Of no interest to me, sir.'

And again Gawain laughed. 'Lady,' he said, 'she is only eight years old! The favour she gave me was the sleeve of her newest dress. I keep it here near my heart.' Gawain slipped his hand inside his doublet and took out a length of sheer blue silk. 'See how small it is against your own slender arm.'

Scarcely able to believe how the world was suddenly brightening around her, Antikonie turned and saw how tiny was the sleeve he held. Amazed, embarrassed, alight with possibility again, she raised her eyes to share Gawain's smile with a coy, up-from-under stare. Then they were laughing together in delight as he told her more of the little Lady Obilot, and how she had persuaded him to fight in her father's cause by the adoring way in which she had offered him her undying love, claiming that she and Gawain were really one person and would always be so.

'So you see,' said the knight, pulling Antikonie back into his arms. 'I do truly love her, but not, Lady, as I feel for you.' Then he lowered his mouth to hers again, and again she felt herself melt as he gazed down into her eyes and said, 'I think your mouth was made for kissing.'

'Your hand, Sir Knight,' Antikonie gasped breathlessly, reaching to prevent his intimate advances, '... it seems no stranger to adventure.'

'It has learned that boldness is often rewarded,' said Gawain.

'Then when it encounters virtue,' she whispered, 'it must learn patience.'

But Gawain was not now about to be deterred.

'Believe me, Lady,' he sighed, 'my birth is as high as yours, and my desires are as strong. I beg you to have mercy on them.' The tenderness of his touch had already turned to passion and, amid the tumult of her own released emotions, Antikonie found herself responding to his urgency even as she sought to resist it.

'I hardly know you, sir,' she gasped, 'and yet ...'

'Yet your heart races as mine does,' said Gawain, holding her closer in his embrace and kissing her again.

Again, without truly wishing to succeed, she tried to pull free. 'Ah, you are hasty!' she gasped. 'Can love strike as swiftly as this? Do you truly love me?'

'Yes, yes,' Gawain urged, his breath hot and close at her delicate ear. 'Can you not feel it?'

And, 'Yes,' she sighed, 'oh my sweet knight, yes.'

They had been alone in the chamber throughout this encounter, and had they remained so, then the victory of which Gawain had already con-fidently assured himself would certainly have been his. But as their embraces grew ever more passionate the door opened and a man came into the room, saying, 'My Lady, your brother has returned.' Then he stood open-mouthed with amazement at the sight of Antikonie in this stranger's arms. 'Who the devil are you, sir?' he demanded.

At the sound of the voice, Gawain looked up across Antikonie's naked shoulder. The man saw and recognized his face.

'Gawain!' he growled.

'You have me at a disadvantage, sir,' said Gawain. 'You seem to have heard of me but ...'

'Yes, I know you, damn your eyes,' the man spoke over him. 'Did I not challenge you at Arthur's court? I know you for a traitor and foul murderer who slew my Lord, Judas-like, while he gave fair greeting. Would you ravish his daughter now?' The man turned back to the door and shouted down the stairway for the guards to come.

Antikonie, meanwhile, was staring up at Gawain, white-faced with shock and dismay, demanding to know whether what the man had said was true.

'I swear it is not, Lady,' Gawain answered, having realized by now that he must have arrived by chance at Ascalun. 'Believe me, there is some error here. I'm no more a murderer than ...'

'... than you were about to ravish me,' Antikonie supplied, gazing into the earnest appeal of his eyes. By now they could hear the din of armed men running up the stone stairs below them. 'I believe you, Gawain,' she said. 'I will speak to my brother. He will listen to me.'

'Stand back, Lady,' cried Gawain's accuser, 'there will be violence here.'

'My sword and shield are below,' said Gawain. 'Would you stick me like a pig while I cannot defend myself?' But Antikonie had seized him by the hand and was pulling him away to another, smaller door. 'Come quickly,' she cried, 'this way,' and she led him up a narrow stairway to a higher chamber where she slammed and bolted the door behind them.

Immediately Gawain saw that there was no other way out of this round chamber. Knowing that the door could not stand for long against a determined force of men, he looked for something with which to defend himself. The walls were bare except for a heavy wooden chessboard that hung from a hook by an iron ring, and a shelf where the black and white figures of stone chessmen were ranged. Already he could hear the ring of chainmail and the clatter of weapons as the guards mounted the stairs outside. 'This will have to do,' he said, taking down the chessboard from its hook. He glanced at Antikonie. 'Are you with me still?'

'I am,' she panted, her eyes bright and excited, 'with all my heart.'

'Then take these stone chessmen. When I open this door, throw them at the guards with all your strength.'

Looking to surprise for some small advantage, Gawain pushed open the door sending one of the guards tumbling back against the others, then he and Antikonie stood together at the head of the stairs, he wielding the heavy chessboard as though it were both bludgeon and shield while she hurled kings and queens, bishops and rooks, black pieces and white down on the heads of the astonished guards. She was laughing as she did so, and crying out in excited delight, 'I think I love you, Gawain. I'm sure of it. I do.'

The guards had fallen back in confusion before the assault when the young Lord whom Gawain had met out hawking appeared at the foot of the stair. 'Out of my way, fools,' he shouted. 'Antikonie, stay your hand. Is that the traitor Gawain who fights there like a tavern brawler?'

'Gawain it is,' the knight shouted back, 'but no traitor, and I defend myself as best I can.'

'You lie, coward. My father the King was foully slain on All Hallow's Eve. His killer gave your name.'

'Then was he both a coward and a liar. I am the victim of slander here.'

Antikonie beseeched her brother to listen to Gawain, but the Lord angrily reproached her for defending their father's murderer. 'Come down,' he commanded her, 'and let me prove him false at the point of my sword.'

'Your challenge would be braver if I were armed,' Gawain retorted. One of the guards growled, 'Cut him down while we have him, as he did our King,' and Antikonie cried out, 'You must kill me first, coward.'

'Do you shelter behind a woman now, Gawain?' scoffed the Lord.

'Give me my sword,' said Gawain, 'and I'll answer for my honour before any man.'

Standing beside him, Antikonie proudly declared, 'You sent this knight to me brother, and I have taken him under my protection. This craven attack on his life wrongs me.' And when her brother asked whether Gawain had charmed her from her senses, she tilted her defiant chin at him. 'He has given me his word,' she said, 'and I believe him. Gawain is innocent.'

'Doubtless he has given you cause to think him so,' her brother replied. 'Your charm is notorious, Gawain, but can you prove your innocence?'

'There is one who will swear I was nowhere near your King on All Hallows.'

'And who might that be?' the Lord demanded.

'A lady of high birth and unsmirched reputation,' said Gawain, with a swift and not altogether comfortable glance at Antikonie.

'Ha! No doubt yet another foolish woman you have gulled!' the Lord snorted. But he too was uneasy with the present stalemate. 'Sergeant, guard this stair,' he ordered. 'Those who love me, come away and give counsel.'

So Gawain and Antikonie were left alone together for a time. Deeply in love with him now she sought reassurances that he loved her too. Gawain held her close, murmuring affectionate words of comfort, while he gazed over her shoulder, trying to think his way out of this tricky corner.

After a brief consultation, the Lord returned with his counsellors. 'We are agreed there may be cause for doubt in this matter,' he conceded, 'but dare you prove yourself no enemy to me?'

'Arthur himself will tell you that my word is proof enough,' Gawain declared. 'But if you ask more then, for this sweet lady's sake, you shall have it.'

'I shall hold you to that,' the Lord replied. At his command one of his counsellors told how, in the previous week, his young master had been defeated in a passage of arms by a stranger knight. That knight had charged him, on pain of his life, either to render himself prisoner before Lady Blanchefleur at Belrepaire, or to spend the rest of his days seeking out the Castle of the Grail.

Gawain laughed out loud at this revelation, and when the Lord asked if he dared to mock his shame, he said, 'There is no shame, for you have been bested by Parzival who is the worthiest of knights. What do you ask of me, sir? Parzival is my friend. I will never take up arms against him.'

'But if you are truly a friend to my Lord,' said the counsellor, 'you will take up the Red Knight's challenge on his behalf and swear to seek out the Castle of the Grail.'

'Ha!' Gawain did not conceal the hint of mockery in his voice now, 'I see you have heard that Montsauvage withholds itself from those who seek for it!'

'Make up your mind,' the Lord answered. 'You can die here if you prefer.'

'Very well,' Gawain assented, 'I accept this charge – but only for love of Parzival whom I have already sworn to aid.' Then he caught a small, unhappy whimper from the young woman at his side. 'And in honour of this brave lady your sister,' he quickly added, 'whose friendship I will sorely miss.'

'But will you not take me with you?' she asked. 'Shall I not fight at your side?'

'Have a care for your pride, sister,' her brother warned.

'I have never been so proud,' Antikonie declared. 'Nor have I ever felt so alive.' Then she turned her eyes on the man to whom she had given her inexperienced heart. 'Did you not say you loved me, Gawain?'

Scarcely able to hold her gaze, he said, 'Lady, if I cared for you less I would be readier to risk your life for the joy of keeping you at my side. But honour summons me to dangers from which a chessboard will not protect me. I beg you, give me leave to go.'

'If I withhold it,' Antikonie demanded, 'will you stay?' And when the knight glanced away, giving her no answer, her face flushed and tears pricked at her eyes. 'I think perhaps you *are* a traitor,' she said then. 'Your treason has injured one who loves you dearly.' She stood, tall and proud, holding him in the fierce reproach of her gaze as she lifted a hand to her shoulder and unbuttoned the sleeve of her dress. 'Here,' she said bitterly, 'add this to the many favours you already wear, and guard your heart well, sir, lest someone carelessly breaks it as you have just broken mine.'

With that she turned away from him and walked down the stairs, holding her head high and fighting back the tears that threatened to overwhelm her.

All that night Antikonie's words rang in the dark places of Gawain's dreams, for they echoed on the bitter accusation that Cundrie had made against him before Arthur's court: that he was incapable of noble love and a traitor to the heart. Had the sorceress been right after all? Was he no more than an insatiable philanderer, doomed now to spend his days in a hopeless quest for the unattainable?

Early the next morning as he climbed into his saddle, Gawain looked up to the tower where Antikonie had fought beside him. In the pale light he saw her standing at the parapet where the breeze lightly blew the veil from her lovely face, revealing the reproach there and the hurt he had given her. Regretfully, the knight lifted his hand in salute, but the young woman turned away without acknowledging him. And so, with uncharacteristic sadness, and a grave foreboding in his heart, Gawain rode off into the dawn.

CHAPTER TEN

THE

SOUL FRIEND

 hat then of Parzival whose wanderings across the blighted land, and countless furious victories in combat, seemed to bring him no closer to the Castle of the Grail?

A year passed, then another, and a third, yet there was not a morning in which he did not wake with the sound of Cundrie's cursing in his mind. Then, on a freezing night of March snow, he fell asleep shivering in his armour, and the figure of his beloved wife Blanchefleur came to him in a dream.

'Husband, they tell me you have become as Gawain,' she said.

'It's true, Lady,' his dreaming self answered. 'The world now knows me for a great knight. Gawain and I are sworn brothers.'

'And you are both false to those who love you,' said Blanchefleur.

'Not so, Lady,' he protested. 'I swear it on my honour.'

'Then why are you untrue to me?'

'Blanchefleur, I shall be true to you until I die.'

'Yet you do not come home. Did you not tell me once that nothing was strong enough to prevent your swift return?'

'I did, and I believed it, but my life is waste unless I find the Grail.'

'What is the Grail?' asked the figure of Blanchefleur. 'Whom does it serve?'

'I don't know,' Parzival cried aloud in his sleep. 'I don't know these things.'

'Then where do you think it lies?'

'I have seen it at Montsauvage,' he said, 'where the Rich Fisherman nurses his grievous wound.'

'How did you come to that place?' asked Blanchefleur.

'I was lost in fog. I let my horse's reins hang free.'

'And trust brought you there! Husband, why do you not keep faith with your heart?'

'Blanchefleur, my Condwiramurs ...' But even as he called and reached out for her, Parzival saw the beloved figure vanish in the mist of dream.

He woke weeping in the bitter wind. His sole desire was to return to Belrepaire, but in the cawing of the rooks he heard a coarse echoing of Cundrie's cry of shame, and he knew he could never face his wife until that curse was lifted. Spindrift snow blew into his eyes. His horse got to its feet, powdered with snow from the drifts. Parzival lifted his foot to the stirrup. His fingers were stiff with frost as he grasped the pommel. Only his will was driving him and for too long he had been driven by his will. But he pulled himself up into the saddle, tugged at the reins and was about to ride on when a memory of the dream returned. It fell across his mind like a shaft of winter sunlight. He saw how far he had lost touch with the simple trust that had once guided him.

Parzival leaned forward and patted the sinewy neck of his horse. 'Well, old friend,' he said, 'all these years you've answered faithfully to these reins, yet I am lost. I think we might both fare better if you choose your own way now.'

He clicked his tongue. With the reins draped loosely from the bit, the patient beast moved off through the snow, treading its steady way hour after hour, until it brought him, later that day, to a secluded retreat in a leafless beechwood where the hermit Trevrizent strove in solitude to make his soul.

Dusk was falling and the hermit was kneeling at prayer beside the fire he had lit in a ring of stones outside his cell. Surprised by the sound of a stranger's approach, Trevrizent raised his gaunt head as Parzival's horse came through the bracken.

'Did I startle you, father?' asked the knight, dismounting.

'Bears and stags may startle me,' – a smile softened the lines of the hermit's austere features – 'but I fear nothing human ... though I pray you, disarm, for it grieves me to see a man go armed at this holy season.'

Laying down his lance and shield, Parzival said, 'What feast is this? I've lost all track of time.'

'The feast of God's love for fallible man,' Trevrizent answered. 'Today is Good Friday.'

'Ah,' said Parzival, unbuckling his sword, 'the day when God died.'

'To be reborn, friend,' the hermit assured him. 'God's love never dies.'

'Were you as familiar with the world as I am,' Parzival answered, 'you might have cause to doubt that, friend.'

But Trevrizent gave a small chuckle at such doleful condescension. 'Do you think I've always worn this cowl?' he said. 'I too have borne arms in my time.'

'Then you know something of the sorrows of the world.'

'And its temptations,' Trevrizent added, studying the knight's grim face by the fitful light of his fire. 'I think you may have fallen into one of the worst of them, Sir Knight,' he said.

'What do you mean?' asked Parzival, discomfited by that searching gaze.

'I mean despair,' Trevrizent said, 'which is the injured face of pride.'

'Or a sane response to times as bitter as these?' Parzival countered.

'Nevertheless it is a great sin.'

'Then am I a great sinner.'

'And in sore need of rest, I think.' The hermit smiled at the young knight. His eyes – they were a clear, tarn-water grey – softened with compassion. 'Forgive me, friend. Come, sit down and warm yourself at my fire while I find you some food. It will be simple fare, but it will sustain you.'

For an instant Parzival recalled what harm had come to him by obeying his mother's instruction always to pay attention to grey-haired old men, but he was so weary, and there was such wisdom and care in the hermit's smile that he could see no harm, and possibly some good, in doing as he was bidden. So he removed his iron armour and wrapped himself in a warm blanket and sat by the fire, eating the food that Trevrizent offered him. There was only plain water, almost freezing from the spring, to wash it down with, but he felt refreshed by its clarity and restored to his strength.

Later, as the fire crackled beside them and the stars glittered in the night above their heads, Trevrizent persuaded the young knight to unfold the troubles of his heart.

'A long time ago I was taught to follow God's light and to shun the dark Lord of Despair,' sighed Parzival at last. 'Yet by faithfully following the one I have only been led deeper into the other's grip.'

'How so?' asked the hermit, frowning.

But Parzival was not yet ready to share more than generalities with this stranger, however sympathetic he might seem. 'I have unwittingly brought death to ... one who was as close to me as life itself,' he confessed hoarsely. 'And then to a knight who was my kinsman too.' With a kind of grim defiance he looked up into the hermit's anxious frown. 'Yes, believe me guilty of these terrible crimes, for it is so. But believe also that I was utterly innocent of their intent. And if you understand that, you will see why I think hope is too frail a plant to withstand such cruel winds.'

'Yet if these crimes were unwitting ...' Trevrizent began after considering his words, but Parzival spoke impatiently across him.

'It makes no difference,' he snapped. 'The guilt grows like a canker on the heart.' He glanced away, stared gloomily into the heart of the fire. 'Nor is that the end of my shame. There is a further fault – one that forever banishes me from the wife I love.'

'Then unburden yourself of it,' Trevrizent urged. 'Tell me, what have you done to incur this shame?'

'Ask rather what I have not done. My crime is that I did not do something – something which I had been plainly told not to do. I was obedient to those I loved and trusted and it brought me only to harm. Tell me what sense there is in that – what glimmer of light, let alone of divine order in the world?'

'Let me answer your question with another,' said the hermit softly. 'How will you become yourself if you do only as others tell you?'

'But the man who advised me was a friend. He meant well for me.'

'Yet in matters of the soul we must sometimes do the very opposite of what friends advise.' Trevrizent was staring meditatively into the middle distance as he spoke, as though into some delicate passage of his own long story. 'Believe me,' he said, 'there are moments when loyalty to the inner light can feel like stepping into outer darkness.'

Parzival puzzled over these disturbing words for a time, not wanting to believe them. 'I think this is a dark answer you give me,' he said at last.

Trevrizent glanced back at him with a wan smile. 'Perhaps this world is not the simple place of light that you would have it.'

'Mine once was,' Parzival declared. 'Everything was clear – as clear as my love for my wife. I long for such innocent simplicity again, for it seems to me that everything else only corrupts the heart.'

Trevrizent stirred the embers of the blaze with a stick, shaking his head slowly. 'We were all born innocent, friend,' he sighed, 'as was Adam himself. But not since Cain raised his hand against his brother can any of us deny our share in the pain and darkness of the world.'

'For which it seems there is no remedy.'

'For which the only remedy is love.'

'However great the suffering, priest?'

'I am no priest,' said Trevrizent softly. 'Merely one who suffers in solitude like yourself. Yet I know our suffering is needful. We are what we make of our pain.'

'Say rather, what it makes of us,' retorted Parzival bitterly.

'No,' the hermit reproved him. 'Love leaves us free to choose. I think you have let pain close your heart. You must open it again.'

Parzival shook his head. His body shuddered under the rough blanket. 'Then grief will overwhelm me.'

'Perhaps not, if you can name it. Can you find words to speak your grief?'

Parzival stared into the fire. Silence was silting at his throat, yet in a life otherwise bereft of hope, the hermit's words offered at least the promise of release. For long moments he fought all kinds of resistance inside himself. His whole body was trembling, though not with cold. At last he heard his own voice like a whisper of frost on the darkness.

'I grieve for a father who never showed me his love,' he said. 'I grieve for a mother whose heart I broke because I myself did not know how to love. And I grieve for my wife whose truth has shown me how to love.'

'Surely such love can be trusted, friend,' the hermit answered him softly. 'Only be true to it and all shall be well.'

But Parzival knew he had barely yet embarked on a true confession of the darkness shadowing his soul. 'There is a greater grief,' he murmured, scarcely able to breathe the words. 'I have vowed not to come to her again until I have found the place of the Grail.'

The knight was not so preoccupied with his own unhappy fate that he failed to sense a sudden, wary stiffening of the hermit's body. Frowning, Trevrizent turned his face away to stare into the fire. When Parzival glanced across at him, troubled by the tense alteration in his manner, the hermit shook his white head, drew in his breath and said, 'No one comes before the Grail unless destiny consents. This I know, who have seen it with my own eyes.'

And Parzival was all attention now. Weariness fell from him. He sat up so quickly that the blanket fell from his shoulder, but he was indifferent to the piercing cold. 'You have been at Montsauvage?' he demanded.

'I have,' Trevrizent acknowledged uncertainly.

'Then tell me of the Grail. Explain its mystery.'

'It cannot be explained,' the hermit answered quietly, '– only experienced.'

'But what is it?' Parzival pressed. 'What is the Grail? Tell me what you can of it.' His tone became more urgent. 'I need to understand.'

For a long time Trevrizent looked into the young knight's eager face, as if assaying the quality of the soul that shone through those troubled eyes.

Eventually, as though a moment for which he had long prepared himself had finally arrived, he sighed, pulled his cowl closer about his head, and said, 'It is the sacred stone that was brought from Heaven by the neutral angels.'

'The *neutral* angels?'

Again Trevrizent drew a deep sigh. 'Have you not heard?' he said. 'There was a war in Heaven once, when the hosts of darkness rose against the powers of light. The whole starry firmament was torn apart in their struggle for dominion. But there were some who would not take sides in that terrible war. It was those neutral angels – they who strove to hold the universe together – who brought the Grail to earth, where it remains under the protection of the Grail guardians. It is the stone of healing – that which has the power to make life whole again.'

'A stone!' Parzival exclaimed in a quiet, wondering exhalation of breath. 'A stone from Heaven!'

'Yes,' said Trevrizent, his own face momentarily luminous in the gloom with the wonder of the thought. 'And in that stone's pure substance are wedded the virtues both of darkness and of light. Such is the singular nature of the Grail, and from that mysterious conjunction flows all the bounty of the earth.'

'Yet everywhere we look,' Parzival frowned, 'the land lies waste.'

'Because the Grail is kept in exile from it,' Trevrizent answered sadly. 'What is this wasteland but the absence of the Grail?'

'But why?' Parzival demanded. 'Why was it lost to us?'

The hermit sat in silence. For several moments, he seemed to withdraw deeper inside the darkness of his cowl. When he spoke his voice was burdened with grief. 'Your question strikes close to home,' he said. 'This is my family's shame. It has come about through the bitter fault of my own brother – Anfortas.'

'You are brother to the Rich Fisherman?' Parzival exclaimed in amazement.

'Say the Sorrowful Fisherman rather,' Trevrizent answered, 'for angling is the only pleasure left to him.' He would have fallen silent again, withdrawn into the austere cloister of his solitude, but now it was Parzival who pressed for speech, demanding with such urgency to learn more of Anfortas that the hermit at last consented to tell the story of his brother's fall from grace.

'Anfortas was the last king named as guardian to the Grail,' he explained. 'It is the holiest and most sacred charge – one that

requires the sacrifice of all worldly ambition and desire. Nor would I
have you think that my brother was weak, for neither the appetite for
power nor the lust for wealth could corrupt his noble mind. Yet
against the claims of love he proved quite helpless.'

'But have you not said that, of all things, love is to be trusted?'

'I have,' Trevrizent smiled wanly, 'but nothing is more difficult
than love. It comes in many guises, and if we mistake its nature we
can cause great harm. Such was the sin – and the sorrow – of
Anfortas. For whether it was through the malign influence of the
magician Klingsor, or simply through his own human frailty – for
the woman was very beautiful – I do not know; but my brother fell
in love with a proud lady who disdained him. He cared for nothing
save to win her heart, and her scorn caused him great suffering. In
his mad desire to possess her, Anfortas forsook his sacred charge
to do her will.' Trevrizent held his head in his hands for a time,
staring into the fire. 'It was for that proud lady's sake,' he sighed
eventually, 'that he fought in single combat against her sworn
enemy Gramoflanz – he who now calls himself King of the Wood.
In that fight Anfortas took a terrible wound in his groin. It is a
wound that festers with poisons from the lance that gave it. It will
not heal.'

'But if the Grail is a stone of healing,' Parzival frowned, 'why can
it not heal the wound?'

'It can,' Trevrizent answered. 'But Anfortas betrayed the Grail. Now
the sight of it is agony to him, though its virtue keeps him alive. But his
wound will not heal until one comes to Montsauvage who understands
the power of the Grail and restores it. And for that to happen there is a
question that must be asked.' Trevrizent shrugged as if with cold.
Parzival heard the heavy release of his breath on the night air. 'I have
heard that one came there who might have asked,' the hermit said with
a bitter note of regret in his voice, 'but he said nothing. So Anfortas

suffers still, and the land sickens with him.' He sighed again, glanced across at Parzival in the firelight. 'And you, friend ...'

'What of me?' said Parzival, scarcely able to draw breath.

'If your name is not written on the Grail you cannot hope to come to Montsauvage. Go home, I pray you. Go home to your wife's love.'

'I do not break my given word,' the knight grimly declared. 'If this Grail can be found, then it is I, Parzival, son of Gahmuret the Angevin, who will find it.'

'What!' Trevrizent exclaimed, his face whitening in the darkness. 'You are Gahmuret's son? Then you are sorely in need of pity and forgiveness. Your mother, the Lady Herzeloyde, was my own sister, and the knight you slew at Arthur's court was my good friend.'

All but stunned with shock, Parzival got to his feet and stood swaying in the fitful light from the fire. The night was cold at his face. He was gasping for air yet each breath seemed to turn to ice in his lungs. Staring down into the hermit's anxious gaze, he released a bitter, mirthless laugh. 'You see it then!' he cried. 'You see how everywhere I turn I'm made God's fool!' He laughed again, scoffing at the maze of stars which seemed in that moment no more than an immense machine designed for his particular torment. 'Well, uncle, what do you say now about God's love?'

'That it is larger than our understanding, nephew,' Trevrizent answered. 'Your guilt is great, yes, but ... I cannot think it lies beyond forgiveness.'

'Out of your charity and noble heart, you may forgive me,' Parzival retorted, 'but I cannot forgive myself. And there is more. Having learned so much of my shame you had better know the whole terrible truth of it. I was the fool who came to Montsauvage and failed to ask about the suffering of the King.'

'You?' Trevrizent gasped.

'I was guided there by the Rich Fisherman himself,' Parzival confessed, his voice unremitting now in the bitterness of his self-accusation. 'He gave me the sword which the Grail-bearer had sent to him. I saw the lance that runs with blood. I sat at the table of the Grail. I felt its radiance and ate of its bounty. Yet I did not speak.'

'Dear God! Here is great cause for grief, my Parzival,' the hermit cried. 'Yet the ways of the Grail were ever mysterious. If you could come there again ...'

'There is no hope, uncle,' Parzival interrupted him. 'I have been searching for many years since then but the place of the Grail withholds itself.'

'Yet you are of the family of the Grail,' Trevrizent urged. 'You are nephew to Anfortas and to Repanse de Joie, the bearer of the Grail.'

'There was another there,' said Parzival with a wistful frown of regret. 'An old man with silver hair who was as beautiful as he is ancient.'

'Titurel. Your great-grandfather who was the first guardian of the Grail. His life is sustained by the precious sight of it and he cannot die in peace until the new guardian comes. All these are your kinsfolk, Parzival.'

'And all have found me unworthy.'

'They have found you young and untried,' the hermit sought to console him.

'Yet I am honoured even at Arthur's court as a great knight,' Parzival cried defiantly. 'Since I left Caerleon I've fought with more knights than I can count and none proved worthier.'

Trevrizent studied his nephew, nodding as he listened. 'You have courage, pride, a powerful will, all the knightly virtues, yes,' he said. 'But the Grail asks more.'

'I've sacrificed my whole life to this quest,' Parzival exclaimed in baffled fury. 'What more can be asked?'

'That which is the hardest of all things, and the softest also,' the hermit answered. 'I mean the gentle strength of a mature and constant heart.'

'And where should one learn that in this fickle world?'

'Perhaps you should leave that world for a time?' Trevrizent said. 'Believe me, nephew, a life of action quickly loses all sense of meaning if it is not also grounded in contemplation.'

Parzival looked round at the hermit's cramped little bothy, the hearth in which the fire was guttering, the night glittering blackly above the bare trees. 'Do you imagine I'll find my lost light in *this* gloomy wilderness?' he sneered.

But the hermit calmly withstood his sarcasm. 'I think you'll never find your light again,' he said quietly, 'until you've found your way to your shadow too.'

'I don't understand that,' Parzival said, reaching for his weapons, determined to move on now, away from this living reminder of his failure and shame.

'How should you,' Trevrizent replied sternly, 'when you recognize only your own virtues and blame all your misfortunes on the world outside?'

'Not without reason,' Parzival snapped back. 'I've done nothing to deserve this fate. I was true to God's light, I was true to what Gurnemanz taught me. I have been true both to my wife and to this terrible quest that keeps me from her. Since I first rode out of the wildwood my every intention has been good.'

'Yet life will not be ruled by our intentions,' Trevrizent said. 'And perhaps that is just as well, for which of us is perfect?'

Parzival had been about to buckle on the sword that Anfortas had given him. Its weight was in his hands as Trevrizent added, 'But then perfection is not asked of us. Life wants us rather to be *whole*, my Parzival. To be wholly ourselves. And for that we must admit our darkness as well as our light. We must strive to hold them together as the stone from heaven does.'

Stopped in his tracks by the hermit's words, Parzival was looking down at the sword he held. He saw how closely he had identified himself with the fierce sheen of its edge as though he himself were no more than a righteous blaze of light. He felt the difference between his own frenzy of despair – its fury and guilt, its bitter, cynical reproach against life – and the serene poise of the white-haired veteran of pain across from him – the man in the simple hermit's cowl, who was holding out a beckoning hand into the gap between them now as he stood in the guttering shadows of the firelight, saying, 'I pray you, nephew, stay with me a while. Let you and I meditate in friendship on these things.'

CHAPTER ELEVEN

THE

PROUD LADY

eanwhile the years had also passed for Gawain, that other aspect of the questing soul, whose restless – some would say *faithless* – heart carried into life the shadow-side of Parzival's undeviating constancy.

One hot afternoon, as he made his dream-like way towards the Castle of the Marvels, he was parched with thirst and sweltering inside his coat of mail when he came upon a spring where a woman sat with her back to him. She was singing to herself as she braided the shining fall of her hair. The day stood tall and blue above her. On the dry summer air the music in her voice rippled as clear and liquid as the spring. Gawain felt his senses suddenly attuned to the rapt, spellbound quality of the moment. The woman turned her pale cheek at the sound of his approach. His gaze met hers and he found himself pierced to the quick by a dark, flashing beauty of such vivid intensity that for a long moment he forgot to breathe.

'Do you stare at every woman that way?' the Lady asked as she made fast the last braid of her hair.

'Only those who command the attention of my soul,' Gawain

answered, dismounting. 'Lady, allow me the joy of your closer company.'

But the woman glanced vaguely away, saying, 'Why should I trouble myself to pleasure you?'

Unused to such cold absence of interest, Gawain was momentarily discomposed and when he spoke it was with an honesty that surprised him. 'Because otherwise you keep my heart from what it thirsts for now, and I might die of it.'

'One slain so easily is no use to me,' the lady scoffed, studying her fingernails.

'Then you *are* in need of service?' he said.

'And if I were why should I turn to you?'

'Because I am Gawain,' the knight smiled, 'and have a name for courage.'

The Lady frowned as if puzzling over this declaration, then gave a lightly dismissive snort. 'The name means nothing to me.'

Again Gawain had to think quickly to regain her attention. 'Then I'm delighted to find myself ahead of my reputation at last,' he said, aware how dry his voice was. 'I have a great thirst on me, Lady. Allow me to drink from this spring then put me to whatever test you choose.'

'Drink,' she invited with casual indifference. Gawain knelt where the spring poured from the bank of the little dell into the stream. He was cupping his hands at the freshet when the lady added, 'But I warn you, knight, my service brings nothing but humiliation.' He lifted the water to his lips, gazing up at this extraordinary woman as he drank. 'Is that to your taste?' she asked.

'Your beauty is, Lady,' he answered, 'and for the sweet reward of possessing that I would face any risk.'

'Then you, sir ...' She paused as if to listen to the faint sound of music that came from beyond the rise of the dell – fiddles and flutes, a tambourine and a drum beating out a quaint, rustic dance.

'Yes?' Gawain encouraged.

'... are the mindless fool I first thought you.' She got to her feet, arranging her skirts, as if she had lost even the slight interest she had shown in his presence.

As fascinated by this lovely woman as he was astonished now, Gawain recovered from the blow – it had felt like being smacked across the cheek with a silken glove. 'Will you not at least tell me your name?' he said.

'No,' the woman answered shortly, then gave him a petulant frown. 'I tire of this tedious place. If you want to be of service, fetch my horse.'

'Gladly.' Gawain got to his feet and looked around him. 'Where will I find it?'

The lady gestured vaguely beyond the rise. 'There is a bridge over there. Walk over it and you will come to an orchard where those other fools are dancing. The beast is tethered there.'

'Will you hold my own steed while I go?' he asked.

'Do you take me for a stable-maid?'

'No, Lady,' Gawain answered, stung by her haughty tone, 'I take you for the mistress of my heart.' But the woman gave no sign of being moved by his reply, so he patted Gringolet's flank as the horse drank from the stream, muttered, 'Wait here, old fellow,' and walked off towards the bridge. He was about to disappear from sight between the trees when he heard her voice behind him.

'You may travel with me, knight.'

He turned, smiling, nodded in reply, then with his heart absurdly gladdened by this first faint sign of her approval, crossed the wooden bridge into an orchard of apple trees where a company of men and women were dancing gaily together. They waved in welcome as he walked among them, calling, 'Come join us. Join our dance. Come dance with us, fair knight.' But Gawain's eyes were already fixed on the dappled mare he had seen tethered by its rich bridle amid a swirl of blossom from an apple tree. Smiling, he waved the dancers aside and walked towards the horse, but when they realized what he intended to do, the dancers stopped to watch and the musicians lowered their instruments. Self-conscious in the sudden silence, Gawain approached the mare. He was reaching to untether it when a man called out, 'I advise you not to touch that palfrey, sir.'

The knight turned and saw the man looming close to him, grim-faced. Still smiling, but with his hand resting closer to his sword-hilt, Gawain said, 'Faith, would you prevent me, sir?'

'By no means,' the man answered, 'but be wise and leave the beast alone.'

'Your advice smacks more of cowardice than wisdom,' Gawain said with a dismissive snort. As he loosened the halter where it was tied at the branch, one of the women who had tempted him to the dance put a hand to her mouth and called, 'A curse on she who brings so many brave knights to their doom.'

Gawain turned his head and fixed her with a stern glower. 'Madam, if you speak of the lady to whom this mare belongs, I'd have you take back that curse.'

'Alas for you, knight,' the woman answered him undaunted. 'You'll find that lady less fair than she appears.'

The men and women stood watching the knight in silence as he took the mare by its gorgeously enwrought bridle and led it through the orchard towards the bridge. One or two of them shook their heads as though lamenting his folly.

Gawain walked on past them in disdain. The mare's hooves resounded on the wooden bridge but he heard the mutter of whispering behind him, and suddenly the whole company in the orchard burst into coarse laughter.

Suspecting some crude joke at his expense, the knight halted and turned, his hand reaching for his sword, but in the same moment the music struck up again and the men and women returned happily to the measures of their dance as though nothing of lasting interest had happened.

Baffled, a little uneasy now, Gawain led the mare across the bridge and down into the dell. When he came out between the trees he saw the lady standing by his horse, Gringolet, and smiling up at a deformed dwarf, who sat perched in the saddle like a grotesque parody of himself. The creature's hair bristled like a hedgehog's coat and two great fangs protruded from his mouth like tusks.

Gawain said, 'It seems I've taken better care of your horse than you have of mine.'

'You were so long about your errand that I'd quite given up on you,' the lady answered with a derisive toss of her head. 'This dwarf was amusing me. He cuts a fine figure, don't you think?'

'I think he's a fine foil for your beauty, Lady. I've seen nothing so hideous since the witch Cundrie came into Arthur's court.'

'Cundrie is his sister. I think his features are the mark of a lecherous mind.' When the dwarf cackled with glee at her words, she said, 'Tell this fool what you think of him, dwarf.'

'That he's a fool indeed,' cackled the dwarf, 'if he came back expecting gratitude. And a still greater fool if he intends to follow you.'

'If you were twice your size, dwarf,' Gawain scowled, 'I'd make you rue that insult.'

'And if I were twice your size,' the dwarf scoffed back, 'I still wouldn't be fool enough to wear *my* brain between my legs.'

Both dwarf and lady chuckled with mirth at the retort. Flushing with anger now, Gawain said, 'I advise you to watch your foul mouth, dwarf.'

'And I advise you to blunt your lust, knight,' the dwarf came back, 'and sharpen your wits.' He dug the little spurs at his heels into

Gringolet's flanks. Seeing his horse chafe at the sharp pain, Gawain released the mare and reached for Gringolet's bridle, shouting, 'Get off my horse, or I'll throw you off it.' But the animal was unsettled now, bucking and snorting even at his master's approach.

'O brave!' cried the Lady. 'Now I see why you have a name for courage. It takes valour indeed to defy a dwarf!'

At that moment, the dwarf spurred Gringolet again so that the horse whinnied as it turned and reared, knocking the knight aside. 'Catch me if you can, fool!' the dwarf shouted, struck the horse across its hind-quarters with his riding crop and, cackling with triumphant laughter, galloped away through the dell.

'Faith, Lady, you keep ill company,' Gawain panted, trying to recover his dignity.

'And it grows worse,' she answered, 'when a witty dwarf is driven off by a self-regarding oaf. And still, for all your boasting, there's only one horse – which is mine.' She reached for the pommel on the mare's saddle. 'Come, give me your hand. You will make as good a mounting-block as any.'

As Gawain clasped his hands to lift her up into the saddle, he said, 'Your ankles are slender, Lady.'

'Not so slender as your chances of winning my favour, footman!' And with that she kicked Gawain away from the mare's side, knocking him off balance, and pulled round the head of her mount.

'Your tongue may be cruel, Lady,' said Gawain, 'but I think the light in your eyes is less harsh.'

'Then you delude yourself.'

Gawain gazed up at her in wonder and dismay. 'I hope not, Lady,' he said, 'for I swear love has never possessed my soul like this before.'

'Ha, do you say so, knight? Then must my fond heart swoon – were it not sure that you've said those words a thousand times before!'

'I have,' Gawain admitted, wide-eyed and breathless at his own truthfulness. 'I admit it freely and to my shame. But I've never meant them before.' He stood, wondering, unfamiliar to himself, yet with a gathering sensation of tender self-disclosure. 'Not until this moment,' he whispered, 'did I even begin to understand what they might mean.'

But the Lady merely looked down at him with a scoffing snort of disbelief.

'I swear it,' said Gawain, '– on my soul's honour.'

'The honour of a self-confessed deceiver! Why should I believe you – even if I wanted to?'

'Because in disparaging my truth,' he answered with a confidence that came only from his own unquestioning devotion, 'you may injure your own. I think there is a destiny between us, Lady. It feels as if both our lives are at risk here.'

'I do not fear for mine,' she retorted. 'I've seen too much of it already.'

For the first time since he had heard her singing, Gawain thought he caught a note of absolute sincerity in her voice. Its harshness was directed against herself yet it gave him greater hurt than any of the barbs she had shot his way. It made his heart ache for her. 'A sad admission for one so fair,' he said. Then his eyes brightened with hope as he gazed up at her. 'But you've seen nothing of life as we might live it together – two proud spirits such as you and I!'

She gave a brief scornful laugh. 'I've had my pick of proud spirits. My single pleasure has been to humble them all. Why should it be any different with you?'

Gawain sustained the fierce dismissal of her gaze. 'Because, to my shame, Lady, I too have wounded many who loved me. But I begin to see how such exploits are an insult to the heart.'

'Then let those who have a heart avoid them,' she answered. 'As for me, I go my ways.' With a click of her tongue she urged her mount into motion and rode slowly away from the man who stared up at her in wonder, calling, 'I think life must have given you great hurt, Lady!'

Without looking back, she said, 'Does the footman set himself up as physician now?' and rode on, but the mare was ambling quite slowly through the ferns, so it wasn't difficult for him to catch up and walk by her side.

'In such a case as yours,' he said, 'I know of one sovereign remedy.'

'Which is love, I suppose,' she answered. 'Pah! A quack's potion! I've sicked it up many times.'

'Ah!' Gawain smiled, 'now I begin to understand. Lady, I think you are afraid of love.'

For a moment she said nothing. Thinking that he had at last found a vulnerable place in her cold armour, Gawain glanced up at her, but met only contempt in those lovely eyes. 'You were more effective as a mounting-block,' she said. 'And more amusing. You know *nothing* about me.'

'Enough to recognize my own soul when I see it,' he said.

'I am no-one's soul but my own. As you'll find to your cost if you cling to me.'

'I shall,' Gawain declared. 'I'll treasure every hurt that you give me till you own yourself mine.'

'Then grow rich in pain – if you live long enough. For be warned,' she stared down at him, 'I measure a man by his deeds not his words.'

'Have I not already asked you to put me to the test?'

'Oh I shall,' she said, 'I shall!'

'Then you'll find there's neither man nor monster that I dare not meet for your sweet sake.'

'But can you overcome your own base self?' the Lady challenged. Then she gave a bitter laugh. 'And harder still – can you endure the dark side of a woman, knight?' With that, she clipped her riding crop across the mare's flanks and cantered away out onto an open heath.

'Your eyes are dark but they are also beautiful,' Gawain called after her. 'I want to know everything about you.'

'Then you have much to learn, fool,' her voice rang back at him on the breeze.

Gawain stood, watching her go. 'You are so proud, Lady,' he shouted, 'that I shall call you Orguleuse.' But this time she gave him no answer. Sunlight flashed off her blue gown as she crossed the heath. A pheasant rose out of the bracken and whirred away, ratcheting its call across the hot sky.

Feeling his heart swell with a desire so intense he was uncertain whether there was more delight in it or pain, Gawain whispered to the warm air, 'And God help me now, for so fierce is your hold on my heart I cannot help myself.'

Then he set off in pursuit of her.

CHAPTER TWELVE

THE

FERRYMAN'S

DAUGHTER

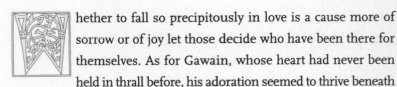hether to fall so precipitously in love is a cause more of sorrow or of joy let those decide who have been there for themselves. As for Gawain, whose heart had never been held in thrall before, his adoration seemed to thrive beneath his lady's scorn. For long miles in the heat of the afternoon he followed on foot in the tracks of her mare, disregarding her jibes and silences, until they came eventually to a magnificent castle which rose in a shimmer of white stone on the far bank of a broad, swiftly flowing river.

As the lady cantered some distance ahead of him to meet the approaching ferryboat, Gawain paused to catch his breath. Looking up at the high towers of the castle, he saw many ladies gathered at the windows gazing back down at him. In a moment of sudden realization, it occurred to him that he had come at last to the Castle of the Marvels. He began to run after his lady to ask whether this was indeed the case, but she was already leading her mare aboard the ferry before he could catch up with her. Twice he called out for her to wait for him, then he heard her voice, deliberately loud, carried back towards him on the breeze. 'Ferryman, that cheapjack at my heels cannot pay his passage,' she was saying. 'Leave him ashore.'

By the time Gawain had reached the bank, the ferryman had already pushed off and was poling his boat back across the river. The lady stood at the stern with an amused smirk at her lips. She was about to turn away when Gawain called, 'When shall I see you again?'

With a wry laugh the woman answered, 'Not till the dark of moon.'

'Then when that time comes,' Gawain shouted across the widening gap of water, 'I promise you a night of sweet moaning, Lady.'

With a haughty tilt of her chin, she lifted one hand and pointed along the bank to Gawain's left. 'Look over there,' she called. 'There's trouble coming.' Gawain turned his head and saw an armed knight galloping towards him round the bend of the river. His lance was not lowered but he was coming on at a furious pace, and mounted on Gawain's own stolen charger, Gringolet. 'If that knight's lance rips the bottom from your hose,' the Lady laughed, 'then those ladies at the windows will have a new moon to stare at.'

When he was within a few yards of Gawain, the knight reined in Gringolet so harshly that the steed rose up on its hind legs, flashing its forehooves in the air. Gawain could see the foam at its mouth and the sweat glistening at its back. 'That horse is mine, sir,' he shouted angrily.

'And that lady is mine,' shouted the knight, throwing aside his lance. 'Defend yourself.' He leapt from the saddle, drew his broadsword and advanced on Gawain swinging the blade through the air. Gawain unsheathed his own sword just in time to parry a blow, then the two men were fighting for their lives under the eyes of the silent women who looked down from the high windows of the castle.

It was late afternoon when the duel began, both men were deft swordsmen and both were strong, so dusk had begun to fall before either of them had won an advantage over the other. Dust rose at their feet and choked the air. Inside their helmets both men's heads were aching with the ring of sword against sword and the clash of shield on shield. Orguleuse had long since disappeared inside the castle so all of Gawain's attention was focused on defeating this fanatical opponent but he was beginning to wonder whether he had the strength for it when he recovered from a clumsy sally with so swift a riposte that the other man was unbalanced. Following through with the full weight of his shield, Gawain knocked him backwards to the ground, kicked away the sword that had dropped from the knight's hand as he fell, then he was standing over him, with just enough breath left to demand that he yield.

His opponent lay on the ground with the point of Gawain's sword at his gorget, shaking his head. 'Kill me, knight,' he groaned. 'I'll not be shamed in the eyes of that proud lady.'

'No,' Gawain answered, 'it was a good fight. Let that be an end of it.'

'Give me death, damn you,' the fallen knight demanded, wild-eyed. 'My life is worthless now.'

But Gawain shook his head and withdrew his sword. 'I'll not kill one who fights so bravely for the same lady as myself,' he said and turned away to attend to Gringolet.

'Then I'll kill myself if I must,' the knight panted.

Shocked by the desperation in his voice Gawain turned back to him and saw the young man drawing a dagger from the scabbard at his belt. The blade was out and reaching for the knight's throat when Gawain cuffed his arm with a forceful swing of his own gauntlet and the two men were struggling bodily again. Only with great difficulty did Gawain manage to wrest the dagger away from him and throw it aside, then he stood, restraining the man with his own powerful arms in a clumsy sort of embrace as he stared into his anguished eyes. 'Are you quite mad?' he panted.

The young knight turned his head away. 'You should have let me kill myself.'

'Go your ways, knight,' Gawain answered. 'You're young still. There are plenty of other women in the world.'

'Do you have eyes for any of them now?' the knight demanded, his voice fraught with despair. There was an almost famished pallor to his face. The two men stood panting, gripped closely together, each staring at a harsh reflection of himself in the other's eyes. At last Gawain pushed him away. 'That lady is mine, I say,' he glowered. 'Resign yourself to it and be free of this hopeless love.'

The young knight turned away, consumed with jealousy and loss. 'Then I wish you more joy of her than I ever found,' he answered hoarsely, and bent to recover his dagger and sword.

Still suspecting that the man might injure himself, Gawain again pushed him away. 'No, these weapons stay with me.'

The knight lifted one hand to his head for a moment, staring at his rival with a bitter mix of pity and baffled fury conflicting in his face. 'Take care, knight,' he said, 'or the Duchess will drive you to madness too.' Then he turned on his heel and walked away.

With a disturbing sensation of watching his own vanquished shadow slink away, Gawain watched the young knight go, then he turned to pay attention to his horse. For the first time he realized that the entire fight had been observed by the ferryman who approached him now from where he'd been sitting by his moored boat.

'You fought well, sir,' the man said, with a wryly cocked brow, 'but this is my field you fought on and you must pay toll for it.'

'Then take that madman's weapons in payment,' Gawain answered. 'I've no use for them.'

The ferryman bent to pick up the sword and dagger and examined their jewelled pommels with a shrewd eye. 'Hmm, they'll fetch more than enough.' His grizzled face broke into a smile. 'Will you lodge in my house tonight?'

'I'd rather you ferried me across that river.'

But the boatman shook his head. 'I will, sir, but not now. That is Klingsor's castle. There's darkness enough there in daytime. I'll not go there by night.'

Thinking that the man was merely angling after more money, Gawain said, 'Name your price. I mean to join my lady there right now.'

'Not in my boat,' the man answered, 'and there's no other.' His refusal was gloomily absolute, but a moment later he smiled up at Gawain with narrowed eyes. 'Shelter with me tonight. You must be weary, sir. And look, your arm is bleeding.' Gawain looked down at his wrist where blood oozed from under his sleeve. Conscious of the stiffness in his sword arm, he saw where the young knight's blade had ripped through the mail to cut the flesh near his shoulder. As if it had merely been waiting for attention, the wound began to smart. Gawain's armour felt heavy about him. His stomach quailed with hunger.

'Come, my cottage is just over there,' the ferryman invited. 'I can stable your horse, and I have a daughter who'll look to your needs.'

So with a wistful look back at where the high towers of the castle disappeared into the gloom, Gawain allowed himself to be led to the cottage. The ferryman's pretty daughter, Elise, tended his wound with salves and bandages, then served him a satisfying meal, but not even her coy banter and quick, flirtatious glances could stave off the knight's great weariness. He withdrew to his chamber and soon fell into a deep sleep, from which he was eventually woken by the chill of dawn.

Thinking of his lady, he lifted the curtain at the window by his bed and saw the castle across the river in the misty light. To his amazement he made out the faces of the women still gazing from the windows as though they had kept watch there, unsleeping, all night. And then, softly, as in a dream, he heard the door of his chamber creak open. Turning his head at the sound, he saw Elise standing in the gloom with her hands clasped together under her chin, and the tresses of her hair unbraided at her shoulders.

'I couldn't sleep,' she whispered. 'I kept remembering the way you fought, and how merciful you were, and it stirred my heart.'

'Child, if your father catches you here ...' Gawain began, but Elise spoke over him, stepping a little closer. 'Oh, he knows where I am,' she declared as if it was the most natural thing in the world. 'I'm here with his blessing.'

'Are you now?' Gawain saw how the curves of the young woman's body were outlined through her nightgown by the light from the window. 'Well,' he smiled uncertainly, 'it was a generous thought, but ...'

'It's a cold hour, sir,' Elise wriggled her bare shoulders. 'And me with nothing but my shift.'

'God, what am I thinking of?' he exclaimed. 'Here, take this blanket.'

Stepping still closer, she said, 'May I not rather share your bed?' And before Gawain could demur, the girl had slipped under the blanket to lie beside him.

'Oh well,' he laughed, 'as you're in already.' Then he felt her soft warmth snuggling up into the crook of his arm. 'But you must lie still,' he added hoarsely. And, when her hip wriggled against his thigh, 'Do you hear?'

'It seems a waste of a soft bed,' Elise whispered. 'You're very warm, sir!'

She sat up, swiftly pulled the shift off over her head, and wriggled down again with the palm of her hand sliding from his chest to his stomach. When he tried to pull away, she pleaded teasingly. 'Don't you like me? I thought from the looks you were giving me downstairs ...'

Again Gawain tried to make a safe space between his naked flesh and hers. 'I do like you,' he said. 'Of course I do, but ...'

'Well then,' Elise giggled, and pushed her belly and limbs much closer.

'Elise, little friend,' Gawain gasped, 'you must lie still.'

She lifted herself up in the bed so that he felt the soft fall of her breast against his skin. 'Don't you want me then?' she asked, gazing down at him wide-eyed. When he didn't answer, her cold fingers slipped down towards his thigh. 'Oh yes,' she whispered, 'I think perhaps you do!'

'Don't do that,' Gawain spluttered. 'Oh God, at any other time I'd gladly have taken you. But now I ...' He sat up in the bed, feeling the chill at his naked back. 'Faith, what's the matter with me?' A moment later he drew in his breath with an audible gasp as the girl's fingers closed around him. 'Elise,' he hissed, *'don't.'*

But her grip gently tightened. 'Where's the harm, sir?' she whispered. 'I know you'll not stay longer than this night ... but we can make the night sweet, can't we?'

She lifted a soft thigh and laid it over his. He felt the touch of her tongue at his chest. The curls of her hair brushed against the skin of his neck. He drew in his breath and slid down into the bed again, his mouth reaching for hers. Smoothly she raised her body over him. His hands slipped down to her thighs and his eyes closed as he felt her mouth fall damply open. Then, in the darkness of his mind, he saw the ladies watching from the castle windows, and his Lady Orguleuse among them, staring down at him with a derisory sneer at her lips. Instantly he pulled away from the girl's probing tongue. 'I can't,' he said. 'I can't. My heart lies elsewhere.'

'But who's to know?' the girl's voice coaxed. 'I'll be no trouble. I promise.'

For a moment longer Gawain wavered. He gasped at the skill of her touch – she was licking his throat now, moving the full span of her hips against him – but in his mind's eye he saw his lady's scornful face again and at once his manhood wilted. Pushing the girl firmly away, he turned his back on her. '*I'll* know,' he said, glumly abashed, and lay frowning into the dawn-lit chamber. 'God,' he muttered to himself, amazed at the numb shock in his voice, 'I can't do it. I really can't do it!'

Lying on her back beside him, Elise pulled the sheet up over her breasts, and pouted at the ceiling. She said, 'It's that proud lady, isn't it?'

'To my pain and sorrow, yes,' he frowned, '– though God knows she'll have nothing to do with me.'

'Then you should count yourself lucky!'

'*Lucky*!' he protested in disbelief. 'If I can't have her I'll go as crazy as the poor fool I fought today.' Present only in his need for sympathy and understanding, he stared down at the girl. 'What do you know about her, Elise? Who is she? Tell me everything you know.' But far from responding to the urgency of his plea, she shrugged away from him with an impatient sigh. 'I'm sorry,' he said, 'I do like you, I think you're very pretty, but ... Talk to me, Elise.' And when she still said nothing, 'Are you sulking?'

'I don't want to talk about *her*.'

'All right,' he said, 'I understand.' And lay in frustrated silence for a moment before lurching up again. 'But at least tell me about the castle over there, and the ladies I've seen at its windows.'

'I can't,' Elise protested anxiously. 'I don't want to. Don't press me so.'

Gawain had detected the change in the girl's voice. Her refusal was nervous rather than petulant now but he leaned over her, trying to fix her with his most soulful gaze. 'Elise, I need to know. Who is this Klingsor? You must tell me what you know. My life might depend on it.' But the girl pulled away from him and sat up, whimpering, with her hands across her breasts. When he tried to shake some sense into her, she began to cry more loudly. 'I can't', she wailed, slipping her legs out of the bed, 'it frightens me.'

Concerned at the amount of noise she was making, Gawain called for her to come back and tried to hush her. 'I didn't mean to frighten you,' he apologized more gently, but she was sobbing still, and a moment later Gawain heard her father's voice in the passage outside, asking what all the commotion was about. 'It's nothing, friend,' Gawain reassured him. 'I merely asked your daughter about the castle and she grew afraid.'

Pulling her shift back over her shoulders, Elise cried, 'He didn't want me, father,' and ran weeping from the room. The ferryman stood in the open doorway, studying Gawain with a grim frown.

Then he said, 'Do you still mean to go there, sir?'

'I do,' Gawain declared, reaching for his hose and beginning to get dressed. 'Why are you both so fearful? What is this place?'

His voice heavy with dread, the ferryman said, 'You are in the Land of Marvels at the Castle of Marvels, about to enter the Bed of Marvels, whereon your end is certain to be death.'

'Then you'd better give me your advice,' Gawain said lightly. He had snorted at the threat, but he could hear his own heart beating in the silence.

'That castle is ruled by the magician Klingsor.' The ferryman's hand rasped across his chin as he studied the knight. 'My advice is to withdraw.'

Buttoning his tunic, Gawain said, 'I know nothing of this Klingsor, but Cundrie the Sorceress has challenged me to free the many ladies held captive in that castle, and the woman I love has entered it. So you can tell me the devil himself rules there if you like – I will still go.'

Gravely the ferryman shook his head. 'This is foolhardy, sir.' But Gawain ignored the man's evident anxiety and continued to dress himself, wincing at the stiffness in his injured arm as he pulled on his heavy coat of mail. Outside a cockerel bragged from its dunghill to the breaking light.

'Very well,' the ferryman sighed dubiously, 'I'll do what I can to help you. There is a shield you must take with you. It will cover your whole body. Once you are inside the castle you must never let go of it, do you hear? Not even to sleep.'

'Don't worry.' Gawain buckled on his sword belt. 'I shan't think of sleep till Klingsor's spell is broken.'

'Are you so sure you'll be in control of your thoughts?' said the ferryman. 'Hear me, sir – trust only to the shield, even though the place may seem quite deserted.'

'Very well, friend,' Gawain smiled at the man's doom-laden manner. 'What else?'

Again the ferryman gloomily shook his head. 'Pass through the halls of that place till you come to the chamber where the Bed of Marvels waits,' he said. 'Lie down on it – and pray!'

CHAPTER THIRTEEN

THE

MAGIC BED

o we not all live in a land of marvels, friends, and does not each of us sleep nightly in a marvellous bed of dreams? For in this strange world how are we to tell reality from illusion, and whether we wake or if we dream? And is there not cause to wonder whether there is a real world out there at all, or do we rather go to meet it as it unfolds around us from within?

Such questions troubled Gawain's mind as the ferryman poled his boat through the dawn mist drifting across the river. He heard the foggy calls of waterfowl, the dip and splash of the pole. Then the castle loomed above them like an emanation of the mist as they approached the further shore. The boatman shipped his pole and caught at a mooring. Gawain clambered onto the jetty hampered by the heavy bulk of the huge shield that the man had given him. Broad enough at the top to cover his head and shoulders, and tapering all the way down to his feet, its scoop of metal was so unwieldy that it was like carrying an iron door on his arm.

'Remember the shield at all times,' the ferryman whispered after him.

'It's so big I can hardly forget it!' Gawain grunted. 'But I thank you for your aid and counsel. Wish me well, friend.'

'I wish you what you wish for yourself,' the ferryman answered, and pushed his boat back out into the water.

Gawain watched him disappear into the mist, then he hitched the shield at his shoulder and stared up at the ramparts. As he passed through the unguarded gate a dense silence hovered across both outer and inner wards. There was no sound or motion anywhere, not even the stirring of a breeze. Everything felt so unnaturally still that he jumped in alarm at the sudden clank of iron when the point of his shield grazed against the stone steps that led up into the central keep. And once inside the keep, the silence grew still denser and more unnerving.

The way to the state rooms stood open, and each painted chamber that Gawain entered felt as though its occupants had withdrawn a mere moment before he passed through the door – yet only his own footfall echoed across the marble floors. Of the many ladies who had watched him from the windows there was no sign. Still less could he see any indication of the dark power that imprisoned them. Had the silence not been heavy with menace, Gawain might have believed that there was nothing to fear in the place but himself.

A spiral stairway in the corner of the great hall took him up to the next floor. Again he passed through a number of empty chambers until, with an echoing sigh of hinges, he threw open the door on to the inmost room.

Staring inside, he released an involuntary gasp of wonder. 'Faith,' he whispered, 'if ever there was a bed of marvels, this is surely it!'

It stood in the centre of the smooth and otherwise bare rink of its chamber – huge and plush, and canopied with heavy brocades that hung from tall oaken bedposts to which, at floor level, were fixed what might have been upright millstones had they not been fashioned from some crystalline mineral that glowed with ruby light. He had never seen such a majestic bed before. It was a bed to revel in, a bed in which generations of bawling infants might have been born, a bed – Gawain suddenly remembered – in which a man might meet a tremendous death.

'Yet must I lie on you, bed,' he whispered.

Hitching the shield awkwardly at his shoulder again, he closed the door behind him and took a step towards the bed. As soon as he did so, the ruby wheels revolved and the stately piece of furniture rolled a yard or two away from him like a wagon. Gawain froze on the spot, astonished by this first, utterly unexpected sign of activity in the whole castle. Then he took another step.

Immediately the bed moved again.

'Do you fear for your virginity, bed?' Gawain laughed uneasily. Again he advanced, again the bed rolled away. 'Lie still,' he whispered as though to a nervous animal, or to a girl he was about to seduce. Then he lunged quickly. Just as quickly the bed moved off, picking up speed, and began to career violently around the room, lurching and turning and flapping its canopy, as though outraged by his clumsy attempt on its modesty. The grinding noise of the wheels and the scrape of the bed against stone walls echoed around the empty chamber. 'Be still, damn you,' Gawain shouted above the din as he chased the frantic bed round the room, twisting and turning in its tracks.

Finding his efforts hampered by the weighty bulk of the shield, he was about to put it down when he remembered the ferryman's warning. He stood, thinking for the moment as the bed banged and crashed about the chamber. Then, holding the shield up, away from the floor, he turned his back on the bed as though losing interest, waited for it to come rushing past him and, at that moment, leapt into the air and threw himself backwards to land gasping on the feather mattress.

At once the wheels screeched to a halt. Gawain lay panting under the weight of the shield. He was congratulating himself on bringing this mad contraption under control at last, when the bed swung round on its axles, accelerated again and crashed its way from wall to wall in crazy efforts to throw him off.

All the masonry of the tower was shaken by the din. It was as if the whole castle was under demolition by a battery of siege engines. Beams might have been falling, stone vaults tumbling down. Jarred by the shock of each violent collision, Gawain lay with gritted teeth, trying to hold on to the clumsy shield that covered his whole body like an iron lid, muttering, 'Dear God, lady! I dreamed of you bidding me to a gentler bed than this!'

And once more the bed juddered to a halt. The echoes rattled and faded. The bed lay there in silence, thinking.

Unable to see anything but the back of his shield, Gawain waited for a few moments, daring to hope that he'd broken the will of this deranged machine. When nothing happened, he lifted the shield to peer round it. Immediately, from somewhere in the canopy above him, a hidden battery of slingshots flung a shower of stones and bolts at him. They struck with an impact so sharp that his flesh was cut and bruised beneath his coat of mail. Bleeding at the lip, half-stunned with shock and pain, the knight opened his dizzied eyes in time to see the door of the chamber swing open with a bang, and a burly, naked figure like a chalk giant strode in, holding a swollen cudgel.

'At least you're not wearing armour, friend,' Gawain muttered, drawing his sword to meet this new threat. 'I have the better of you there.'

But the ogre merely snarled as he brandished the cudgel twice about his head, and the snarl deepened to a deafening growl. When Gawain blinked to clear his head, he found himself facing not a man but a huge, famished lion that opened its red throat in a roar, and with a single flick of its massive paw all but sent the shield flying from his grip. Unbalanced, the knight was knocked back across the bed. With another ferocious roar, the beast was on him, and there was no time to think before he was fighting for his life. He could taste the hot stink of the lion's breath as the tongue and fangs flashed over him. He felt the gash of its claws through his coat of mail, and the warm gush of his blood from the wounds. Yet among that frenzy of talons and teeth, the coarse smother of its mane at his mouth, and the splash of blood about his eyes, Gawain sensed that the animal was somehow kin to his own passionate soul. The knowledge of it seared through him with vivid, overwhelming force in the very instant when a last, desperate thrust of his sword-blade pierced the lion's heart, and he himself – gasping under the weight of its death throes – swooned out of consciousness from loss of blood.

Some time later – it might have been minutes or days, he had so little sense of the passage of time – he was briefly drawn back through the surface of the black, bottomless pool that was his mind by the sound of an old lady's voice calling as if from a great distance, 'Sir Knight, Sir Knight.'

He opened his mouth, coughed on a trickle of blood, and managed to say, 'What do you want? Who is it?' before his words blurred into a groan of pain.

'God be thanked,' said the voice above him. 'We thought you dead.'

Gawain struggled to open eyelids that might have been clotted shut with blood. When his vision briefly cleared, he saw four familiar faces gazing down at him with anxious concern. Vaguely he tried to smile. His bruised brain tried to remember names but before he could quite recall who these ladies were, his vision blurred and swayed and he fainted away.

When Gawain woke again his entire body was glittering with pain. He looked around and found himself in a different chamber, lying on an ordinary bed. There was no sign of his weapons and armour or of the great iron shield. His wounds had been tended and bandaged by some careful hand. He saw that he was no longer bleeding, and his next thought was for the proud lady who obsessed his soul. Wincing at the pain the movement caused him, he got up from the bed, shook his head to clear it, and set off in search of Orguleuse.

A small door led him out to a spiral stairway. He was about to go down when he thought he heard sounds of movement above his head, so he went up instead, higher into the tower. On the next floor he entered a round chamber that was quite empty except for a curious mirrored pillar in the centre of the room. It was richly wrought with many gems, each of which glittered with a sparkling radiance. Coming closer, he saw that what he had taken for mirrors were in fact magnifying lenses arranged in a series of screens. Each of them opened up a different view on the surrounding landscape.

As though staring through a magic casement, he could see the bend of the river below the castle, and the ferryman's cottage. He could see the blowing heath across which he had followed his lady the previous day, and the meadow where he had fought and defeated his rival for her love. As he walked round the pillar, other prospects were revealed beyond the immediate vicinity of the castle. His eyes ranged across thick woods, a deep river gorge, and hollows and far summits paling hazily to the horizon. He watched two swans descend towards a mere where they alighted on their own reflections. Then, at a closer, lower level, his eye was caught by a movement in one of the lenses. When he looked more carefully he made out the distant figures of a knight and a lady approaching the castle.

Gawain was staring at them in brooding fascination when someone spoke at his back. 'Sir Knight, you should be resting still.'

As he turned, another voice said, 'Your wounds are not yet healed. They will open again.'

Gawain found himself looking at the four queens who had gazed down on his torn and bruised body after his fight with the lion. He saw at once why he had thought their faces familiar. The woman who had just spoken was his mother, Sangive. Beside her stood his grandmother, the Lady Arnive, wife to Uther Pendragon, who had been abducted by a magician many years before and never seen since. And at either side of the older ladies stood his two sisters, though neither showed any sign of recognizing him. Gawain cried out in amazement. How on earth had they come to this eerie place? He moved to embrace them but all four women seemed distracted and confused.

'What is your name, Sir Knight?' asked Sangive.

'Mother, it's me, Gawain!' he answered, perplexed. 'Don't you know me?'

But Sangive stared at him as at a bewildering stranger. She said nothing, merely glanced like a nervous animal to the older woman at her side.

'Grandmother? Sisters?' Gawain turned to the others. 'Surely you recognize me?' They too stared at him through strangely glazed eyes. 'What are you doing here?' he pressed them. 'Why don't you answer me?'

Then another voice spoke at his back. 'Peace, Gawain. You will only disturb them.' The voice was hollow in that vaulted chamber, and though its tones were less strident than the last time he had heard them, it sent a shudder through him still. He was speaking the hated name even as he turned to face the hideous, bristled, boar mask of her face. 'Cundrie!'

'Yes, Gawain. So you followed me after all?'

'As you knew I must.'

'And you have acquitted yourself well so far – though judging by your wounds it's been a close-run thing.'

There was a hint of mocking laughter in her voice still, and

Gawain was not to be appeased by her more conciliatory manner. 'Why are the women of my family here?' he demanded.

'Where else should they be in times like these?'

'They should be at home, at peace. What have you done to them?'

'This is none of my doing. They are in Klingsor's power, which remains unbroken.'

Gawain turned to the four queens again, trying to shake them from their trance. 'Mother, it's your son. Speak to me. Sister?' Then he glanced back at Cundrie in frustration. 'Why don't they know me?'

'Tell me, Gawain,' the sorceress replied, '– are you quite sure you know yourself any more?'

'What witchcraft is this, Cundrie?' the knight demanded impatiently. 'What is this damnable place?'

'You are in Klingsor's castle. This chamber is his spying-place. The mirrors on that pillar show all the land for six miles around. From here his power reaches out like a cold shadow on the heart of all who do not resist him.'

'Who is this Klingsor?' Gawain demanded. 'Tell me more about him.'

'He was once a knight very much like you,' said Cundrie. 'Now he is a magician who works great evil in the world. A long time ago he was castrated for raping a queen. He's been taking his revenge on womankind ever since.'

'Then it's time he was stopped. Tell me, where I can find him?'

'He is everywhere,' Cundrie laughed, 'but you cannot see him. No one sees that prince of shadows unless he chooses to reveal himself. Yet all the women in this castle are held under his enchantment.'

At that moment the Lady Arnive approached Gawain, reaching out a hand that trembled as it touched his arm. Her face was worn from long years of lonely grief. 'Sir Knight,' she entreated him, 'we look to you for our release.'

'If it's in my power, Grandmother, you shall soon be free,' Gawain sought to encourage her. 'But first I have to find the power that makes you suffer so.'

'Then perhaps you should look in the mirror,' said Cundrie.

Gawain's eyes turned to where she pointed. He gazed back into the curious, jewelled screens on the pillar and at first saw only the pale ghost of his own reflection. Then his heart jumped like a salmon at a leap for beyond that reflection, almost as though enclosed inside it, he could now make out the face of the lady who approached on horseback with a knight at her side.

'Orguleuse!' he cried.

'That lady is the Duchess of Logres, sir,' said his mother, staring fearfully into the lens, 'but you have named her well.'

'Is that Klingsor with her?' Parzival demanded.

'We have never seen him,' said Gawain's elder sister. 'How can we tell?'

'Whoever the man is,' Gawain growled, 'he is riding with my lady and must answer for it. Where is my armour and my horse?' Turning to leave the chamber, he winced at the sudden flash of pain from a wound that the lion's claws had torn across his chest.

'Peace, knight,' said his mother, seeking to restrain him. 'You are in no condition to fight.' But Gawain pushed her impetuously away, his pain and stiffness utterly overwhelmed by the tide of jealous fury building inside him. 'No one rides at that lady's side while I look on,' he panted. 'I need my weapons. Cundrie, what have you done with them?'

But when he turned to look for the sorceress, he found that she had vanished as quietly as she came.

CHAPTER FOURTEEN

THE

KING OF THE WOOD

awain left the chamber and hurried down the stairs, searching each room until he found his coat of mail with his helmet, sword and buckler lying beside it. Aware that blood was already beginning to seep from the bandaged wound at his chest, he armed himself and hurried out of the castle to where the ferry-man waited for him by the wharf.

On the far bank of the river, Gringolet neighed at his approach, frisking in the sunlight. Gawain put his foot to the stirrup and gasped with pain as he pulled himself up into the saddle. Dizzy-headed, scarcely able to hold himself upright, he took the lance and shield that the ferryman offered up to him, and wheeled his horse to face the knight who was now cantering across the meadow at the side of Orguleuse.

'That lady is mine, knight,' Gawain shouted. 'Defend yourself.' Then he clanged shut his visor, lowered his lance and spurred his mount to the charge. Driven by jealousy and rage, and ignoring the alarms of his bruised and bleeding body, he urged Gringolet into a furious gallop that brought his lance smashing into the visor of his rival's helmet with all the force he could command behind it. The knight was knocked from his saddle and fell with a crash of metal to the ground where he lay, twisted and jerking like a damaged toy. Gawain's own body had been further injured by the shock of the impact. For a queasy moment, he thought that he too was about to fall from the saddle. Only with difficulty did he rein in his mount, and turn back across the silent meadow to claim the lady as his prize.

A dazed smile lit his face as he made out her beauty in the morning light, but before he could catch his breath to speak she met him with a bitter greeting. 'By what insolence dare you name me yours, fool?'

'By right of arms as well as of my love,' he answered hoarsely. 'This is the second knight I've vanquished for your sake.' He looked down at his fallen rival. 'Who is this man?' he asked. 'Is it Klingsor?'

'Klingsor!' the Lady scoffed. 'Do you imagine *that* fiend can be toppled by a lucky stroke? Klingsor has subtler means of fighting than this knockabout child's play with sticks and shields.'

Discomfited by her scorn, Gawain said, 'I'm glad at least to learn you are no friend to him.'

'What woman could be?' Orguleuse answered, '– least of all myself.' Then she glanced down at the fallen knight in contempt. His body lay quite still now but for the thick trickle of blood oozing from his broken helmet. 'No, this sleeper is just one of a hundred fools I could rouse against you if I chose.'

'I think this one has just died for you, Lady,' said Gawain, and saw her face blanch as he looked back at her.

'No,' she said, shaking her lovely head, and swallowing as she spoke, 'he died because his foolish desires conflicted with yours.' She glanced away from Gawain's grave gaze, fighting back emotions she had no wish to feel. 'This is not the first such death,' she added coldly.

'Then make it the last,' Gawain urged her angrily now. 'If there's any justice in the world I've already won you for myself.'

'What kind of justice?' she retorted harshly. 'The justice of the tavern brawl? Do you think I'm a mere drab for brutes to bandy over? Is it my fault if men think they can impose their will by violence? Pah, you're all the same! It no longer even amuses me to watch you kill each other.'

'Then put an end to it,' Gawain said. 'Admit yourself mine, Duchess.'

'So you know who I am?' she said. 'Then you should also know that I do not submit to claims of ownership.' Her gaze was proud and fierce, almost savage in its assertion of her sovereignty, but for the first time she noticed the blood leaking through Gawain's hauberk, and that his lips were white with the strain of holding himself in the saddle. 'I see you were badly wounded on the Bed of Marvels,' she added, a little less harshly as she chivied her mare into motion. Then, as if regretting a momentary weakness, she snorted coldly again. 'A pity that you learn nothing from your pains!'

'I learned that the bed was hard to catch,' Gawain smiled ruefully as he urged Gringolet to follow, 'and that when I caught it, I would get no peace!'

'Ah! So there is a glimmering of a brain under that iron after all – though a wiser man might have known not to cling so tightly to his shield.'

'Had I not done so,' Gawain protested, 'the bed would have killed me!'

'Are you sure of that?'

Surprised by the question, wondering just how much of this troubling woman he had yet to understand, Gawain said, 'I'm sure only that half the world seems to be under your spell, Lady – and that you hold us all in scorn.'

'Not all,' she corrected him. 'There was one who came ...' The Duchess took a deep, wistful breath on the sunlit air. 'I could have loved him, I think ... And he was more than a little in love with me too, but ...' – again she sighed, avoiding her companion's discomfited gaze – '... he resisted.'

'Then he was either a saint or a fool!' said Gawain gloomily.

'Perhaps. In any case he was a husband. And deeply wedded to the wife he had left at Belrepaire.'

'Parzival!' Gawain exclaimed. 'That knight is my sworn brother. He once told me I'd find no lasting meaning in life till I learned to value the truth of a woman's love.' His wan face brightened now. 'Lady, this gives me fresh hope.'

'Why so?' she said. 'You and Parzival are very different.'

'But I find that you lied to me when you told me that you had no heart. I had almost begun to believe you, but now I think that if you love Parzival as I do, then in time you may learn to love me too.'

'I said I *could* have loved him,' The Duchess glanced away from Gawain's eager smile. With a harsh light in her eyes she stared into the distance. 'I'm no longer made for love,' she said. 'My heart is as cold as ash except for a single unextinguished desire.'

A less infatuated man would not have found a glimmer of encouragement in her words, but this was the first time that Gawain had heard Orguleuse utter so much as a hint at a continuing appetite for life. Instantly he seized on it.

'Name it,' he demanded. 'Tell me what you desire.'

'No.' She turned the full ferocity of her gaze on him. 'Go home and lick your wounds. Do not imagine there is some easy way for you to win my love.'

'I suspect that nothing will ever be easy for me again,' Gawain answered more gravely now. 'But as God is my judge, I do love you, Lady. Nakedly. With all the truth I have, and without reserve. If you will not have that love at least let me serve you. What is it you desire?'

Moved despite herself, the Duchess glanced away from the

compelling honesty of Gawain's solemn gaze. It took a moment or two for her to resume an air of apparent indifference and when she spoke, the edge of her voice was less sharp. 'It is a trifling thing,' she prevaricated. 'It is ... no matter.'

But Gawain heard the hesitation. He said, 'Now I think you do lie, Lady.'

'For your own sake,' she replied impatiently. Avoiding his eyes again, her gaze fell on the place where the blood oozing through his chainmail had stained his green surcoat. 'Look, you are bleeding still.' Instantly she repressed the involuntary note of anxiety in her voice.'Your wounds embarrass me. Leave me now. You're in no condition to serve me.'

But if Gawain was light-headed now, it was not only from loss of blood. 'If you're trying to break my pride,' he said, 'know that only death will stop me. What is it you want?'

'It is ...'

'Yes?'

'No more than a branch off a certain tree.'

'Faith,' Gawain laughed wryly, 'you make it sound as harmless as lying on a bed!'

But the Duchess's face was pale and grim as she wrestled with a sudden tumult of conflicting emotions. 'That tree is in a place guarded by the man who ... the man who robbed me of all happiness,' she declared at last.

'So your desire is for vengeance?' said Gawain.'Is it Klingsor you speak of?'

'No, but one close to him,' she frowned. 'His name is Gramoflanz. Klingsor himself is untouchable – his dark magic makes him so. But Gramoflanz is his ally and agent in the world. He dares to call himself King of the Wood. But those woods are mine. He claims both my lands and my self as his by right. But he is none of my choosing.'

The bitter pride flashing in her gaze fired Gawain's heart with a new access of vigour. Immediately he demanded to know where this Gramoflanz might be found, but in that moment Orguleuse seemed less scornful of him than concerned for his welfare. 'Consider your wounds,' she said. 'You lack the strength for this ordeal. Leave me, I say. Leave me while you still live.'

'Did I not say there was a destiny between us, Lady?' Gawain insisted.

There was a long moment of silence in which she saw that neither derision nor discouragement would deter him. In her own gaze, something too tremulous to declare itself as hope contested with a flickering anxiety. She wanted to reach out to him but could not permit herself to do so. She wanted to speak but feared that words might betray the long-unfamiliar stirrings in her heart. And when Gawain urged her again to tell him where he could find Gramoflanz, she too knew herself confronted by her destiny.

She led him in silence to a place where the river plunged in a steep torrent through a gorge. Reining in her mare at the brink of the cliff, she pointed to the rough terrain on the far side. 'The tree I spoke of is a broad oak at the centre of that grove. A single leap would take you over.' Again she concealed her feelings behind a withering show of scorn. 'But you've proved your folly often enough. I need no further evidence.'

Gawain was staring across the gorge at an ancient oak grove ringed by stones. The opposing edge of the drop was a smooth jut of outcrop rock perhaps five feet higher than the ground on which his horse stamped its hooves. The gap between was wide. He could hear the sluice and clatter of the torrent where the river swirled and frothed into a deep hollow some thirty feet below. As far as the eye could see there was no safe crossing.

Biting his lip against the pain of his wounds, he tugged at the reins and took Gringolet back several yards from the edge. The air felt wild about his head. He sensed that he was nearer to death than he had ever been.

'This is madness,' his Lady cried. 'A leap like that will open your wounds.'

'Your words are crueller than wounds, Duchess,' Gawain said quietly as he turned again, readying his mount for the jump. He gazed at her with an intensity that might have been trying to fix the memory of her beauty in his mind for all eternity. Then shouting, 'Remember me,' he dug his spurs into Gringolet's trembling flanks.

In the instant that his brave mount leapt into space, Gawain knew they would not reach the other side. For a frantic instant the horse's hooves scrabbled at the stony edge but found no purchase. Pulled back by their unbalanced weight, both horse and rider plunged into the river far below.

Already weak, and hampered by his heavy coat of mail, Gawain was pushed along in a swirl of black light. His mouth and nostrils were crammed with water, his head bursting with noise. He was being swallowed by the river and on the point of drowning when the current drove him into collision with the submerged trunk of a fallen tree. His hand broke the surface and snagged against a bough. Reflexively he snatched at a branch and found the strength to drag his own dead weight along the trunk to the shore, where he lay gasping and choking for a long time, watching his blood leak on the stones.

Eventually he got to his feet and looked around. He had been swept round a bend in the gorge to a rocky culvert where the cliff fell less sheerly. There was no sign of his horse, but he saw how, with a further expenditure of effort it ought to be possible to clamber on foot up to the ridge. The climb might kill him where the fall had failed, but with a vague sense of how preposterous his obstinate valour was becoming, he decided that he would rather die trying to serve his lady than let what was left of his life drain away like a stuck pig.

Drawing his sword, and using it for support, Gawain staggered to his feet and began the climb.

Almost an hour later he passed through the ring of stones to stand under the oak tree at the centre of the grove. Lifting his sword, he hacked at a thin bough until it came away in his hand.

At the moment the green bough left the tree, a voice behind him growled, 'That tree is mine, knight.'

Swaying a little from the effort, Gawain turned to find himself confronted by a burly figure holding a massive axe. His armour was green with verdigris, and his helmet wreathed in oak leaves with a peacock feather for a plume. Long, tangled hair, the colour of winter bracken, hung about the man's brawny shoulders. He squinted at Gawain from his cocked head. A smile twisted his lips above the matted beard that flowed like foliage from his chin.

'Do you deny me this branch?' said Gawain.

'I do,' the man's voice boomed, 'but if you wish you can gamble your head for it.'

'Then defend yourself,' Gawain panted, but he was staggering as he advanced across the grove, and his vision was blurred.

Gramoflanz merely chuckled at his defiance. 'You can scarce stand, let alone fight,' he scoffed. 'Go home.'

'I take pity from no man,' said Gawain, '– least of all one who has injured my lady.'

'Ah, so the Duchess has sent you!' Gramoflanz sneered. 'Well, you're not the first. Look around you.' A sweeping gesture of his axe pointed out what Gawain's dizzied eyes had not taken in before – that from the boughs of the surrounding trees hung the dried remains of many human heads. 'I warn you, sir,' he snorted, 'the woman is mad. You'll find no joy in that cold heart.'

Gawain stood in a patch of sunlight, trying to focus his blurred eyes. 'If her heart is cold, Gramoflanz,' he said, 'I think it's because you made it so. What have you done to her?'

Gramoflanz shrugged his broad shoulders. 'There was a man she loved. I took off his head.' He looked around and with another casual gesture of his axe indicated a blackened object dangling from a bough like a wizened fruit. 'It's that one, over there. He was as pretty as you once,' he grunted. 'His death made me King of the Wood, and by rights the woman is mine. But she'll not give herself – even though I kill every fool she sends against me. Only one ever got away from me, and he lives to regret it.'

'As you shall not,' Gawain shouted, dropping the oak-branch as he lunged towards Gramoflanz with the point of his sword. But he was so weak and dizzy by now that he almost fell, and Gramoflanz merely stepped aside in a nimble dodge, swinging the flat of his axehead against Gawain's back with a controlled force that declined, as it might otherwise have done, to smash the knight's spine. 'It's too easy,' he laughed. 'When you have help, challenge me again. Till then, farewell.' Lifting the axe to his shoulder, he turned to go.

Panting where he stood, Gawain pushed his free hand against the open wound at his chest to staunch the bleeding. 'I am Gawain,' he gasped, 'and I need no help.'

'Gawain!' Gramoflanz exclaimed, turning to inspect his challenger more closely. 'Ah, so you've come at last! Well, I see you're as valiant as Cundrie promised. But there's no honour in killing a man who's already half-dead!'

'And none to me if I return to my lady without that branch. Stand and fight!'

Gawain made another desperate lunge. Again Gramoflanz stepped deftly aside to avoid the thrust. With a scornful laugh, he twice swung his axe within an inch of Gawain's head, then he snorted, and turned away. Frustrated and humiliated, Gawain shouted after him, 'You must fight me, coward.'

'Then heal yourself that I might do so honourably.' Gramoflanz bent down to pick up the severed branch of oak-leaves and tossed it across to Gawain. 'Here, take the branch if you think it will do you any good. Meet me at the Castle of Marvels in two weeks' time. And tell the Duchess I demand payment in full this time. I'll settle for nothing less than your head and her hand.'

'Be warned,' Gawain gasped, 'I'll fight the harder if she watches.'

'Good! I look forward to it. Bid Arthur himself come and watch my sport.'

'He'll come to watch me pluck that peacock feather from your plume!'

Again Gramoflanz laughed. 'You have spirit enough. We should have been comrades, you and I. Look, here comes your horse. Let me help you mount.' But Gawain shook his head. He stood for a moment, steadying himself against Gringolet's shiny wet flank, then he put his foot to the stirrup and pulled himself up into the saddle.

'There is a bridge some miles downstream,' said Gramoflanz. 'Come, I'll keep you company there.'

But Gawain had no desire to consort with his Lady's enemy, and was in any case uncertain that he could stay upright for so long a ride. Declaring that he would return the way he came, he urged Gringolet back towards the edge of the gorge. The horse shied nervously for a moment, but then saw that he was looking down onto the other side and had the advantage of height this time. Responding to his rider's urging, Gringolet made the leap and easily cleared the gap, but the impact of the landing left the knight swooning with pain.

Gawain was only just clinging to consciousness when he came upon the Duchess wandering through the wood on foot, leading her mare, distraught.

'Here is the branch you asked for, Lady,' he said.

'But I thought you were ...' Orguleuse stared up into the knight's pallid face. For an astonished moment her face brightened with a surge of relief that was close to joy, then her heart quailed when she saw how much blood he had lost. Dropping the reins of her mare, she hurried towards him.

'Gramoflanz treated fairly with me,' Gawain hoarsely sought to explain. 'I shall fight with him soon ... when these wounds are healed.' She was about to answer but he silenced her with his own urgently uttered words. 'Do not mock me for the delay. You have humbled my heart, Lady, and taught it patience, but I ...' His voice faltered as he felt coils of black light swirling up inside him. The glare of sunlight through beech leaves dazzled his eyes, there was a roaring in his ears. 'If I do not live ...' Gawain was saying, 'I bid you never use your great beauty to shame another knight,' and he had barely uttered the sad entreaty when he collapsed from his saddle like a felled oak.

Orguleuse reached out her arms to break his fall, then she leaned over him where he lay groaning on the ground. Tears poured from her eyes as she cried, 'Oh my dear, my dear, forgive me.'

The breath gasped out of him, blood trickled from his lip. For a terrible moment she thought that he had died, but the lids of his eyes opened as he felt the soft splash of her tears at his face. 'This is a strange change, Lady,' he murmured with a wry smile. 'Perhaps I may have reason to live after all ...' Then his eyes closed again, and consciousness abandoned him.

He woke again to the sound of his lady's weeping. She sat beside him in the glade with her blue gown torn where she had ripped the silk to make fresh bandages for his wounds. He saw Gringolet grazing peacefully in the afternoon sunlight that shafted down between the trees.

'Why do you weep, Lady?' he asked.

Her distraught face looked across at him with a stare of wondering disbelief. Then she was holding him gently, soothing his brow with her hand as she said, 'I weep for all the hurt I have given you ... I weep for my own shame. I weep for all those who have already died for me. And I weep for Anfortas who suffers grievously still.'

'Anfortas?' Gawain frowned in bewilderment. 'What have you to do with the Rich Fisherman?'

'Anfortas loved me,' the Duchess admitted through her tears. 'He loved me beyond all reason. And I used him as I used all the others. It was for my sake that he forsook the Grail. It was I who sent him out against Gramoflanz. He took his wound from the poisoned spear that the foul castrate Klingsor had given to Gramoflanz out of hatred for me and all womankind. And ever since that day my life has been worthless. Nothing but pain and madness and a cause for grief – as you have learned to your great cost.'

'No, Lady,' Gawain answered her softly, 'it is more, far more, than that. I know that you have made others suffer because of your own intolerable pain. I know that Gramoflanz killed the man you dearly loved. He bragged of it when we stood in the grove together.'

Then, as if Gawain's words had at last uncovered her secret wound, Orguleuse laid her head at his shoulder and was sobbing uncontrollably.

For a long time they sat together, far beyond words, in the shafts of sunlight moving through the beech trees' shade, while she released all the pent-up years of grief. Overwhelmed with compassion for her sorrow, Gawain felt his heart swell with loving tenderness for the suddenly vulnerable woman in his arms. Held close in his embrace, she heard the beating of that heart.

After a time the tears flowed more quietly and she found the breath to speak again. 'That man was my husband,' she said. 'I loved him with all my heart. But when he was killed I forgot how to love. My hatred for life became as bitter as Klingsor's. It left me as cruel and as cold. I've been in the grip of that cold madness ever since, capable only of hate and scorn.' She looked up at Gawain then through a blur of tears. 'I might have remained so for ever had not ...' But then, as if assailed by some inwardly consuming crisis of belief, or by a sense that, after all the harm she'd caused in the world she must remain for ever unforgivable, she glanced away, leaving the thought unspoken.

Gently Gawain put a hand to the soft skin of her cheek and turned her face towards him. 'What, Lady?' he pressed.

Trembling, Orguleuse drew in her breath. Lowering her eyes under the intensity of his gaze, she whispered, 'Had not one come who loved me dearly enough to brave all the hurt that raged inside me.' Then she looked up into the face of the wounded man who held her. 'Oh God, you see me as I am, Gawain. If you have any love left for a creature such as I, then I am yours.'

'I think you forget,' Gawain smiled, '– I too have given great hurt in my time. I think we deserve each other, you and I.'

Then it was hard to say which of them was the more joyful, or the more incredulous, as they delivered themselves over to a loving embrace, in which he whispered, 'To me, Lady, even your darkness shines.'

Many breathless kisses later, she dared to ask, 'Then shall we be faithful to each other, Gawain?' And at last, with a clarity and truthfulness such as he had never previously known, the knight took her face gently between his hands and gladly answered, 'With all my heart, Lady, with all my heart.'

CHAPTER FIFTEEN

THE

DARK BROTHER

o Gawain and his Orguleuse returned to the Castle of the Marvels where they found that the shadow of Klingsor had been lifted through the power of their mutual love, and all the ladies freed from the cold spell of his enchantment. Joyfully Gawain's mother and grandmother and sisters recognized the true nature of their champion, rejoicing in the transformation that love had made both in him and in the lovely Duchess of Logres, who proved as gentle now as she had been harsh before.

Messengers were sent out to King Arthur bidding him come to the Castle of the Marvels where he would find his long-lost mother restored to him, and where he might preside over the combat between Gawain and Gramoflanz. The knight's wounds had begun to heal by the time the appointed day approached, but his Lady was growing ever more anxious at the thought of him once more putting his life at risk for her sake.

'I care only about you,' she pleaded. 'Let Gramoflanz keep what else he has of mine so long as I have you. Withdraw and stay safe with me.'

But Gawain laughed away her apprehensions, saying that he had so much to live for that she need have no fear of losing him.

'Come, lie down again,' he smiled at her, 'for this is truly a bed of marvels now!'

When the day of the fight dawned Arthur and his company had not yet arrived. Gawain woke early that morning and, having armed himself, took Gringolet out onto the field to exercise him. Satisfied to find all his own limbs in good condition, he was putting the horse through its paces when he looked up and saw an armoured knight approaching at a gallop through the morning mist. As the figure came closer, Gawain made out the green oak-wreath at his helmet and saw the jaunty dance of his peacock-feather plume.

'You're early, Gramoflanz,' he muttered softly to himself, shutting his visor. 'It seems that Arthur will miss your humiliation after all.' Then he couched his lance and spurred Gringolet to the charge.

Through the slit in his visor he saw his opponent hurtling towards him, the lance-point aimed unwavering at his chest. Gripping his shield more tightly, Gawain swayed slightly as they came together in a clash of fearsome violence. He heard the clatter of the lance-point at his shield, felt the shock of the blow in every bone as his own lance glanced off its target, and for a moment he thought he might fall, but with every muscle straining, he kept his seat and swept on past. When he reined in Gringolet and turned the horse's head, he saw that his opponent was still firmly in the saddle.

Gawain's breathing sounded hollow inside the helmet. Facing into the sun now, he saw its light dazzling off the wreathed helmet as he urged his horse to a second pass. Somewhere distantly he heard the sound of drums and trumpets in the castle, but his attention was fixed on the armed figure already bearing down on him across a meadow that still glistened with dew.

Again they clashed, again both lances remained unbroken. Neither knight fell. The horses sweated and steamed.

Summoned by the sounds of alarm, Orguleuse reached the parapet of the castle in time to see the knights careering towards each other for the third passage of arms. She gasped out loud at the fierce splintering of lances. Her hands were at her mouth as both horses came ungirthed and fell screaming to the ground, tossing their riders aside in the fall. Seconds later, both men were on their feet, approaching one another with drawn swords.

They fought in grim silence, the air ringing with the clash of steel, each man knowing himself up against so formidable a contender that neither could afford to waste energy in futile shouts or threats. Rarely had two strengths been so equally matched, rarely had the skill shown by one swordsman been so perfectly countered by the other. The sun rose in the sky, the heat of the day grew more intense, and still the two men circled and hacked at each other, sweating and gasping for breath as they looked in vain for some weakness in the other's technique, or any slight advantage that might force the duel to a conclusion.

Both were so intent on this fight to the death that neither noticed the approach of Arthur and his company across the meadow. 'Great God! Here is fierce fighting, Kei,' said the King to his seneschal who rode beside him.

'It looks as though Gawain has his hands full,' Kei replied. 'And look up there, Lord. As usual he seems to be surrounded by women!'

Kei had pointed to the parapet where Orguleuse and the ladies of Gawain's family looked down on the fight with increasing anxiety. In the same moment when the King called out, 'God be with you, nephew!', the Duchess was fervently whispering, 'Dear God, give him strength!' But it seemed that prayer would not be enough, for Gawain's chest wound had reopened under the stress of combat, his strength was ebbing and he was forced to give ground under a fierce, swingeing assault. Sensing victory, his opponent found new reserves of strength, coming on so swiftly, and with such reckless violence, that Gawain was knocked off balance, lost his footing and fell backwards to the ground.

The breath was slammed out of him. He could feel blood hot and damp inside his hauberk. Through the slit of his visor he saw the flounce of the peacock-feather plume against bright sunlight as the man who had beaten him lifted his sword high above his helmet, steadying himself to strike.

In the same dizzy instant, from where he lay panting in the grass, the fallen knight heard the anguished sound of his Lady's voice carried across the river on the still air. 'Gawain!' she cried. And again, 'Gawain!'

Unable to defend himself, regretting everything that would never come to fulfilment between them now, Gawain waited for the blow to fall. The sword-blade glinted a moment longer in the light, then it came down – but slowly and without force, as its wielder stepped back, lowering the weapon across his chest. A hoarse, exhausted voice echoed inside the oak-wreathed helmet. 'Gawain? Dear God, is that you?'

Then the knight let the sword fall to the ground and lifted off the helmet with its peacock-feather plume.

Gawain focused his blurred vision and found himself looking up into an agonized, familiar face.

'Parzival?' he exclaimed.

'Gawain, my brother, dear friend,' the other answered. 'Oh God forgive me, had that lady not cried out ...'

'Parzival, Parzival,' Gawain chuckled in exhausted disbelief, 'do I hear you speaking to God again? Faith, no wonder I couldn't get the better of you!'

Then Parzival was leaning over to help his friend to his feet. He grasped him in a warm embrace as he said in a voice aghast with the thought of how close they had come to disaster, 'To kill you would have been to kill myself.'

At that moment Arthur rode up to join them, astonished to discover that the men he had watched trying so hard to kill each other were his own most favoured champions. 'How has this mischance come about?', he asked. But it soon became clear that he himself had the answer in his train.

That very morning, on his way to the Castle of the Marvels, Arthur had come upon the battered figure of Gramoflanz. Demanding to hear his story, the King learned that Parzival had fought with him the previous day for the sake of his uncle, Anfortas, the wounded Fisher King of the Grail. Having defeated Gramoflanz, Parzival had commanded him to give himself up to the Duchess of Logres. Then, as a sign of victory, he had garlanded his own helmet with the oak wreath and the peacock-feather plume, and it was for this reason that Gawain had mistakenly attacked him.

Now, on the field outside the Castle of the Marvels, Gawain and Gramoflanz came face to face again. 'It seems that Parzival has left neither of us in much shape for sport,' said Gramoflanz with a rueful grimace as he displayed his own smashed sword arm and bandaged head.

'For my Lady's sake, I'll be ready to fight when you are,' Gawain answered.

But not long afterwards his Lady appeared with Cundrie the Sorceress at her side. Once she was quite sure that her lover was unharmed, Orguleuse turned in appeal to Cundrie, and matters were immediately taken out of the hands of the men.

'Well, Gramoflanz,' said Cundrie, 'this is no longer Klingsor's castle. Gawain and this lady have lifted his spell, and now it seems that Parzival has broken your power. Do you still call yourself King of the Wood?'

'No, Cundrie,' Gramoflanz conceded. 'When Parzival bested me I vowed to return the sacred grove to its true sovereign, and yield myself to her mercy.' He turned to look at the Duchess, sustaining the scalding glance of hatred in her eyes. 'I cannot ask forgiveness for the great pain I have given you,' he acknowledged, 'but my life is yours to dispose of as you will.'

For a long time the Duchess studied the man's proud, defeated face, evidently struggling with a conflict of emotions in her own agitated heart. 'I cannot grant you forgiveness any more than you can ask for it,' she said at last. 'But there has been enough fighting and too much death. Keep your life, Gramoflanz, and if you have the heart for it, do as Parzival and my Lord Gawain have done – put it in the service of the Grail. For in our pride and folly you and I have brought great harm upon that mystery.'

'Wisely spoken, Lady,' said Cundrie, then she turned her boar-mask gaze on the man who stood adoringly beside the Duchess, holding her tenderly with one arm. 'And you, Gawain – in answering my challenge I think you may have found a noble love after all. Are you truly worthy of it?'

'I shall strive to be so,' declared Gawain smiling, 'for this adventure has brought me richer rewards than I imagined. I have won the love of this lady, and in all the perils that awaited me, only the dearest of friends could beat me down.'

'More than a friend, Gawain,' said Cundrie. 'You and Parzival are soul-brothers, and what each of you has separately achieved – Parzival in his solitude, and you through your adventures of the heart – has served also to strengthen the other's soul.'

'Then this is indeed an hour of great joy!' King Arthur exclaimed.

'Truly so,' said Cundrie. 'Come, King, your mother and sister await you in that castle. It is a time for celebration now!'

And so, amid great rejoicing, Gawain and his lady were wedded in the Castle of the Marvels. The once-haunted halls of that place were filled

with light and laughter and music as the knights in Arthur's cavalcade and the ladies who had been freed from Klingsor's enchantment
feasted happily together. Only Parzival stood apart from that joyful
company in a corner of the chamber where the joyful company were
dancing.

After a time Cundrie came to join him there. 'So your life is not
yet free from sorrow, Parzival?' she said.

'No, Cundrie,' he sighed in answer. 'Nor can it be till I come again
to my wife at Belrepaire.'

'Which you have sworn shall not happen until you have done what
you left undone in the place of the Grail?' She studied him shrewdly
through narrowed eyes. 'Yet I think you are much changed since I
saw you last.'

'My soul has been schooled in patience by the time I spent with
the hermit Trevrizent.'

'Ah!' Cundrie smiled. 'So do you do as *he* says now?'

'I'm less a simpleton of light than I once was,' Parzival answered her
smile. 'I know that if there is to be any meaning in my life it won't come
from blind obedience to others,' he added more solemnly. 'It will rise,
like a living thing, out of my own encounters with experience.'

'Even the painful ones?'

'Yes. It took me a little time, but I've come to see that I'm answerable for my own pain too.'

'Then you are changed indeed.'

'But my name is not yet free of the shame you laid on me.'

'Yet you have stayed faithful to the service of the Grail, and have
avenged the terrible wound that Gramoflanz gave to Anfortas.'

'Vengeance does not bring healing,' said Parzival sadly. 'Nor has it
brought me any closer to the Grail.'

'Do you think it is only space that has kept you from
Montsauvage?' Cundrie asked him. 'Has your journey not also been

through time? What if all the battles, ordeals and obstructions you have met were necessary for you to become the person who might attain the Grail?'

Parzival frowned and glanced away. 'There are times when I doubt that the Grail even exists.'

'Perhaps the Grail is not a thing to be found, or an absence to be mourned,' Cundrie answered. 'Perhaps it is not the Grail that vanishes, but we who are estranged from it? Perhaps it is a presence patiently waiting your attention?'

Parzival looked back at her, frowning. 'Or perhaps it's no more than a figment of a dream?' he said. 'All I know is that I've been fighting my way towards it for years, and the fighting only seems to deepen the wound.'

'But perhaps you have not yet gone deep enough to meet your most intimate opponent? Come with me, Parzival.'

And the sorceress led the bewildered knight away from that hall of revels, up a spiral staircase to the chamber in the high tower where Klingsor's magic pillar glistened in the shadows with a gem-like radiance. 'From here,' she said, 'you can look out across all the lands of the Grail.'

Parzival stared in wonder over the wide horizons revealed by the many lenses, and though he saw many plains and hills and forests he had crossed in his travels, nowhere could he make out what he most desired to see. Sadly he turned to look at Cundrie. 'There is still no sign of Montsauvage.'

'You think not?' she said. 'Then do you see a knight encamped over there, on that far hillside?'

Parzival looked where she pointed and saw an armoured figure tending to his horse on the brow of a hill. A pennon fluttered from his lance and when it unfolded in the breeze, Parzival made out the sign of a crescent moon with a single star beside it. 'I don't recognize his banner,' he said. 'The man seems a foreigner to me. Is he a Saracen?'

'He is,' said Cundrie, 'and of royal blood.'

'Who is he?' Parzival frowned. 'Where does he come from?'

'Perhaps you should ask him, for that prince stands between you and the Grail.'

Parzival studied the figure in the mirror more closely as though he were the guardian of some secret that he urgently needed to know, but he could make out nothing more than a sturdy, armoured presence bedding down for the night beneath the stars – a figure that would have been much like himself were it not for the exotic nature of his trappings. Then he heard the voice of Cundrie saying, 'Sleep now, Parzival, and go out and meet him tomorrow.'

'Dear God, Cundrie,' Parzival sighed wearily, 'is there no end to fighting?'

'Not till the last battle has been lost and won,' said the sorceress, then she turned away, leaving the knight alone with his thoughts.

With a heavy heart, Parzival rode out in the dawn light to meet the stranger knight. Concealed in iron arms, both men advanced as if by common assent towards the moment when they confronted each other at either end of a narrow pass. High above them the sound of a buzzard's cry pierced the air.

'What do you seek in these parts, Saracen?' shouted Parzival.

'A lost father,' the Saracen answered, his voice huskily accented inside the hollow of his visored helmet. 'I ride in Love's service, knight.'

'A noble cause,' Parzival called. 'But I ride in the service of the Grail, and you stand in my way.'

'And you in mine, Christian,' came the defiant reply.

The Saracen's pennon fluttered in the breeze, the sign of the crescent moon and star glistened in silver against the green of his shield.

Parzival heard the restive stamp of his horse's hoof against stone. 'Who are you?' he called.

'One who has never given way,' shouted the Saracen. 'Stand aside.'

'For no man, Infidel,' Parzival shouted back. 'Look to your defence.' And he spurred his mount once more into the violent ritual of arms.

The two knights clashed with terrific force, but neither fell, so they tossed aside their splintered lances and dismounted to face each other, sword against scimitar, on the stony ground. Sparks flashed as blade struck blade. Shields clattered and rang. For a long time they fought, sweating inside their coats of mail, eyeing each other through the narrow slits of their visors, neither contender yielding a single stride of earth. Yet the balance of strength was such that the longer the contest lasted the more the two knights seemed to become a single complex animal strangely warring with itself, or like two impassioned lovers fused in the ever-deepening intimacy of a fierce embrace.

At last, in a desperate gasping after fresh energy, the heathen prince shouted out his strange battle cry – 'Zazamanc.' With a sudden access of strength he lunged against Parzival, who lost his balance and fell skidding to the ground. Swiftly the Saracen lifted his scimitar and brought it slicing down, but Parzival rolled away and the blade struck the earth at the very spot where his neck had been only an instant earlier. Before the Saracen could strike again, he sprang, shieldless, to his feet, and stood, panting, aware how close he had come to death. And in that moment the beloved face of his wife flashed into his mind. Her name leapt like flame to his throat: 'Blanchefleur.'

The cry rang out across the morning air, reaching up into the blue expanse of the sky, and in far Belrepaire the heart of the Lady Blanchefleur leapt as though the actual sound of his call had reached her. Feeling the deep draw of her husband's love, and the urgency of his need, she rose to her feet in her chamber, whispering, 'My Parzival!' and the courage of her own loyal soul reached out across unseen distances to strengthen her husband's heart.

As if sensing the power of this sudden, strange communion, the Saracen let his concentration slip. When he lifted his gaze he saw Parzival's sword – the sword that had been given to him by Anfortas – swinging in a sheen of light towards his head.

Time seemed to move more slowly. Knowing that he was watching his own death-stroke fall towards him through the air, the Saracen prepared his soul. And then – as though a stone were thrown into a frozen lake – even as the sword crashed against his iron helm, its blade shattered into harmless shards of light. And it was Parzival who stood shocked and utterly defenceless now.

'Praise be to Allah, the wise, the all-merciful!' the Saracen whispered.

Far above them, the hawk's cry pierced the air. Then there was silence.

Parzival closed his eyes. With a wry smile of acceptance he recalled how, long before, his cousin Sigune had foretold that the sword of the Grail would hold good for a time, then break in the hour of need. Well, it had broken now, and despite his many victories, and for all the huge number of men he had humbled and killed, his Grail quest had ended in defeat.

For Parzival too time was slowing down. Calmly, as though held and contained by his wife's undying love, he unlaced his helmet and took it off, reflecting that at least there would be no more fighting, no more killing – only these final seconds of strangely blissful peace in which, as when he had been a boy, he listened to the sound of bird-song and tasted the simple air.

For the last time Parzival breathed in the light. In that moment nothing separated the world within him from the world without.

There was nothing to be done, no fretful urging of the will, no time for ambition or regret. It was as if his silent, receptive presence had become an empty vessel through which only the pure, impersonal surge of life itself still briefly flowed.

Then he opened his eyes and saw the eyes of his opponent staring back at him through the slit of his visor.

'You fought well, Christian,' the Saracen panted. 'Never have I been pressed so hard. Had your sword not broken, my name would not now be written in the Book of Life.'

'Then before you finish me, knight,' said Parzival, 'I would know the name of the champion who has vanquished me.'

'No,' said the Saracen, 'there can be no talk of victor and vanquished here. I am too proud to let the lucky blow that spared my life bring to an end a life as valiant as your own. I think that in this battle we have both lost and both won.'

And Parzival watched in wonderment as the Saracen scabbarded his sword.

'Then I know you for the most magnanimous of knights,' he said, blinking in the sunlight, scarcely able to believe, '– but I still don't know your name.'

'My name,' said the Saracen, 'is Feirefiz Angevin.'

'But the title of Angevin is mine!' gasped Parzival. 'By what right do you take that name?'

'By a son's right. My father is a Christian like yourself, and the son of a king. His name is Gahmuret the Angevin. Do you know where I will find him?'

'Not in this world, prince,' Parzival answered amazed. 'My father is dead.'

Now it was the Saracen's turn to gasp in surprise. '*Your* father?'

'Dear God,' Parzival exclaimed, 'Cundrie told me I had a brother I knew nothing of. She said he was a champion whose glory far outshone my own. She said ... my brother was mottled like a magpie, being both black and white.'

'Take off your helmet, Feirefiz.' The ringing command had come from an outcrop rock high above the place where the two knights stared at each other in bewilderment. Both turned their heads at the call, and they saw Cundrie gazing down on them. 'Show your brother your face,' she said.

Feirefiz lifted his visor and took off the dented casque. And for Parzival it was like gazing into the dappled shadows of a pool, for despite their parti-coloured skin, the noble features he saw reflected there were strangely like his own. And in that moment of recognition both knights saw how in the other's face was scored a living memory of the father that neither had known.

'You are both Gahmuret's sons,' said Cundrie, 'though by different mothers, both of whom were injured by his pride. Yet the wrong done by the father can be made right by the sons, and in confronting each other you have each overcome your self.'

Again, in the high blue of the sky above their heads both men heard the piercing cry of the hawk.

'That was the last battle,' Cundrie called down to them, smiling. 'The time of the sword is over. It is the Grail that calls you now.'

CHAPTER SIXTEEN

THE
QUESTION AND
THE STONE

nly a few moments earlier Parzival had been readying himself for death, and so entirely unexpected was this sudden alteration in his circumstances, that it felt almost as ·though a kind of death had happened. Yet it was no black door through which he had passed, but a loop of light, for everything that had seemed to curse his life for years was falling away, and in its place a radiant new life was beckoning.

High on the rocks above him, Cundrie – the boar-masked sorceress who had publicly condemned him to a life of shame – smiled down at him now as a kindly minister of grace. 'I have had word from Trevrizent at Montsauvage,' she said, 'and you, Parzival, are blessed above all men, for you and your wife have been named to the kingdom of the Grail.'

In a place far beyond speech, scarcely able to take in the import of her words, Parzival gazed up at Cundrie in a trance of wonder. Then he became conscious of his dark brother Feirefiz standing beside with arms open to take him into a warm embrace. Parzival opened his own arms to receive him. The two brothers who had come so close to ending each other's life stood for a long time clasped together, their eyes brimming with tears of joy. But as he felt the gathering strength of their mutual love, the thought came into Parzival's mind that he was the younger of the two, and the least worthy.

Looking back up at the sorceress, he said, 'Did you not once say that my brother is the elder son, Cundrie? Surely this great honour should be his?'

From where she stood on her high rock, Cundrie shook her bristling, boar's-mask head, smiling as she said, 'The Grail is not of the father, Parzival. Nor can it be inherited. It is in life's gift now.'

At those words, Feirefiz put his hand to Parzival's shoulder, smiling with affection at the amazement in his face. 'It seems that this is your mystery, little brother,' he said. 'Yet it would give me great joy to witness it.'

'Then come with me!' Parzival exclaimed. 'For too long you have been lost to me. Now that I've found you I would have you always at my side.'

'Spoken like a true brother, Parzival,' Cundrie cried, 'for the truth is that without your brother you could not have come to the Grail.'

'Will you lead us there, Cundrie?' Parzival asked, but again the sorceress shook her head. 'You will find your own way now, and I have other work. Klingsor's power is broken for a time, but he is dear to me, and I must seek him out in the shadows where he hides. Good friends, farewell.'

She raised her hand in salute, there was a brief alteration in the light, the blue haze of the day seemed to shimmer round her, and when their eyes recovered from its dazzle, the brothers saw that she was gone.

So Parzival and Feirefiz rode on together, recounting the stories of their ordeals and adventures across the years, and feeling their love and admiration for each other grow stronger with each mile that passed. Each came to recognize in the other qualities and perspectives without which his own life could not be complete, and they began to understand how that lack had filled them both with a nameless yearning all their days. Now it was as if each felt himself restored to the singleness of his own being by the other's presence at his side.

With that knowledge they fell at last into companionable silence and became alert to their surroundings once more. When they came out of woodland onto the sunlit shore of a mere, Parzival recognized the place where he had seen the Rich Fisherman angling from his boat. They rode beside the quiet waters of the mere until they came to the cleft in the rocks, and when they reached the summit of the cliff they were looking down on the place between the river and the woods where the gleaming white ramparts of Montsauvage rose from the moat in the hazy light cast by the late afternoon sun. The bridge was raised, and the moat so still and windless that it offered an immaculate reflection of the Castle of the Grail.

Scarcely able to believe the good fortune that had brought him back to that mysterious place, Parzival raised his eyes to the parapet, from where the voice of an unseen sentinel called down. 'Who approaches there?'

Immediately Parzival recalled how Montsauvage had been the place of his disgrace and failure. Was it really possible that he might be received back inside its great hall with honour now? He glanced at his brother, took in the smile of reassurance there, and was further heartened by the thought that his friend Trevrizent was waiting to greet him beyond those walls. He remembered what the patient hermit had taught him about the war in heaven – how the bright angels and their darker brothers had struggled for dominion, and how there were some who had refused to take sides with either the powers of darkness or the lord of light. It was to those courageous neutral angels – those who had striven to hold the universe together – that Parzival owed allegiance now. It was they who had appointed his family as guardians of the stone that alone had power to heal the wounds incurred in that disastrous war, and he was not the only one to have failed in that sacred charge.

After all his long years of travail, he saw that it was not only Anfortas either, but all the fallible men and women walking between earth and heaven who were the bearers of such wounds. And so, acknowledging himself no more than one among them, he raised his head and answered proudly, 'I am Parzival of Wales, son of Lady Herzeloyde by Gahmuret the Angevin, and Lord of Belrepaire. I would speak with my uncle, the Rich Fisherman.'

'Who rides with you, Widow's son?' the voice demanded.

'This is my dark brother, Feirefiz, from whom I will not be parted.'

'Then fair welcome to you both,' the voice replied without hesitation. 'The Grail bids you enter.'

Across the still air of the moat came the rattle of chains and the creak of a windlass as the bridge was lowered. They heard the scrape of iron against stone and the portcullis began to rise. A fanfare of trumpets sounded as the two brothers rode over the bridge and into the outer ward.

They were met by pages who disencumbered them of their weaponry and saw to their horses. Then Trevrizent was at the door of the keep to welcome them. His austere head was softened by a hopeful smile, though not even he seemed immune to the air of anxious trepidation in the glances of all who had waited so long for this moment. Warmly, he and Parzival embraced each other, then to a gathering murmur of expectation, the brothers were ushered into the darkened chamber where Anfortas lay.

The air around his bed hung heavy with the fragrance of terebinth and musk and the aromatic herbs with which his attendants had sought to sweeten the stench of the Fisher King's wound. Approaching him through the hall's vast silence, Parzival heard the whirr of his breath and the gasping wince of pain as he shifted his weight, casting about for comfort in the gloom.

'What noise there?' Anfortas groaned. 'How long must I lie like this? Has this rotting flesh not suffered enough for its sins?' Then opening his haggard eyes he became aware of a presence looming over him, and the tender touch of a hand at his shoulder. He raised his head to see more clearly. 'Ah, is it you, nephew?' he sighed, and though the agony caused by the movement flashed across his face like silent lightning, he reached out a trembling hand.

Parzival took the hand between his own. He looked down in sorrow on the anguished figure. The iron-grey locks of the Rich Fisherman's hair had grown longer. They hung about his shoulders like a woman's now, and Parzival saw what he had failed to observe on his first uncertain visit to this bedside: that this man was truly his uncle, for something very close to his mother's fine-boned beauty was plainly visible in that ravaged face.

He felt a pressure at his hand tugging him closer. Tenderly, Parzival leaned over to hear what Anfortas wished to say, and his heart swam in its blood when he made out the words of the Rich Fisherman's entreaty. Uttering the one thought that held any consolation for him now, Anfortas was whispering, 'If there be any mercy or pity left in this life, bid them keep the Grail from my sight so that I may have the death I desire.'

The words expired in a blizzard of pain. His eyes gazed up in beseeching silence for a moment or two longer, then his head fell helplessly back against the cushions of his bed.

Already Parzival's eyes were blurred with tears. As he stood by his uncle's suffering body, he was remembering the father who had abandoned him, and the mother he in turn had abandoned. He remembered how he had brought death to his kinsman, the Red Knight, with the ignorant javelin he had hurled. He remembered the anguish of the starving women and children among the blackened ruins at the siege of Belrepaire, and the bodies of the dead he had found in the sacked farms all around that city. He remembered how the once lush land had been laid waste by war and greed, by the seemingly insatiable lust for land and power. He recalled the grief of Gurnemanz for his dead sons, and how, unable to accept her own inconsolable loss, Sigune had cherished the rotting corpse of her lover. He was thinking about all those who had suffered in his cause, and of the many brave knights that had been injured and killed by his own furious pride. With a pang so excruciating that he might have been acknowledging it for the first time, Parzival felt all the grief he had encountered since he first began his long journey into exile from true innocence of heart. And in that same moment of anguished illumination, he saw how – mile after mile, day after day, battle after battle, until he had finally met defeat at his brother's hands – that guilt-driven journey had taken him further and further from the one true source of joy and meaning in his life.

Reflecting on his pride and bitterness, and the wilful error of his ways, he found himself wondering what the wound was at the heart – or in the mind – of man that kept him for ever in exile from what he most desired.

And there, in the immediate presence of the Fisher King's intolerable suffering, he felt utterly powerless that, for all his manly strength and proven valour, he had nothing to offer but compassion now.

Parzival lifted a gentle hand to soothe the pain that seared in wave after wave across the wounded man's brow. His own body was trembling with grief. In the immense, attentive silence of the hall he heard himself whispering, 'What ails thee, uncle?'

And it was as if the whole, mysterious Castle of the Grail exhaled. For hearing the tenderly uttered question, Anfortas opened his eyes. The measure of his breathing altered, and his skin that had been as grey as any shroud began to suffuse with colour as the lips of his wound were softly sealed.

Parzival stood transfixed as he watched this miracle of healing taking place before his eyes. In the same instant the whole chamber glowed luminous with the radiance of the Grail. When the knight looked up he saw the stately procession of maidens bearing the Table of the Grail into the hall, and behind them came the graceful figure of the Grail-bearer herself, Repanse de Joie, holding between her hands a silver chalice in which gleamed the stone. As she came closer, Parzival saw how bands of light and darkness were silently revolving about the stone like night and day. He was standing magnetized by the sight, when he heard the voice of Feirefiz whispering, 'Brother, is it permitted for one who is no Christian to witness this mystery?'

'I'm sure that it must be, brother,' Parzival answered, 'for I have seen the Grail before and marvelled at the bounty it gives. All Nature's increase is there, so I think that this stone from Heaven must be a living emblem of the earth itself, which is mother and father to us all.' Yet even as the brothers gazed upon the stone, they saw its nature change, and what had gleamed with mineral brilliance only a moment before was palpitating softly now.

'Brother,' whispered Feirefiz, 'is the Grail not very like the human heart?'

'Yes, brother,' Parzival quietly replied, 'and that too is common to us all.'

And still, as Parzival stood in wonder at the vision, the Grail was changing until it seemed a heart no longer, but the soft, protective chamber of a womb in which unborn twins, one male, one female, were floating at peace. A moment later that vision too had passed, and Parzival's astonished eyes were gazing into a glassy, translucent vessel where he saw the figure of a knight standing with a lady at his side.

At first he took them for his mother and father reunited, then he saw that both figures were at once within the Grail and outside it – that the image was also a reflection. And when, perplexed by this further evolution of the mystery, Parzival turned his gaze away from the still-changing Grail to see the source of what was mirrored there, his heart overflowed with gladness. For there was indeed a woman present at his side, a woman whose face was older than the one he remembered but made still lovelier by the patient years between. She smiled at the blurring bewilderment in his eyes as she reached out her hand to his, saying, 'Welcome home, my Parzival.'

'Blanchefleur,' he whispered quietly in answer. 'My Condwiramurs. My love.'

And so at last Parzival and his lady entered into that earthly kingdom which is the region of the heart and the ever-mysterious presence of the Grail. And through their meeting in the joyous freedom of their love, there flowered the promise of a whole land flourishing again.

For I, Wolfram, poet of the heart, maintain that when a life is so lived that the world's favour is won without dishonour to the soul, then this is surely fruitful toil. And if there was a war in heaven once, then we who are neither wholly good nor wholly bad, we who consist both of shadow and of light, we sad, wounded creatures standing between earth and heaven, striving to be whole – can, if we are truly human, choose to be among the healers too.

AFTERWORD

WOLFRAM'S PARZIVAL: A MYTH FOR OUR TIME

any years ago, fondly believing that it might further my adolescent ambitions to become a writer, I went to university to study English. I hadn't realized that the English faculty wouldn't be teaching us to write: it was teaching us to *read*, and to read critically, and in ways that soon persuaded me that no writing I might do could ever withstand such ferocious scrutiny. So my literary ambitions withered and it took me the best part of twenty years to recover belief that my imagination might have something to say for itself after all. When that happened, I found myself recalling a decision I'd made at the start of my second year in college.

At that time most of my contemporaries eagerly took up the option to study modern authors. I too was excited by the troubled and exalted visions of Conrad, Eliot, Lawrence and Joyce, but I chose to work instead on the period from 1066 to 1385 and became an amateur medievalist. I already knew and loved the poetry of Chaucer and the Gawain Poet, and was acquainted with Langland's *Piers Plowman* and many of the lyrics and ballads, but even so my reasons for setting out on this year-long pilgrimage through the literature of the early Middle Ages were far from clear to me. I just knew I had to go.

During the course of that year I read many medieval romances, from the exquisite lays of Marie de France, through Chrétien de Troyes' witty and insightful adventures of the heart, and on to the virile, turbulent prose of Malory's *Morte d'Arthur*. It was through those enchanted stories that I started to gain a larger perspective on the kind of interior landscape that had first been opened up to me many years earlier by my entranced reading of Grimm's Fairy Tales.

That landscape had nourished aspects of my childhood imagination that went unanswered by the mucky streets of my home in the industrial north. Now, as an undergraduate newly awoken to the problematic life of the mind, I began to glimpse in its contours something that had largely been banished from serious consideration by the post-holocaustal world, for it was like studying a map of the soul.

Now I've no doubt that there was an element of escapism in my appetite for those old stories, but I can't believe I'm alone in thinking that the attempt to escape from what William Blake called 'mind-forged manacles' is a fairly sane response. And I feel just as sure that – intuitively at least – my imagination was beginning to understand how the themes explored by the medieval romances might have a direct bearing on some urgent, unsolved problems of our own troubled times. I think that was why I cared about them. And I *know* that was why, much later, they would encourage me to shape similar stories of my own.

Nowadays I would go so far as to suggest that the romance writers of the 12th Century were laying down an agenda for the development of western consciousness that was as crucial for the welfare of its heart as that of the ancient Greeks had been for the sharpening of its intellect. It's an agenda with which we're still struggling today, and on which – if the dismal state of mutual misprision between the sexes, the degraded condition of the planet, and our ignorance of the unconscious forces which propel us towards calamity are anything to go by – we have made, generally speaking, far too little progress.

The themes of that agenda can be briefly resumed under four related headings:

the need to renegotiate the balance of power between the masculine and feminine principles (and not only in outward relations between the sexes, but inwardly, as aspects of our individual being, whatever our biological gender);

the need to renegotiate the relationship between civilization and the natural order (in particular the need to recognize that renewal often comes out of the wilderness, and sometimes in ways we don't recognize or consciously desire);

the need to renegotiate the balance between the ambitious claims of the ego and the larger, more exacting claims of the soul;

and the need to renegotiate relations between conscious awareness and the neglected resources buried in the dreamworld of our unconscious shadow-side.

In a sense, the last heading subsumes all the others, and perhaps for that very reason many of the romances were overtly cast in the form of dream books. Even the ones not presented in that way tended to take the form of dream-like journeys between the everyday world of social reality and a mistily ambiguous otherworld where the big transformations happen. These days we have to remind ourselves that, for the courtly medieval audience, knights and castles and tournaments were the stuff of social realism. The otherworld was something else, and it's possible to regard accounts of strange adventures there as merely a more or less sophisticated form of courtly entertainment. They certainly were that, of course, and all the more enjoyable because of it, but I prefer to take a larger view, one that takes them seriously within that visionary tradition of western writing which has always valued the wisdom of dreams and which insists on the primacy of the imagination in the shaping of our world.

Generally speaking, that tradition has been more openly championed by poets than by prose writers, particularly in recent times. But as Margaret Anne Doody shows in her splendid book *The True Story of the Novel*,[1] the narrative tropes of the medieval romance have much in common with those of the modern novel as well as with such ancient prose fictions as *The Golden Ass* of Apuleius. So much is this the case, she argues, that the distinction between romance and novel is far less severe than has been suggested by those critics who regard the social and psychological 'realism' of the novel as a more mature mode of story-telling than the romance with its unabashed taste for marvels.

In any case, when I set out to be a novelist, I knew where the springs of my own imagination lay. Two of my novels[2] were consciously conceived as contemporary variations on ancient Gawain stories, and when, some years ago, I was approached by the BBC to write radio drama, I turned to a related source for inspiration. The result, a two-part play broadcast by Radio 4 over three hours on Easter Saturday 1995, was called *A Stone from Heaven*. It was a free adaptation of Wolfram von Eschenbach's narrative poem *Parzival*, but during the course of writing it I found myself possessed by the curious sensation of having embarked on a heavily-fictionalized form of autobiography. The more I progressed with it, the more strongly I began to feel that Wolfram wasn't just telling my own story but also that of many of my contemporaries.

Like Parzival, many of the children born around 1939 were separated from their fathers by war, and left in the anxious company of mothers frightened by the violence of the times. Much the same thing had happened to our own parents 25 years earlier at the start of the First World War. It was as though we had inherited their affliction and there has never been a day's peace across the planet since 1939. In fact, our view of life has been so largely shaped – though it would be more accurate to say *distorted* – by the atrocious history of the twentieth century that there is a sense in which, to a more or less terrible degree, we are all now casualties of war.

My generation grew up in an increasingly materialistic society where the standards of masculinity were set by an aggressive patriarchy organized into companies that carried on their trade with martial zeal. (Consider how many knights are now champions of business!). Almost nothing in our education was designed to give us an understanding of the feminine perspectives that might be available to men, still less of the activity of a masculine spirit within women. We knew almost nothing, that is, of the role of the unconscious in shaping our experience. Nor, for many of us, was there any vital sense of a spiritual dimension to life. The history of industrialized slaughter in both World Wars, together with the ever-imminent possibility of total destruction through thermonuclear conflict, had left most of us convinced that the existence of a benevolent God was beyond belief. The scientific world view seemed to make a nonsense of many religious claims and, apart from its use to describe a particularly stirring form of music, the word 'soul' had no apparent referent. If there was any meaning to life – and that itself was an open question – then it was entirely self-created.

So we set out on our journeys into adulthood, armed with a bright weaponry of rational logic, defended by our scepticism, and possessed of large ambitions – for love, for success, for wealth, for happiness and perhaps even for fame – yet largely ignorant of our own nature and utterly estranged from any vital sense of the sacred. Whether we were 'idealists' trying to change the world or 'realists' accepting and working with its injustices, we were each questing for a viable sense of personal meaning in what a selective reading of TS Eliot had long since shown us was a Waste Land time.

We were also on a collision course with those refractory, undomesticated aspects of life that flourished outside our tightly managed scheme of things. Such anyway was the case with me, and it was only through the changes brought about by such collisions that my perspectives began to widen. Emerging from them in a renewed effort of self-recognition, I saw that the insights of Wolfram's *Parzival* might offer a relevant myth for people in such an errant condition.

Of course others had seen it so before me. In his *Memories, Dreams and Reflections*,[3] CG Jung spoke of the importance of the story in his own life, recording how his memory of his father was 'of a sufferer stricken with an Amfortas wound' that would not heal. Likening his boyhood self to a 'dumb' Parzival witnessing this suffering, he admits that 'like Parsifal, speech failed me'. Laurens van der Post[4] has suggested that the story of the grail quest resumes in dramatic form Jung's theories of the lifelong quest for individuated consciousness, though it was Jung's wife Emma who made a detailed psychological study of the tale in collaboration with Marie Louise von Franz.[5] And approaching it from a different angle, the great mythographer, Joseph Campbell, saw in Wolfram's *Parzival* 'the earliest definition of the secular mythology that is today the guiding spiritual force of the European west'.[6]

My own sense of the continuing power of this story has been reinforced by the time I've spent using its themes as a stimulus for writing workshops at Dartington and elsewhere. Participants in those events were asked to monitor memories from their own lives that were aroused by listening to the incidents of the story, to explore them in conversation, and then to write out of an imaginative fusion of their own experience with motifs borrowed from the tale. It's a technique called 'midrash writing' after a rabbinical method of exploring untold parts of scriptural stories through imaginative improvization, and it can produce startling results.

One man came to the workshop because a dream had told him to think about 'wolfram'. As an engineer, his only association had been with the metal of that name – tungsten (which means 'heavy stone' in Swedish). It was only when he'd chanced upon a translation of Wolfram's *Parzival* that the wider implications of the dream came clear to him. Having done no imaginative writing since his school days, he was far from relaxed about trying again now. But I have an unforgettable image of him reading aloud a moving piece, written from the point of view of Parzival's horse, in which he reflected on his own failures of trust and his often injurious reliance on the will. Another man found himself writing out of the still livid wounds of a twenty-year marriage to what he called 'a man-hating woman'. After several intense hours of imaginative work with words, relating Gawain's story to his own – he came to the realization that, whatever else their conflicts might have meant for her, his ex-wife had been desperately mirroring the rage and anguish of his own long-neglected soul.

There were women at those workshops too, each of them finding through the images of the story new ways of examining the ambitions and confusions of their own questing spirits as well as of confronting the pain inflicted on them by the illusions and insensitivities of men. Much of the value of the work came from dialogues between men and women across the gender divide as they reacted, positively or otherwise, to the archetypal figures of the story, and found their way towards a larger, more compassionate attention to each other's experience.

Of course, any good story can be made to work this way but, for some of us at least, the very form of the Parzival story seems to offer a metaphor for life as a mythic journey into meaning through the liberating spaces of the imagination. And there are particular qualities to its themes and motifs which can encourage us to approach that journey in an adventurous spirit of self-renewal.

A good place to start is with the acceptance that the people in this story are not presented as the kind of fully-rounded characters we expect to find in a novel. They are less individuals than archetypes, each representing in dramatic form some important element in the structure of the human psyche, and the interplay between them offers a working model of the human soul, revealing the contradictory aspects of its nature and its often painful struggle to reconcile them.

Once this is recognized then the Parzival story can be read in the way that certain schools of dream analysis suggest we should try to read our dreams. Using this method we don't identify solely with the figure who seems to represent us in the dream, but with all the other figures who appear there too. The assumption is that each of them, along with all the impersonal motifs and situations of the dream, illustrates some not-yet-conscious aspect of our nature with which our dreaming mind wants us to become better acquainted. Thus when we dream about our fathers and mothers, our spouses, lovers, friends and enemies, it's not those actual figures, living or dead, who have chosen to spend part of the night with us, but symbolic representations of them that have a vital part to play in the unfolding drama of our interior life.

Having grown up in an age that tends to think literally, we are poorly educated in this kind of thinking. 'If dreams mean anything why can't they just say what they mean?' is typically the positivist's response – a response which fails to realize that dreams do exactly that, though the language they speak is that of the imagination. Its syntax is subtler and more flexible than that of rational logic, and its vocables are drawn from the timeless store of symbols. It is, in fact, our native language, though our schooling has largely estranged us from it. But, as with all languages, one grows fluent by practice, and once we make the effort to see through literal appearances in this way we maximize our imaginative use of the resources that the unconscious spontaneously offers. At the same time – and this goes to the heart of the matter – we are reminded that our personal lives are continuous with the life of everything around us, that the presence of everything else is the condition of our own existence, and that for all our experience of ourselves as separate and isolated individuals, we are also members of one another.

In our own time, Lawrence Durrell has attempted a mode of story-telling which encompasses this kind of insight. The various characters of his *Alexandria Quartet* and *Avignon Quincunx* seem to meld and flow into one another as the novelist calls the existence of the discrete ego into question in order to explore the poetics of the soul. But a more direct parallel to the emblemology of the Parzival story might be found in the Major Arcana of the Tarot Deck. Each of the symbols depicted in that vivid procession illustrates an elemental aspect of human experience. The order of their sequence dramatizes the gradual education of the soul, from the condition of untutored Fool, through an initiatory cycle of changes, to the integrated wisdom of the wiser Fool.

Parzival's history clearly follows that trajectory. He begins as the uneducated green man, more or less a wilderness creature, perfect in his simplicity and, as far as the world is concerned, a hopeless fool. The obedient innocence of his youth cannot cope with the ambiguous impact of experience. He is gradually matured by the ordeals he undergoes until he achieves a compassionate wisdom won from knowledge, grief and silence. But an important part of that journey is delegated to his soul-brother Gawain, whose erotic adventures act out those aspects of life that Parzival has left unlived.

Rather than puzzling over a discontinuity here, it makes excellent sense (as Edward C. Whitmont[7] suggests) to think of these two figures as twin aspects of a single soul – aspects which are in conflict with one another, yet both of which are necessary to its wholeness. Without access to Parzival's loyalty of heart, Gawain is a mere libertine; without Gawain's amorous encounters, Parzival remains a solemn prig. But the two natures can be reconciled only through a crisis of consciousness that the story presents as armed combat.

In much the same way, Parzival only attains the grail when, after a life-and-death struggle that extinguishes his hitherto triumphant ego, he is united with his dark brother, Feirefiz. That is to say, he approaches the state of wholeness only when, through hard-won self-recognition, he assimilates the values associated with his previously unconscious shadow-side.

Just as the male figures of the story are confined within the variously inflected archetype of knighthood, so the female characters are barely differentiated as individuals. In ways that must seem quite dismal to the evolved feminist thinking of our time, they remain maidens in need of rescue, for example, or prophetic hags. But as I suggested earlier, it's more profitable to read them not as portraits of women but as elemental constituents of the human psyche – the beleaguered values of the soul and the power of the intuition among them – and to consider how the various aspects complement one another.

The demure figure of Condwiramurs, for instance, remains only partially realized at the time of her marriage to Parzival. Her own otherwise unexpressed life – the rage at being abandoned by her husband, her fury at his bone-headed commitment abroad to what (were he less driven by his will) might have been found with her at home, and her own ambiguous, sometimes promiscuous feelings about men in general – all these bitter passions are acted out on her behalf by the Lady Orguleuse. Yet the Duchess herself will find no peace until her own injured heart dares to open itself to the risk of love again.

The word 'behalf' gives the clue. Without each other's energy to complement their own weaknesses and strengths, Parzival and Gawain are, at best, only half themselves, and much the same is true of Condwiramurs and Orguleuse. The structure of the story seems to suggest that to approach wholeness as a person, whether male or female, one is required to assimilate all of these different aspects into a conscious unity which tries to leave nothing out of count, however stressful the contradictions. That this is a process fraught with difficulties is clear from the general context of strife, loss and injury – particularly sexual injury – in which the principal characters of the story pursue their destinies. That context is both generational and cosmic in its reach, for as the story unfolds we discover that conflict on earth mirrors the divisive conflict in heaven, and the wounds of this conflict will be passed on from one generation to the next until an evolutionary act of consciousness opens up a genuine possibility for renewal.

For this reason, Wolfram's story, unlike Chrétien's, begins not with Parzival but with his father, Gahmuret. Long before Parzival is born, Gahmuret loses his own father to the violence of the times yet he is driven by a restless ambition to emulate his father's martial accomplishments. He shows only a casual concern for the feelings of his distraught mother and finds it impossible to sustain a mature relationship with either of his two wives. Having lived his father's life, Gahmuret dies his father's death, passing on to his sons responsibility for all that has been neglected by the narrow preoccupations of his self-glorifying career.

For a time it seems as if the cycle must repeat itself. Despite all his mother's neurotic efforts to protect him, and perhaps because of them, Parzival sets out into the world in much the same cavalier way. His crass encounter with Jeschute amusingly caricatures his father's callous way with women. Sigune's inability to let go of her lover's rotting body mirrors the manner in which Parzival's own neglected soul metaphorically carries his father's corpse about with him – a dreadful emblem of that masculine vitality which has fallen into decay and must somehow be revivified. He has to find ways of coping with the mockery and authority of the world, yet his efforts to emulate the one-sided achievements of his absent father bring the youth into collision with everything that he has inherited through his mother. His ignorance of the values associated with his feminine side is vast. He doesn't know that his unfeeling departure has left his mother dead behind him. In his eagerness to prove himself a knight he doesn't know that his first act has been to kill a kinsman. Nor is he aware that he has a larger destiny than that of a mere crack-jouster, for not only must he redeem both his own and his father's failures of the heart, he will have to find a way of healing the sexual wound that blights the family of the Grail – a family of which he does not yet know himself to be the spiritual heir. Meanwhile the dumb obedience with which he conforms to the expectations of those around him only brings Parzival into increasing conflict with the claims of his own essential nature.

As the story unfolds, he will be made aware of the extent to which he is the prisoner of his own ignorance, yet the access of knowledge brings with it such pain and derangement that it seems as if consciousness is itself a kind of wound. If so, it is a wound for which the only cure is greater consciousness, and in his quest for that, Parzival will encounter forces far more impersonal than those embodied by his relatives and friends.

Because almost everything in our education conspires to identify the separate ego as the centre of consciousness (with reason as its trusty sword for keeping anarchy at bay) we tend not to believe in such impersonal powers these days. Wizards and witches, monsters, ogres, angels – all have been relegated to the nursery, and even there they are entertained only as 'figments of the imagination'. So imperious is the fallacy of literalism, we forget that it is by means of such unsettling figures that the imagination mirrors hidden aspects of ourselves – aspects that will break out, resentfully, angrily, violently, if they are ignored. Stories like this one wisely bring them back into play, reminding us that what matters is that we recognize their powers and find skillful ways to deal with them.

The further Parzival and Gawain venture beyond the known world the more urgently do they encounter the problem of harnessing the raw, amoral energy of such figures in service of higher values. But the jaded civilization of Arthur's court has already lost its sense of purpose and direction. Even its formidable defences are porous to the haunted wilderness of the otherworld. And it's from there that both the challenge and the possibility of renewal come.

To begin with, it comes in the form of Parzival himself, the roughly-clad green man, barbarously armed. But he covers his wildness with the Red Knight's armour, tears himself free of his roots and, taking Gurnemanz for his mentor, becomes a conventional knight. Living as his father lived, forsaking his wife for adventure, he is on a collision course now with larger, more impersonal forces.

Anfortas, the Rich Fisherman, lies in wait for him. The Grail Castle looms on its savage crag. Divested of his armour and dressed as a woman, Parzival the wanderer is admitted to a dream-like ritual of wonders. He is given a sword – bright symbol of the penetrating intellect – that will break when he most needs it. He is shown the bleeding lance and the table of the grail. He sees Anfortas unable to stand or sit or lie for the grievous wound in his groin. Everything seems charged with an energy that is both sacred and sexual, yet that energy is arrested, impotent, unfruitful. Later we will learn how Anfortas was given that wound, and about Gramoflanz who gave it to him – the usurping King of the Wood who has, through violence, seized control of what belongs by right to the feminine principle. And we will learn about the shadowy castrate Klingsor, whose malevolent enchantment holds the women of the kingdom in thrall at the Castle of the Marvels and has cast this blight across the lands of the grail. Like Parzival we dimly discern a mysterious pattern of relationship between a sexual wound, a lance that bleeds and a cup of generation. But like Parzival we find it hard to bring them through into consciousness, to speak about them. And so silence prevails, the dark powers win again, the possibility for renewal fails. But nothing is quite as it was before. Sigune may still grieve over her decaying lover, but the unconscious has sprung open like a wound. Soon blood is everywhere.

Later we may come to ponder the connection between a tender, three-night long initiation into married sexuality, a pattern of blood on snow, the inability to take advantage of a ferryman's willing daughter, and a magic bed where raw animal energy has to be overcome and transformed if a spell is to be lifted. Our guide in these matters of the heart will be the hideous sorceress Cundrie, the boar-tusked guardian of hag-wisdom, who has burst into the arrested castle of the mind with threats and challenges and scornful demands that we wake up from our immature dreams of conquest, that we try to become fully human.

Here in the dark feminine, rendered angry and monstrous by neglect, is the transforming power-source of the story. Yet Cundrie will be assisted in her endeavours by a quietly reflective male figure, one who has turned his back on the life of action and delivered himself over to solitary contemplation. He too is a wilderness creature, living away from the violence and temptations of the world, striving to make his soul. The hermit Trevrizent may not himself be the spiritual prince who will bring renewal to the blighted land, but without access to his hard-earned wisdom that prince will never find his way back to the Castle of the Grail.

So here we come to it at last – the question of the grail. What are we to make of its arcane mysteries, and, as I asked in the Preface, can such a promiscuously applied symbol still have value for our sceptical times? To approach an answer, let me take, in the time-honoured tradition of knights errant everywhere, a somewhat roundabout route.

Perhaps the most extraordinary achievement of Wolfram's poem is the powerful act of the imagination by which it enfolds the story of the evolution of an individual human soul within a larger, cosmic myth that offers metaphorical insights into the evolution of consciousness itself. *Parzival* is a story about renewal, the kind of renewal that comes when, and only when, apparently irreconcilable powers are brought to reconciliation – when contradictions have received their complete expression, fought each other to a standstill, then reperceived one another, no longer as hostile opposites but as polar complements.

This is always how something new gets made for life. We take for granted the fact that it happens biologically when the often-conflicting powers of male and female come together and a child is born. We find it harder to conceive how, by a parallel inward process, an individual soul might renew its vitality through the difficult reconciliation of its contrary elements. And, as the epidemic violence of history daily reminds us, we find it harder still to imagine how a similar process might hold true for the social, political and spiritual conflicts of the age – though the problems there are, of course, vertiginous in scale. Yet it is to all these possibilities that Wolfram's story speaks, and it speaks to them through the creative power of the imagination.

But what is the imagination? In a time that puts a premium on information we tend to regard the imagination as little more than a useful complement to other, more rationally accountable instruments of knowledge – a kind of talent that we can have too much of or not enough, one that is usually considered to be the enchanted province of the gifted. But there is a larger, more profitable view of the imagination – one that recognizes it as the means by which, with a greater or lesser degree of psychic energy, all of us perceive and construe our world.

To contemplate how differently a Roman Catholic priest and a Darwinian atheist, for example, conceive of human nature and the world it inhabits, is to begin to appreciate to what degree our sense of reality is a function of the imagination. Neither interprets the world as the other reads it, both would claim access to truth, and each regards the other's view as falsely mythological. What both seem to demonstrate, however, is that we don't only live inside the received world of the natural order: we also inhabit a world of stories – myths by which we try to make sense of the way our inner world comes into collision with the outer world. And if it is through our myths about them that we imagine ourselves and our world into being, then a great deal will depend on the kinds of tale we credit.

The more partial and divisive the story, the more partial and fissive our view of the world and our scope within it. The wider and more inclusive its embrace, the more open we can afford to be. Thus a bad story can have disastrous consequences, as witness the myth of racial purity by which the Nazis authorized appalling crimes, caused atrocious suffering, and incidentally perverted the generous spirit of Wolfram's *Parzival* by dragooning its emblems to its own evil cause.

By contrast, as Ted Hughes puts it, in the truly great stories 'the full presence of the inner world combines with and is reconciled to the full presence of the outer world. And in them we see that the laws of these two worlds are not contradictory at all; they are one all-inclusive system; they are laws that somehow we find it all but impossible to keep, laws that only the greatest artists are able to re-state.'[8]

Wolfram's *Parzival* is such a story, and all the more so because it holds together two different aspects of the imagination: the inventive aspect by which new vision is conceived, and the ethical aspect which enables us to empathize with others and thus ground our understandings in compassion. In Wolfram's story, the invisible champions of the imagination are the neutral angels – those who refused to join the war in heaven that threatened to tear the universe apart. Whatever sources he was drawing on, and there are elements that relate it to pagan, Christian, Kabbalistic and Islamic traditions – Wolfram's gnostic myth of the grail as a sacred stone from heaven is staggering in the reach of its vision. For a universe where one is forced to take sides, where one spiritual power can triumph only at the expense of another, is unacceptable to an imagination large enough to understand that truth is found only where contradictions meet.

This, in Wolfram's vision, is the place of the grail. This is the virtue of the stone, and everything in his story heartens us to live with the tension of such ambiguity. Thus the powers of both light and darkness are built into the fabric of the stone. Both a black queen and a white queen are needful to produce a true champion of the grail. Both black chess pieces and white are needed for Gawain's defence at Ascalun. Parzival (whose very name is a play on words meaning 'pierce through the middle') follows his inner light until it leads him into utter darkness, and only then does he begin to find his way back to the Castle of the Grail. And before that journey can be completed, Parzival himself, the champion of light, must yield to his dark brother Feirefiz whose skin is dappled like a magpie, being both black and white.

It seems that only when that which has split apart is brought back together, and everything has been afforded its rightful place in the complementary scheme of things, only then can the wound in consciousness start to be healed – that is, be made whole again. And this is not a problem capable of a solely intellectual solution. For though the healing presence of the Grail can be evoked only by the asking of a question, it is a question that is prompted by a motion of the heart.

Earlier I suggested that Wolfram's story offers a map to the landscape of the human soul, but there is something in its emblemology of opposites which seems to correspond to the very fabric of our bodies too. We are twofold creatures, our brains, torso, limbs and organs are delicately stitched into a sturdy and fragile unity from almost symmetrical halves. Even the single heart itself is made up of left and right-hand chambers like that vessel called a pelican in which the alchemists strove to solve the problem of the opposites and thereby attain the philosopher's stone, the elixir of life itself. Foremost among the apparent contraries that the alchemical process sought to reconcile was that of matter and spirit, body and soul, and there are many alchemical references in Wolfram's text. He certainly had a poet's understanding of the hermetic connection between the vessel and the stone on the one hand, and the human heart and soul on the other. And he may have had an initiate's understanding too.

In their marvellous book, *The Myth of the Goddess*, Anne Baring and Jules Cashford luminously relate the emblem of the grail to Gnostic and Kabbalistic alchemy and to the processes of renewal and rebirth which were celebrated in the ancient mystery rites of the goddess. 'What is the Grail then,' they ask, 'but the inexhaustible vessel, the source of life continuously coming into being, energy pouring into creation, energy as creation, the unquenchable fountain of eternal being?' In affirming the particular power of Wolfram's vision of the grail, they add, 'There had been other images of the source of creation, but no myth before this had linked that image to the spontaneous outpouring of an individual heart.'[9] And here we approach both the heart of Wolfram's particular genius and its resonance for our time.

The wound that must be healed in the grail story is a bodily wound, a sexual wound, but it mirrors that dualistic splitting of the mind which is the price we have to pay for our consciousness of ourselves as separate beings. Our analytical powers increased enormously with the evolution of such consciousness, but it also estranged us from the wisdom of the heart and from authentic experience of that sense of unity with the world around us which is the deep ground of our being. In search of the self, we cut ourselves off from the primal union with the mother and set out on our quest armed with the sharp sword of the divisive intellect, but the world turned centrifugal on us and we are uncertain now how to find our way back home.

Writing in a time when the power of the church and a hierarchical system of government claimed to offer a coherent picture of the universe, Wolfram confronted a predicament common to many of us today: the anxious awareness that the way to authentic being cannot lie in obedience to external authority, but has to be found through each individual's loyalty to the often contradictory truth of personal experience.

It may not always be a reliable guide but, for many of us, it's all we have, and often enough it leads us into dissidence with the powers that be. Whether coded or not, Wolfram's account of the sources of his story (he claims to have got it from the astrologer 'Flegetanis' in Muslim Spain through the Provencal and therefore possibly Catharist poet 'Kyot') places his imagination in heretical terrain. The prelates of the Christian church have no place in his story, and the power of his vision brought him to an almost Taoist understanding that all the fury and mire of human complexity must dissolve into a receptive emptiness of heart before renewal can take place.

Such a vision makes each life an individual project of the imagination – a gnostic process of self-discovery and self-transcendence, and one which is deeply grounded in the compassionate awareness that we live in the plural, that we are answerable for one another.

So when Parzival asks what ails his uncle, he is also implicitly asking, 'What's wrong with us, why can't we hold it together, why do we cause such injury in the world?' And because his attention is focused not on his own plight but on that of another, he is immediately admitted to the presence of the Grail. Which is to say that the renewing energy of life itself comes to meet him in joyful response.

But all the ancient mysteries have been profaned these days. There are no such accessible rites of passage, no universally accepted myths. It's a time for openness, for sceptical questioning, a time where nothing can be taken on trust. In such a time the activity of the analytic intellect has put enormous powers at our disposal, yet most of us feel paradoxically impotent within a scarily fissive world. Our technological skills present us with choices for which we are ill-prepared, and ingenious things get done in the name of scientific enquiry which leave us ill-at-ease. We find it hard to trust in the virtue of our politicians, our judges, our religious leaders, our doctors, our artists, our intimate relationships, the food we eat, the water we drink, sometimes even the air we breathe.

Some of us recoil from the uncertainty and bewildering moral relativities of this situation into the consoling absolutes of one or other form of fundamentalism – each of which tends to be violently opposed to another. Meanwhile much of the population of the earth erodes the natural environment in a struggle for profit or subsistence, and in the prosperous north-west, like a deep bass-note trembling under everything, there is a sense of impending disaster. We know we've got things wrong. We don't know what to do about it. And so, apart from occasional upsurges of charitable outrage, we shut our eyes against the suffering and aridities of a wasteland time, and hope for the best.

Yet this is not the whole picture, for we also live in a time when two hopeful and apparently contrary motions of the human spirit are seeking to converge.

The first of these is the widespread need for the discovery and assertion of personal identity that has emerged in recent years. For all the vanities and delusions that may attend the many various regimens of self-development, there has never previously been a time when so many individuals have made such a vigorous commitment to the difficult process of self-transformation. Each of them is a knight errant seeking their own path through the dark wood, and in the process they are discovering new, imaginative ways to come together.

At the same time, as the fine flower of our sense of environmental crisis, we are witnessing an unprecedented increase in our ecological understanding. And with it has come an ever-increasing awareness that we are all in this together, and that our decent survival as a species finally depends on the welfare of the entire planetary community.

Furthermore, the kind of thinking required and encouraged by these perspectives is of a subtler order than the old 'objective' positivism. Subject and object, self and other, inside and outside, can all now be perceived as part of a single inclusive field. Whether we like it or not, we have seen that what we do to the other we do also to ourselves, and the accompanying evolutionary shift in consciousness seems to be from egocentrism to ecocentrism, from the divisive perspective of the separate ego to the confluent perspectives of the soul.

Like all transitional times ours is an age fraught with perils and possibilities, but so high are the stakes these days that the outcome is full of doubt. Perhaps what is needed in such a time is a vital response from the imagination. For don't we need to keep the intelligence that reaches us from the outside in living relation with the insights arising from within? Don't we need to temper our talent for invention with a compassionate awareness of how things stand with others than ourselves? Don't we need to remember that, of its very nature, the imagination is a faculty that seeks to hold contraries together in creative tension rather than letting them split off into destructive conflict, and is therefore a resource sorely needed by many warring couples, divided families and embattled communities?

Fortunately, like the ability to dream, it is also a faculty to which we all have birthright access, though it will prosper only to the degree that we take pains to keep it exercised. So a great deal, as I suggested earlier, will depend on the kind of stories we choose to tell each other.

Eight hundred years ago Wolfram von Eschenbach composed a narrative poem which examples us all in imaginative endeavour. The magical stone for which its hero seeks is itself an emblem of the transforming power of the imagination. For properly understood, magic *is* the activity of the imagination – that power which conjures doves out of darkness, redeems the tormented soul from its cabinet of knives, and brings about change in ways which seem to defy the rational mind.

Like all true myths, Wolfram's *Parzival* is a lively oracle of change. The presiding spirit of its vision – startling in its invention, wryly humorous in tone, anti-fundamentalist in its metaphysic, and widely tolerant in its embrace – engagingly demonstrates the gains that can be made for life when an individual sets out in quest for an authentic sense of being. Following his heroes through the landscape of the soul, the poet bravely explores the range of his creative power in ways that are enriched by a hard-won, deep-searching knowledge of the self and by compassion for others. So the question this fable poses to the imagination is not, 'What is the meaning of life?' Rather it seeks to ask, 'How can we best live our lives so that they feel rich in meaning?' And in this, as in so many other respects, Wolfram's *Parzival* remains a contemporary story and a salutary myth for our own troubled and exhilarating times.

Afterword

Notes and References

1. Margaret Anne Doody, *The True Story of the Novel* (Fontana Press 1998).
2. *The Chymical Wedding* (Picador 1990) offers a contemporary variation on the story of Gawain and the Green Knight, while *Alice's Masque* (Picador 1995) improvizes around his encounter with the Loathly Lady.
3. CG Jung, *Memories, Dreams and Reflections* (The Fontana Library, 1967).
4. Laurens van der Post, *Jung and the Story of Our Time* (The Hogarth Press, 1976).
5. Emma Jung and Marie-Louise von Franz, *The Grail Legend* (Coventure, 1986).
6. Joseph Campbell, *Creative Mythology* (Penguin, 1976).
7. Edward C Whitmont, *The Return of the Goddess* (Arkana, 1987).
8. Ted Hughes, 'Myth and Education' in *Winter Pollen* (Faber & Faber, 1994).
9. Anne Baring and Jules Cashford, *The Myth of the Goddess* (Viking, 1991).